Galen's Legacy

HENRY ALLEY

RATTLING GOOD YARNS
PRESS

Rattling Good Yarns Press
33490 Date Palm Drive 3065
Cathedral City CA 92235
USA
www.rattlinggoodyarns.com

Cover Design: Rattling Good Yarns Press

Library of Congress Control Number: 2022931973
ISBN: 978-1-955826-64-8

First Edition

Also by Henry Alley

Novels

Through Glass

The Lattice

Umbrella of Glass

Precincts of Light

Men Touching

Short Story Collections

The Dahlia Field

Literary Criticism

The Quest for Anonymity: The Novels of George Eliot

July, 2022

To Lu and Dai,

With many thanks for
being such great friends
and neighbors over
the years.

For Austin

Love,

Hank and Austin

CONTENTS

Part One
Clearing Away

The morning he got out of prison, Galen was met by Ophelia his sister and Jacob his son. Ophelia, being a florist, had flowers, of course; Jacob, ten years old, small and round, just hugged and kissed him. Galen stooped down, and felt the fragility of his child, and thought of his own father. It was St. Valentine's Day, Ophelia's biggest day of the year. Both Ophelia and Jacob had visited Galen faithfully, and both had fought to prove his innocence.

Standing upright again, Galen felt bungling and fragile and porous—like a vase, but like a bull in a china shop at the same time. Ophelia pressed some long-stemmed yellow roses toward him. For just a moment, her eyes misted up as she was caught once more by the sight of him. She apologized for the other members of the family not being there. However, his daughter was not among the apologies.

Galen had been hoping to see his father—he had given up on his daughter—still, his father had never visited him in prison. Standing in front of the formidable structure, with all this space around him, he was dismayed that his sudden sense of freedom, almost dizzying, could be dampened already. He threw his shopping bag of clothes in the back seat, followed by what books they would allow him to take with him. No one cared about the old Harcourt Brace *Mrs. Dalloway* in the prison library—it was Mylar covered and showed off a bunch of yellow roses, besides. They were glad to see it go. Yet the Billboard encyclopedia of *Rock Movers and Shakers*, which had been a present from Ophelia, Galen had had to fight to take with him. And it was rightfully his.

They got into her Cadillac, '67, a lavender one with fins, a collectible for their milieu, the early 1990s, which Galen always saw as celebrating collectibles.

1

Jacob sat between him and Ophelia on the front seat. "Look, look. I colored this in school," he said, showing him. It was Jacob's version of a Get Out of Jail Free Card. It sported a lean, tanned, sinewy man like his father sprouting blue wings and flying beyond a cell door. His aunt and himself were waving pom-poms in celebration in the background. In real life, Ophelia was not large, as she was here, just very blonde, and always emitted a sense of irresistible bounty. So to others, she was larger than life.

"That's beautiful," Galen said. "You always thought I would get out and get out soon."

Jacob pulled at his sleeve—Galen was wearing an old sport coat, part of the post-prison package. "I'm never going to let you go in there again." Because the structure was still in sight. Galen interpreted this as, "I'm never going to let you out of my sight again." Galen heard stories about men being restored to their normal lives and their dogs following them around from room to room.

"I promise I'll never go in there again. And how could they ever make a mistake like that again, with Andrew and you and the computer tracking them down?" Galen asked.

Jacob still held on to his hand and looked him up and down.

It was the touch. Galen squeezed back. It was like acquiring a second skin—or losing the one he already had. In prison, no one had touched him. When Jacob and Ophelia and sometimes her husband Andrew had visited, Galen had wanted to reach through the glass and caress Jacob's cheek or Andrew's biceps. Galen had to breathe in deeply as he sat in the moving car. He felt close to passing out again but this time because of the contact.

Jacob tugged at his sleeve. "You look thin. I think they made you thin in there. We'll get even."

Galen did feel thin, slight, as though the breeze had blown him straight out of prison and into this car. In many ways, the prison, as prisons are built to do, had ground him down. Still, a physical therapist back behind bars had checked over his workout routine once, seen he had done weightlifting, which counterbalanced the heavy running around the yard and said, "Well, that will keep you from drying up to dust and blowing away." Nevertheless, there was this presence and pressure of Jacob's hand. It reminded Galen of when his uncle was dying and the man had held on to his hand, his face showing the struggle, and then had eased. "Come back," Galen had said under his breath.

Ophelia, who had been uncharacteristically silent, said, at last, "There's something coming up when you get home. We're all in an uproar about it.

Mother especially. The Hotel's been off tilt ever since it got wind. So please try not to be too upset."

"Ophelia, what is it?" he asked, thinking it was his daughter, Teresa, who had kept him out of her life all this time, or that it was his actual father, Gregory, the bellman. The man they kept at the back of the hotel.

"A letter came for you two days ago from Uncle Eugene," she said.

"Uncle Eugene?" he asked. "That's impossible."

"Well, somehow the letter was miss-sent before he moved from California back up here," she went on.

"That would have been three years ago," Galen said.

"Yes, yes. And someone, probably looking at who it had come from, had written 'Deceased' on it, rather than looking at who it was addressed to." She was taking him in across Jacob, and not attending to her driving. Her formidable blonde hair reached to her lap.

"That would have been when he had first gotten ill," Galen said.

"That's right," she answered. "I know it's hard for you to think about Eugene right now, but I wanted to prepare you."

Jacob pointed to the grand bucolic clouds floating above the flooded fields. The frost was lifting from the fences. "Dad, you don't want to miss those. Clouds, clouds."

"Yes, it's been a long time since I could just look at clouds," Galen answered.

"But you know the general rule," Ophelia went on, "is not to talk about Uncle Eugene. At least at Mother's house."

"Different rules at my place," Galen said. "I mean, I will have a home." He was holding up a finger emphatically, despite the shabbiness of the sport coat, which eclipsed all his gestures.

Jacob's face lit up even more. "A house? Just for us?"

"But you are living at Mother's place now," Ophelia said to Galen. "And we're glad you are." Again she looked dismayed and at a loss for words.

"Well, when I get a house," Galen said, "we'll talk about Uncle. Constantly."

"For real?" Jacob asked. "A house of our own for real?"

"In any case," she concluded, "there may be a new will somewhere. That, at least, is what AIDS House and Gay/Lesbian Liberation are claiming, and that Eugene's house may go to them. And now here's this letter that's come."

A letter. Galen felt a foot on the landing. What he had been waiting for. A spiritual foot, a ghostly foot. Something that he had thought would never come. Comfort, solidarity, a sense of home, of maybe a real parent in the offing once again. Whatever was in the letter, whatever Eugene said, it was bound to be better than the terms of his deathbed. His uncle—the strongest man in the world, the gayest man in the world, at least back then—had come back to Carleton Park from a glorious life in Los Angeles and San Francisco—to renege on being gay and die. Galen had been kind. Galen had been a good caregiver—had tried to see to all the difficult business of his death, when Ophelia and Christabel his mother had run out of steam—but inwardly, privately, he had been scornful and devastated.

Jacob burrowed his head into Galen's shoulder, and, kissing the top of Jacob's head, Galen had a sudden sense of shame, very much like what had visited him in prison. Great unworthiness about being a father and yet being an ex-con (even though he was innocent and had been restored, as they said, to his normal life), in fact, having two children. An admission of cluelessness—how in the world do you raise a boy, anyway?

When the exit to the small berg of Bradleyville, just prefatory to their own Carleton Park, came up, Galen said, "Do you mind if we stop at the ARCO before we get home? The men's room? They kept me waiting all that time for you to pick me up. I couldn't get back to the lockdown to pee."

"There's time," she said.

But. Oh, I forgot, he said to himself as he pulled himself out of Ophelia's Cadillac. It was an "AMPM Mart," not far in name from the Midnight Mart that had brought him all that grief. And the interior was overwhelming—splashy multi-colored drinks on posters, innumerable gum, innumerable candy, and a whole blue center with stacks of water with the wrap-around label saying "Hydrazone." Jacob had followed him in, and then made a b-line for the candy section.

Galen had to call the cashier to come with the keys to the men's room.

"Remember, Buddy, we're just a hop-skip-and-a-jump off the freeway, so it's a five-minute limit"—flashing the keys. "No offense but you can't imagine the kind of riff-raff we get trailing in here." The man was long-haired, young, sweet, and bushy in his beard.

"I'm not just a freeloader," Galen said. He pointed through the window. "My sister's out there getting gas right now." And the Cadillac Fleetwood blinded Galen a little in the emerging sun.

The cashier unlocked the door. "Like I said, no offense. Anyone can see you're no freeloader. It's just the rules are the rules."

4

Galen used the urinal. But in washing his hands afterwards, he stared at his reflection. Dried his hands and looked at them. Are these mine? I'm no freeloader but ne'er-do-well—for sure. He stared at his reflection. He looked craggy and thin, just as Jacob had said —like a man who had been sent to prison for a crime he did not commit.

There was this matter of going to prison. He had been to the bar that night of his arrest. Just before. He had been drunk. Had been with someone. Had been with his latest. Leo. Who had been the reason for the end of Galen's marriage, the man he drank with, caroused with, shared a dark life with. Someone closeted, anguished, and altogether irresistible. Someone from Mayfair, the redneck sister city, someone apparently rooted, but someone who could never accept the kind of life they were trying to build for themselves. A carpenter, thin, wiry.

He and Leo had never lived together, but they were making plans to just before what happened at the Midnight Mart. The two of them had gone dancing that night, the way they always did on Saturdays. They had some sort of ritual surrounding it. Leo would park in front of the hotel, and they would go off, in the blissful, neoned night to the bar.

But that night, after dancing, after making love in Galen's upstairs room, he had followed Leo back to his Mayfair home for a little more drinking. That's when the Midnight Mart came. Afterwards. After he had been at Leo's. For he had not been able to get enough. He wanted to go into complete oblivion because of his grief over Uncle Eugene. Fear of darkness again. Fear of demons. Fear of closeness. Which Leo charged him with that night anyway. "You never, never want to *be* with anybody." Then Galen had left and gone into the Midnight Mart.

And then the trial had come. And at first, Leo had visited him in jail. But then when Mayfair started getting vicious, when it started bringing his friends and then his boyfriends to the stand, Leo had vanished. Nowhere to be found. The slender, muscular brown-haired carpenter had just crawled under a rock—when his body had been so wonderful in bed, with beauty in his face, richness in his beard.

Galen's trial had been ugly. The prosecuting attorney tried to show that Galen, after going into the Midnight Mart and finding no one there—nothing but an open cash drawer and a missing clerk—had actually returned home and phoned the police to cover himself, to make him look like a law-abiding citizen, when in reality, they said, he had committed the robbery. Well, Galen had been drunk then, so he had not been in the greatest position to defend himself. He knew that. But he strictly remembered "buying" a six-pack of wine-coolers (peach) by selecting them out of the bin, laying eight dollars down on the glass counter, seeing the cash drawer open and then phoning from home. When the police had finally come, they found the knocked-out clerk in the storeroom, who attested to a man of Galen's description having bound and gagged him; the police also found the empty till but no money lying on the counter. Why there had been a gang of hoodlums hanging under a tree just outside—who never had paid attention to anything in the past but this time "noticed" Galen go in and probably rob the drawer—Galen could not understand. One of them had been a Marlon Brando look-alike. But, again, Galen had been in no position to defend himself. No position.

The police did a lab study of every article involved and came up with a small disputable fingerprint on the masking tape which had served to bind Alex's (the clerk's) wrists. The little disputable thumbprint had been enough to turn the tide against Galen, especially the moment they had all learned he was gay. The jury, after all, had been a Mayfair jury—Mayfair being homophobia city for years, the evil twin (on this issue) of Carleton Park.

Later, it was disclosed that Daws, the prosecuting attorney himself, was a secret drag queen by night, and the *Carleton Park Daily* ran stories to feature him. *The Daily* did more than that. It tracked down the hoodlums who had been more than encouraged to testify and found that one of their gang had been curiously spending a lot of money the night after the robbery. When a reporter got to the door, the Marlon Brando look-alike panicked and headed for the fire escape, and a reporter ran this investigative story the next day, too. Meanwhile, his sister Ophelia, following on another tack and putting two and two together, too, called up Marlon Brando's mother and, finding her a "lovely woman," who had in fact used Ophelia's scrupulous bouquets on many Christmas occasions, got just enough information to confirm that Marlon had been the member of the gang to spend all the money. Meanwhile Jacob went for help from his Uncle Andrew, who got on the computer with Jacob and, accessing an up-to-then unknown database, discovered the methods used to "encourage" the witnesses for the prosecution had been illegal. He then took this, via Christabel, to Galen's lawyer, and successfully got a reopening of the case, just when all the other pieces were dropping into position.

Mayfair was scandalized; Mayfair was disgraced. They did not want Galen out of prison, and here he was, coming out strong in Carleton Park, the city next door.

Galen, still at the mirror, knew full well the cashier with the bushy beard would be pounding on the door, saying his five minutes were up. But he wanted to say he hoped this letter, literally dead letter, from his uncle would be long and good and edifying, because he was staring straight into his life without any guide, any mentorship, any opportunity of being shown how to be a father. And he must have that opportunity. Because he was sober now and couldn't just dumbfuck his way through anymore. His father would be at the hotel, but he would still be an assigned servant, a dependent, after the divorce, on Galen's mother and not capable of giving any advice.

The mirror nearly left him praying.

"Dad," Jacob said, when Galen came out, "can I get this gum? It's only ten calories a stick."

Galen held the pack and looked at it, and again the colors of the AMPM Mart nearly engulfed him. Hi-Chew Grape Sensationally Chewy Fruit Candy. Purple was everywhere. But Jacob had gotten him at a good time. Right now, he would have bought his son anything. Galen paid the seventy-five cents out of the folding money the prison had given him. He'd be damned if he wouldn't get more than that once he got a little guidance. He intended to pull his own weight and his children's.

Going out the door and opening the gum, Jacob said, "If I save a few pieces for the bullies, maybe they won't come at me anymore."

Galen bristled. "Bullies? Have they been hurting you?"

"No, not yet, but they said they would."

"You don't buy bullies off with candy," Galen said. "We'll talk more about this."

Ophelia ushered him and Jacob back into the car. "You know," she said, "we're nearly there."

Feeling slightly chastised for delaying them, Galen saw that Carleton Park was coming up at last—his sister took the exit—a little city, gilded with light, just down the highway from this prison, a place he had reimagined so much, too, in his mind, a refuge in an already idealized Oregon valley, a rich backwater of the Northwest, rainy and green, dotted with mist, which came from the mountains and the sea. Maybe this town was, at least in part, what had been promised in the two notes, or better, messages, he had been sent in prison, saying, flatly, "Everything is going to be all right." Just like that twice—folded up, blank otherwise, unsigned. As if he would soon be back to hiking up the iron-flecked cliffs or watching the diamond of the minor league ball games fill up with twilight, night after night. But more important, he'd have the instinct about the right thing to do.

Green seemed to be all around him; they were starting their descent into town.

"Tell me one thing," he said to them. "Did either of you send me any notes while I was in prison?"

"Notes?" Ophelia said eyebrows up. "Of course I sent you notes. Valentines."

"Christmas cards," Jacob added. His hand had gone back to his, but he seemed surprised that his father might have forgotten.

"Roses and candy," Ophelia said.

"Bakery stuff," Jacob went on.

"I didn't mean gifts," Galen said, trying to stop them.

Jacob was smiling, too, patting his father's side. "I wish you had eaten more of the bakery stuff."

"The gifts came with notes," Ophelia explained. "Don't you remember?"

"Yes," Galen put in, "that I do remember. I mean notes by themselves. Mysterious ones—ones that meant a lot to me no less—that just said, plainly, 'Everything's going to be all right.' They were unsigned."

"No," Ophelia answered. Jacob shook his head. "But that's wonderful," she went on, as they entered an empty ramp. "Wonderful!" She lifted her hands again, this time from the wheel. And as if in coordination with her last word, Carleton Park appeared to one side of the beltline freeway, with forested hills and valley, the perfect place for crocuses to arrive—and, of course, every other flower which Ophelia might summon.

The downtown unfolded before them, neatly, as though dealt to them from a brightly colored deck of cards. the New Amsterdam Hotel and Manse Restaurant housed in its corner came up like the King and Queen. The hotel was brown and square, seven modest stories high. A ribbon of stone scrollwork encircled it at the top. Lace curtains shaded its windows, drooped there easily, like eyelids before sleep. And of course, Ophelia's Flowers was right there beside it, with its glass annex of an extended greenhouse.

It was comforting to have the aging spring shadow of that building over him now. He had always thought of the New Amsterdam Hotel as more than just a hotel; it was an intimate constellation of lodging, restaurant, seamstress shop, florist, and pharmacy, not necessarily gathered under one roof, but working constantly in cooperation with themselves on the same block—ever since he had been in high school. He felt comforted by that system now. He could give himself over to a complete renovation by each make-over unit, restaurant, seamstress shop, florist, and pharmacy, after having been beaten up by witches, flying monkeys, and red poppy fields. At first, his mother, apparently a widow, had taken in mending in the old boarding house where Galen had first grown up. But her dream had been to replicate a hotel like her uncle's over in Amsterdam. Then, a few years later, somebody else's financial disaster did drop it right in her lap. Now the "Sorceress Seamstress"

just off the lobby and next to the gift shop, could mend a suit in the morning, outfit the guest by afternoon, and send him or her off with carnations from "Ophelia's Flowers" by evening, along with saline nose drops scurried in by the pharmacy, in case they were allergic to the flowers. They even had (as did the model Vondel Hotel in Amsterdam) an old-fashioned house doctor, who paid calls right to the rooms with a black satchel. Galen saw it as a small city unto itself, and still holding Jacob's hand, he leaned against the seat and felt his whole body travel through the hotel's various healing stations and stratagems.

But they were getting out of the car. Galen felt lucky that, by speaking up, he had held on to his wonderful idea that someone mysterious had sent him those notes. Let the idea be that on some special secret plane—as though in the courtyard, the ghost of Uncle Eugene had sat down on a stone bench and written them, having gotten word from a Dutch angel that Galen's heart was sinking behind the prison walls and needed help right now. Direction.

With the idea of meeting his mother and father in the next few moments and realizing that "jailbird" was the last thing he wanted them to think, he drew the flowers together and straightened the sport coat—rather sheepishly, along with everything else. He felt the tight prison shoes very suddenly—he couldn't wait to get to his own closet and find some of his own. Everything he was wearing was actually a part of a whole booty of consolation prizes from the Law, used, begrudged, and handed down. He folded up his sport coat—neatly. Then tossed it in the trash can just at the curb.

"Dad," Jacob said smiling, slamming the car door for him. "You look Dutch."

"That may be because I feel," Galen answered, "just like Rip Van Winkle."

In getting out in the driveway of the hotel-side home (a comfortable, two-story bungalow, with a certain wrap-around effect), he faced his uncle Eugene's mansion just opposite, affectionately called the Estate—locked down for now—but even so, he could sense in its nine o'clock windows something living, something waiting, an imminence to be reckoned with. Ophelia's flower shop, next to the hotel, showed, in green neon, a bouqueted maiden, all in silks, waltzing across a bridge. "Ophelia, Your Scrupulous Florist."

Jacob took his hand again and led him to the porch. Since Galen's other arm was loaded down with luggage, Ophelia threw the door open, and there his mother Christabel stood, in her blue-windmill-patterned Holland apron and with her sewing over her shoulder. She was crying some. She gave him the semblance of a hug. He hugged her in return heartily, to her dismay.

But once again, with the decided absence of his father, Galen felt deeply disappointed. "Nice to be home. You can't imagine what it was like—"

"Well, then," Christabel interrupted, "we don't have to talk about it, then."

"Why not?" Galen asked, looking down at Jacob, who had his arm around his leg. The shadows of their Dutch living room crossed their faces like the sun's patterning of lattices on curtains.

"Because it'll just depress you." Her arms were akimbo, as if she were giving orders to servants.

"It won't depress me at all," Galen said. "Let's do talk about how brave I was. How wonderful I was. My ears aren't burning enough. Let's talk! Let's talk!" He dropped his luggage down. "Remember, I'm supposed to be restored to my normal life, but that doesn't mean wiping out that happened." Yet on some level, he feared she might have a point.

"It's something to be forgotten," Christabel said. And as she spoke, the grandfather clock in the hallway tolled. It was the Big Ben of the Family. Also, the Westerkerk, from Amsterdam. "You have enough on your mind as it is." Galen remembered that this was a family that refused to talk about the past. Nevertheless, the clock went on sounding.

"Ah, there's our special chimes," she said, "even though they do not make themselves truly felt until midnight."

There was a little bit of arcane English in the family—for that was what Christabel had been taught in Holland as a little girl, and it had filtered through to everybody. And even to the choice of some of the children's names. Nobody named anybody Ophelia, but Christabel did.

"I understand there is a letter here for me," Galen said.

"There is much mail here for you," Christabel said, his arms folded. "It's stacked on your bed in your room. You literally won't be able to sleep until you've looked at it."

"I mean Uncle Eugene's letter that Ophelia told me about," Galen said. Jacob patted his leg.

Christabel went to the desk, pulled at the ring clinched between the lion's teeth, and took out a letter with such care Galen would have thought it was a sick or fragile fledgling. Obviously it brought some melancholy about her brother. "We are anxious to hear whatever he might have to say."

And Galen felt delighted that she spoke of him in the present. As if Eugene had another spring to live. Galen could remember that other spring—when his uncle had come to board with them that first time over

10

thirty years ago—and Carleton Park had eventually kicked him out. With Galen soon following. All that time, his uncle had protected him, been his advocate.

"As you probably know," Christabel said, "we're all concerned about what Eugene actually intended for that mansion. We need the property as a parking lot." She stood in front of the mahogany staircase as if to block it. "Once it's demolished."

Galen felt the letter. It was thin. And said—for they were all waiting, obviously, for him to open it then and there—"I'll get back to you." And went up the stairs, followed by shopping bag-toting Jacob.

He left Christabel and Ophelia astounded. A private time for himself?

Ophelia, a little hurt, waved goodbye. "I was glad I was able to pick you up." She was misting up again.

Galen turned on the stair. He waved the yellow roses, which he still had, along with Jacob's drawing. "Ophelia, I'm sorry. Thank you very much. I'm just distracted."

"All the other flowers are being sent up there," Ophelia called after him.

Up in his room, he was surprised to see that his presence had been completely scoured out. His pictures (more of Rembrandt, van Gogh, Vermeer) lay on the bed, in a stack, like new linen, along with his mail. And his bulletin board had been cleaned off. Everything was in a pile on the dresser. Clothes—his—hung in the closet, but not in any familiar order. Galen was prepared to see that the world had gotten on without him but not that the memory of him had been wiped out. Somehow the room stood, rather frighteningly, for the way his own memory worked these days. Gaps constantly. And out of nowhere. Rip Van Winkle.

He opened the letter.

March 2, 1987

Dear Galen,

I'm writing to you, even though I will soon join you and your mother up in Carleton Park. I'm doing this because I feel like I am my "whole self" here in San Francisco, at least for the moment, and I don't know what I will become once I'm in hospice in your home. Carleton Park, much as I love it, has a way of making me forget who I am. Also, they're about to put me on a new battery of medications which may make me weird. Void, a better word.

When I was last up in Carleton Park, I went through my house and got my life in order. All my journals are in the bookcase. There is one piece which I would particularly like you to have and that is my "Almanac." Also, I have included, in the bookcase, my exact directions about what I would like done with the house. I want you to be my executor as far as this last bit goes. Everything else I own has gone to medicine and care for this dread disease. We can discuss this when we come up but expect me to be disoriented. And perhaps not too articulate. I am having trouble keeping even this straight, even though I have waited for days for a lucid couple of hours. I am too proud to tell you how long it's taken me to write just this much.

In any case, thank you, Galen, for all the love you've given to me over the years. You have been a loving nephew.

Galen had to sit down, reading that.

Everything in my estate should go to you, but, alas, there is not a great deal to pass on. I would like it to go to some gay cause. I shall never forget the days I had with you in Seattle and our special time in Amsterdam. If it isn't too presumptuous to say—you've been like a son to me.

Take care, Galen, I love you, and I'll be seeing you soon.

Love, Eugene.

P.S. Look to your father and don't take him for granted. In his own way, he's looked out for you. When I was last up, I discussed my will with him.

Galen felt that was simply another kick, the first one being that he had been in prison—that Uncle Eugene had said he loved him, and Galen had never said it back. He had always meant to, during all those deathbed scenes, but there had been too much else to think about, particularly if his uncle was going to hang on for the next moment or not. He had not even gone into much reminiscence. And he wanted that now! And if he had just known about this letter, he would have had the guts to say, "I love you"! Maybe Eugene had been waiting, wondering why Galen had been so silent. But he hadn't had the letter. He hadn't had the fucking letter! Who had delayed it? He'd hunt them down and nail their ass. He'd kick ass and take names—clear around the world, if necessary. A regular cosmic violation had happened here. Maybe it had been his family, or some drunk at the post office. Maybe even the prison warden, if the letter had attempted to reach him there.

Galen stayed on the bed and started crying. Jacob, who had been standing with some fear at the window, came up and patted him, but Galen felt this was too much to lay on him, and asked him to go play his tapes for a while. He'd be with him in a moment.

Jacob obeyed, but only reluctantly.

"Are you sure you'll be all right?"

"Yes," Galen said, "I'm sure."

Alone once more, he considered—if only he could have his uncle back, it would salvage all he had suffered. At this moment, it didn't seem like a lot to ask. Just one man back from the dead. Just one. But then he reflected that maybe he was. Maybe "everything is going to be all right" had come from this same pen. The two folded notes were in his backpack, both postmarked "Carleton Park." He tore his pack open. He held them against his uncle's handwriting, knowing full well nothing could come of it, because the notes were printed. He looked at his uncle's envelope—not printed, either, but in cursive. And "deceased" was not written on it, but just "not here." And the address was not this bungalow home address, but the hotel.

And then there had been that part about Eugene consulting with his father. Considering his father's usual condition even back then, how could anybody consult with him, a drunk, about anything?

Jacob crept back into the room, looked at him with dismay. "Really bad news from Uncle Eugene?" he asked, handing him his crumpled handkerchief.

"Oh no," Galen said, using it. "It's all right, I just missed him."

"Oh," Jacob answered. "Are those other letters from him, too?"

Galen blotted his face with his sleeve. "I don't think so. I'll tell you what. Why don't you try to go find your grandfather and tell him I'm here. Then we'll go for a walk."

"Just us?" Jacob's face was like the moon again.

"Just us," Galen said, ruffling his hair.

"But maybe first I'll put on a tape."

Galen took off the pinching shoes and put on his casual slacks. He could hear it—Jacob got "Rock Me, Amadeus" going on his stereo.

"I love how it says, 'Rock Me, Amadeus,'" Jacob said, making his voice even higher as he came back in. "This song is old—but it's going to be worth a lot in a few years."

They went downstairs to the main floor again. Still no signs of his father. Together he and Jacob went out into St. Valentine's Day. They left a note saying they'd be back in just a few minutes. The hyacinths were out in the grounds collaring the hotel, and the flowering quince, separating the household from the grand building, was budding and blooming out in pink, now, as Ophelia's sign, strangely on at this hour, took her tentatively across the bridge again, in green. He had dreamed last night that all of Carleton Park had gone into snow, and certainly there was none of that, but, still, there was an edge of iciness on the wind which seemed to fluff up the primroses, as he peeked into the courtyard of the hotel, to see if everything was intact.

The fountain bloomed still, with water pouring out of the stone maiden's vase. Somehow all spokes of this holiday seemed to converge in this courtyard of golden forsythia and white viburnum, and although Galen reminded himself that he would probably be asked to go back to maintaining this place—he was a gardener by profession—he wasn't going to think about that now. At that moment, he saw the pond flower once more, this time with the reds of the mottled goldfish, which Jacob was pointing to.

Ten o'clock. He did have a Galen's Landscape office they could walk to, but they wouldn't. Not right now. He was asking Jacob what it was like living with Yvonne, that is, with Galen's ex-wife and Jacob's mother, and then with Christabel while he'd been in prison.

"It wasn't cool," Jacob said. "It wasn't very cool at all with Mom."

"Do you prefer Christabel?" Galen asked, pointing back to the hotel.

"Yes, Christabel, Christabel," Jacob answered, his high voice going up even a little higher, as before.

Crystalline clouds of February, free of rain for once, white, were darkening the earth and tips of the buildings before flying off. Which way shall we go? Downtown or toward the University? Maybe just toward the old dime store, the last of the Woolworths, down on what is left of the mall. Maybe we'll just have a look in at the window. Or maybe I'll buy some tulips to give back to Ophelia. Or get cokes for us in Woolworths's cone cups. But eventually he must see his father, no matter what. The opportunities to do so many things just spilled themselves in front of him.

They headed on toward the center of town—quiet, because of the redirected traffic. One major street had been closed down and another one opened, and Galen could see, from his ex-convict's perspective, that it had only made things "worse" in the sense that now all traffic was directed away from the businesses, his own storefront included. There was the little isolated "Milton's Books" and vegetable and fruit stand and the ragged Mayflower Theatre, but still scrolled with stone too, still art deco, and then brief parks with brief rhododendrons and the overpowering smell of flowering Daphne.

They stood directly staring into the Woolworths window, which was covered with cupids and featured the old-fashioned punch-out valentine

books. And then the candy in Aisle Fourteen! Fiery-hot hearts in red boxes and vanilla hearts, too, wrapped in fiery foil. Which delighted Jacob. And the flowers, tulips and daffodils, real and otherwise, which dotted the whole store. The only gift equal to this that he could think of—was the Gay Pride Parade he'd seen in San Francisco back in the 1970s, his first one, full of color and confetti. With his uncle beside him.

They went inside Woolworths and Jacob bought one of the valentine punch-out books, in celebration, again, of the reunion. Next they would go to see his father, the mystery guest.

◆◆◆

It was his father who stood in the doorway of Galen's bedroom, as Galen answered the knock. He had flowers, too. He leaned in across the threshold, as though he were a shy beau holding a bouquet. Outside, Ophelia's neon was still going: "Your Scrupulous Florist." Green, definitely green.

"I'm sorry," he said. "I saw your light was on. Obviously, you were asleep. I'm sorry. I thought you were up." He turned to leave.

"Come in," Galen said, shy also. "How are you? I was looking everywhere for you."

"Oh, I've been busy all day," his father said. He ventured in and sat in the one chair in the room. He, too, seemed bolt-upright and at military attention. Of course, he always sat that way, the few times he ever did rest. Maybe that was the pose Galen had been trying to strike earlier this morning. Close-up, his father looked even better in his chocolate uniform, thin and spare, and so extraordinarily agile and fit for his age.

"You're looking very good, Dad," Galen said.

"Oh yes, well, I think it's the new stationary bike I have," he answered.

"In your room?" Galen asked.

Gregory's room was just that, a room—with a bath down the hall. He hadn't been there either when he and Jacob had gone searching.

Gregory smiled with his head hung low. "Yes. I've got one corner all laid aside for it. You must come and see it sometime. It's quite a spectacle. Some men have sports cars. I have a bike. It doesn't matter that I don't move at all. It's really worth looking at. I mean the way you'd spend time looking at a Ferris wheel or my electric fireplace."

Immediately Galen could feel his heart on the rise—maybe his father meant it this time—that he actually wanted him to stop by, but immediately the wake subsided, hid, wary because of the past. "I would like that."

15

They stared—at the flowers; there was no other choice. "I brought these for you," Gregory said. "They're not very good. They're all red for Valentine's Day"—tulips—"not like something you'd get for a personal celebration." He looked around. "What you have here is more what the day demanded."

"What you've got there is beautiful," Galen said, taking them the way his father always carried the luggage—as though they'd break. "I'll treasure them."

"Oh"—he waved them aside—"they're just a little something I picked up from Ophelia. She took me on a tour of one of her greenhouses the other day. These were something I could afford. You know, she's quite serious about her flowers but wanted to give them to me for free. I wanted to pay." Gregory was pounding his palm.

"I know," Galen answered.

Galen tried to put them—they were in a pot and a little withered—in a special place in the room, as though he favored these over all the rest. This was no easy task, since the small room seemed almost 100 percent flowers already. Ophelia had brought them in later from friends and well-wishers. Cupids done up in amaryllis that looked like pink and yellow conches were leaning against forget-me-nots, fashioned almost as Christmas wreaths, suspended from golden chains, linked with laburnum. These were the demands of St. Valentine's Day Eve, the sweetest of the year, a magic time—greater than those on Christmas or New Year. Amidst all this, Galen did manage to find a spot of honor.

"Well, I really must be going," Gregory said, obviously not having anything more to say.

"Oh, don't rush off," Galen answered. And really meant it. "You just sat down."

It became very clear, then, that Gregory had allowed himself just this much emotional room. Ten minutes up and then ten minutes back. With tulip delivery in between. Ten minutes, but now they were at eleven minutes, and Gregory hadn't gotten through the door. Goodbye, sentiment.

He just stood there, his father fingering the petals of the tulips, which were now on the bookcase. "Like I say these aren't very good. They don't at all express—. You see some of them are already dropping off. You see, I was—very worried about you. And I'm so glad"—he started to cry—"it worked out. You don't know how worried I was. And then I didn't do anything. Like before."

The resonance of Galen's time in prison was striking like a chime. He didn't know what else to do but to go over and hold him.

Gregory hugged back for a moment, and then wiping his eyes, gently pushed him away. "No, enough of that. I never came to see you. Too drunk."

"Please," Galen said.

"No"—his father was waving his hand like the uniformed man he was— "I didn't come up here to unload. Just to celebrate. You've got enough to think about."

"Don't you think I ever think about you?" Galen asked. "I think about you all the time."

"I'm not worth it," Gregory said, still on recoil. "Please save your energy for someone that deserves your attention."

But he did deserve his attention. His father was thinner, more run down to his essence. The man had been through the fire of alcohol. He reminded him of himself, before he had gotten sober. The man looked fit but withered.

Galen stepped back. "Well, if you have to go, you have to go. I'll check in on you in the next couple of days. But you don't need to worry about me anymore. I survived prison fine."

"I can see that—I can't tell you what that means." His eyes were frightened again for a moment. "I had to be sure."

Pulling himself straight, he almost saluted, like a soldier in an opera, or, all right, the doorman of a hotel, before opening a BMW door.

Galen shyly patted his shoulder as his father began a retreat. "You will tell me if there's anything I can do?"

"What you can do?" His father's grand and craggy face became all attention. "That's the question I should be asking you. Goodnight, Galen."

As the door closed, the name hit him—he had to think it—"like a bell." He couldn't remember when he had last heard his father address him directly. "Galen."

He lay on his bed again, wondering if he would sleep.

In his mind, comforted by the dark of the bedroom, up and down those stairs, Gregory went until the man scaled a tower—St. Nicholas' in Amsterdam, until the whole construct started chiming. The bellman. Then Gregory was Quasimodo and speaking to pigeons, that fluttered off in iridescent blue, and then he turned into a statue with a scythe rolling on wheels before a Viennese clock face. Suddenly Galen was in a strange city trying to find a way home, but he couldn't get packed, and he had no flight reservations. He kept getting lost in a huge airport with no ticket windows. He knew that if he got home he would find his father at last.

But then he dreamt he and his uncle went right into the prison library, with the light coming through the bars and slated blinds and saw the men hanging out in the psychology section—hoping to find something, anything, about being gay and that being all right. And together they approached them, and Eugene said, "Hey, guys, it's all right—try this on for size." And showed them a special book on the shelves, a gay version of some great romance, which suggested that for centuries this was what men had been thinking about anyway.

And they went into the showers, where, under guard, Galen had spent so much time trying to soak away his tension and fury. There Eugene parted two men who were trying to make it before being found out, and then led them to safety.

They went into the laundry, where Galen had worked for six months, in the suds of prison blues and greens, and where, appealingly, the big-armed men had bent over the large tubs of water. Here, for two minutes together, Eugene stopped the din of the machines, and Galen could say to the worker next to him, "I'm here because I am a man. I started out a man, born into Oregon, and somehow that got me here."

"So that's your reason?" the man asked. "That's your excuse?"

"It's not an excuse," Galen answered. "It's a fact."

"Well," the man smiled, "my fact is doing drugs."

"Done that, too," Galen told him. "Or at least alcohol."

"Well, see that, then, as your reason," the man told him in an actual conversation he had had, once on the inside. "Otherwise, you'll go crazy, being here and thinking you're not guilty."

"What difference does it make?" Eugene told them. "Standing here arguing over who's guilty and who isn't?"

And they, he and his uncle, went into the mess hall. Eugene put down a doily and silverware from Bloomingdale's or Frederick and Nelson's at every chair. On every table, he put a vase of flowers from Ophelia's Scrupulous Florist, and the men, when they filed in, were not in prison greens but in tank tops and leather vests.

They went into Galen's own cell, and they could see Galen trying to sleep on the narrow bed, and Eugene lit up the postcards on the wall, and gave Galen more dreams of dreaming about Amsterdam. Together they were climbing the stairs of Anne Frank house, which they had done when Galen was young, one slow step at a time. The way narrowed for the two of them, until they were pitched forward to see the upper window which viewed the Westertoren, with its friendly clockface, promising Anne and everybody else that the safe world would return—its spires seeming to form some monument in a graveyard, and yet very much alive because it tolled and brought in healing, advancing time. And Galen, standing and watching himself lying on the bunk, saw his body settle into the dream of walking with his uncle. He said there were so many days when I thought I would only be serving out my sentence—ten years, and the best I could do was hold on to some vision. Whether of the hotel or the Westertoren, I didn't care. My mind would then go into the syntax of great-uncle's souvenir book, saying that "the walls of the Oregon State Penitentiary are charming indeed and may be viewed from a variety of angles, many of which appear to be friendly. Prisoners sometimes adorn their cells with picturesque relics, and have been known to value them more than their fellow inmates, which constitute a thought to be explored hitherafter."

But even though I had all of this!—all of this from Eugene!—I had to live day after day explaining to myself that I was not guilty, that that was the fact I had to live with in order to keep myself going, not to capitulate, not to give in, not to do subservience, just do my time, for whatever reason, just do my time, the way the Franks did their time, and whenever the first opportunity came, open the window and see the church clock tower, at whatever opportunity, open a window, open a window! Open a window! Even if it is the full ten years, even if justice miscarries again and again, and all the discreet lawyers along with Christabel and Jacob and Andrew and Ophelia can't change things one iota, get a view, open a window. Yes, because somehow this is all starting to seem very much like my childhood when being anything but macho was wrong and if you weren't that Marlon Brando look-alike who ended up being the one who robbed the Midnight Mart, then you were supposed to say you were guilty. If you didn't grease your hair and beat up the kid next door, you were guilty. But I didn't say I was guilty then, and I won't say I'm guilty now.

And Eugene took him into the mess hall at night, with the chairs in a row and the tables cleared away. Then the men were shown an old film, a sixties one, where a gay man proves to be a stool pigeon who lives by night in a bar and who causes the beautiful hero to commit suicide because he squeals on their old affair. But then something arrived on screen very different this time—it was, in fact, the scenario as Eugene had originally written it, on commission, where the gay man does not rat, and the protagonist does not commit suicide at all but, in fact, leaves his wife. Galen had known it was true, because he had been in Los Angeles when Eugene had been writing it. And Eugene had been devastated when Hollywood had refused the revision.

As the two of them, Galen and Eugene, moved from floor to floor, cell to cell, office to office, Eugene took notes for more revision, and handed them to Andrew, who had materialized suddenly, and said, "Here, change this," and the whole prison turned into something that was a cross between a circus and a hotel and the whole of Amsterdam.

◆◆◆

When Galen had first seen Gregory (he had been in high school by then and spending all his summers with Eugene), he could not stop looking. What was it? There had been something in keeping with a picture, a photo in the family archives. (Christabel had kept most of them shut away by then, but the resonance carried from somewhere.) Tap the bell, and Gregory would appear, smiling, silent, reliable, but usually (Galen would come to learn) just the least bit drunk. He had a problem. But he could manage going up and down stairs. Strong as a horse but something of a souse. And with a vivid history. Which evidently no one knew anything about.

Except Ophelia, maybe, who was in college by then. She seemed to be in on something, and so Galen had approached her finally, one day. "That face of his rings a bell," he said.

"Literally," she said.

He was out walking with her on Campus Road—out in the country, but eventually leading to the University. She was taking some classes in botany and walking to school these days. It was spring; she was noting all the wild roses. Already getting ready to marshal them.

"Like in a photograph album," Galen insisted.

"He's our father," she said, not meeting him eye-to-eye—uncharacteristic of her. She wore her blonde hair short back then.

"Our father is dead," Galen insisted. And in fact he had been told that ever since he could remember— "Your father died in the War. Missing over Burma."

"Well, he's surfaced," Ophelia said, frowning. Her words came slowly. "Mother didn't want to tell us she had been married to a drunk. So she just made up a story."

There was more to it than that. There actually had been a critical period of time when Gregory had been missing in action, but he had come back. Then Christabel had secretly divorced him as per agreement, and picked up as though nothing had happened. She had been bound and determined to start her life over, a false widow, without any attachments to the past. So kept his return to the U.S. a secret. But when he had shown up again, years later, to take the one job he could actually handle, she had hired him on, provided it did not disturb the family. She had been married to a pharmacist by then, a prescription addict who also sold pills on the side, a man she had later divorced as well.

With Ophelia there in front of him, he had been furious. "Galen"—she touched his sleeve—"try to be as kind to him as you can. You can imagine how he feels."

Still, he rushed away, not stopping until he had reached home and had confronted Christabel. "Yes, it is true," she said, completely worried but acting unruffled. "He ruined his whole life—he was a brilliant astronomer, discovered a few things around Pluto—and he tried to ruin mine. So I let him go. When he popped up again, we needed a bellman, so I took him. He likes being around you and Ophelia, but he makes no claims." She repeated Ophelia. "You need to understand him."

Galen had not known what to say or do. He felt shame and pity—that a man could be so beaten, apologetic. He knew of stories in his high school that were almost as bizarre as this one. He had a friend, for example, who, with his mother, had had his father committed. Thus very suddenly, Galen found all of the anger side of him cooling, especially with him knowing even back then that he himself might have a problem with alcohol. A few weeks later, he went up to Gregory as he was trimming up the courtyard (crouched, with large clippers) and said, "Dad?" and Gregory had smiled, "Yes," and had taken his hand for a moment.

"You mustn't take me too seriously," his father had gone on.

"I do, though," Galen had answered, "and I want you to talk to you."

"I'm not good on that"—his father had taken up the larger clippers, snipping the hedge that didn't need it. "Small talk, I mean."

"Then let's make it big talk, then. Starting back when we thought you were all dead."

His father's back was to him. "That's all gone, all gone." There was a spot of sweat in the middle of his shirt just below the shoulders. The fabric was mailman's gray.

Galen thought, I need to piece you together.

Later, after that, Gregory's availability had come and gone with the moon and alcohol. Galen had learned to accept him as the kind man (once his father) who carried luggage up and down stairs, parked cars, and worked the flowerbeds. It had been heartbreaking, because Galen as a child had made up many, many stories about reunions with his father, and this certainly had not been one of them. He also had wondered why he had been so slow to pick up what Ophelia had known and figured out already. I'm like Rip Van Winkle, he had thought back then, as he did now, but for different reasons.

The way Galen had been as a child and the way he was now seemed in perfect unison. Awkward, sleepy, out of it most of the time, but wanting to get back in. He remembered John Fogerty's "Centerfield"—about hoping to play once more. Still thinking of Gregory in this flowery landscape, he nevertheless felt comforted by the fact that at least his image of him never changed. Up one flight and then down another (frequently the elevator), until Gregory slept in his room at the back. No doubt that was what Gregory was doing now.

◆◆◆

He was still surprised he awoke in his own bedroom. And for the first time since maybe childhood, he was sober.

In prison, Galen had been struck by how much banging and commotion there was, from the early hours on. In the days of drinking, sleep had only been a leap from a cliff into a shallow pool of oblivion, with little breaking of the surface until the alarm. But now, here and in prison, he seemed to float onto the shore of wakefulness very gradually, picking up whatever sounds were in the tidewater—the dinging buoy, to and fro through the house—and becoming those sounds.

When he heard Jacob down the hall, he got up with him, and went downstairs and saw to his son's breakfast. For his entire history with Jacob had included Christabel as the main attendant—meals, clothing, seeing him off to school. So, now it seemed of major importance that he pour his son's cereal for him. He even added, as centerpiece, the pot of tulips Gregory had given him.

"Dad, you're pouring my cereal!" Jacob said.

"Happy to do it. Mother, do you know where all my diaries are?" Galen asked her across the table. "There were five five-year books all in a row on the top shelf of my closet."

"I put them away for safekeeping in the cedar chest," his mother said. "When I let out your room."

"I looked there," Galen said. "Nothing."

"Impossible," Christabel said. "No one knew they were here except me. Let me think about it. They can't be lost."

He loved it when she said that. Hadn't heard it in years. Can't be lost.

"In Holland, we used to pray to St. Anthony, too," Christabel said, her creased, heavily powdered face enclosed in worry. "Just let me think about it. It will surface. Twenty-five years of your life is important."

"I'd like to think so," he answered.

"Are you going to sue because they sent you to prison?" Jacob asked.

"Yeah, it's already in the works—the first stages." Galen was already happy to show he was on top of his new life. Practical at this moment, which he had never been before. But he knew he wasn't on top of anything, that his shoulders were starting to stoop again.

"Money," Jacob said. "Enough to buy all the computers in the world. And to send Dad to the doctor, if he needs one." He emphasized his smile and nodded, as though he were someone thirty years old. Galen was aware now that his son was watching him closely to see if he was eating.

"Galen," his mother said, "you don't want any more publicity. Please. We had to do everything in our power to keep the reporters away from the door yesterday. And they ended up harassing me still." She put her hand to her temple. "I had to lie down."

"There will hardly be much going into by the press," Galen answered. "Maybe a day or two, and that'll be it. As far as I'm concerned. But I have to do something about those coerced witnesses. We just can't let that pass."

"What will you do with the money if you get it?" Christabel asked. "And how much is it?"

"We're hoping three-quarters of a million," Galen answered. "That's the asking price, but that's not what we're going to get." He could sense it, now, sure as he could sense the season of spring all around this house, and in the flower beds of the hotel—and in Eugene's across Holland Avenue of this distinctly Carleton Park street—the family was surprised that he was taking action. They were surprised he was standing up for himself, the way he hadn't at the trial. Were more likely even more astonished that he was willing to risk his orientation being hammered on in the *Carleton Park Daily* once more, for the newspaper, which had taken, in fact, a sympathetic view, and had been instrumental, of course, in getting his release, still also called Galen a "decided outsider" and "gay bachelor." He wondered if the family noticed he was sober, which he had become in prison. Steady hands. And more or less steady on his feet, despite the stoop, which meant that he was much more than a "decided outsider" or "gay bachelor."

"Well, money is just money," Christabel said, coming back in with more scrambled eggs on a plate. "And when you make your decision, you'll simply have to decide whether you want us paraded in front of the public eye again. I for one will simply not have my past gone into one more time—particularly my poetry."

"It's nice to hear you mention your poetry—but I won't do anything beyond standing up for myself, if that's what you mean," Galen answered. "And I'd like to do something with Eugene's house."

"Dad, will you wait for me today?" Jacob asked. "Wait for me before you go into Uncle Eugene's mansion?"

Galen gripped his shoulder. "You expecting something big?"

"Yes, yes" Jacob answered. "I'm something big. Like we're going to get our own house, and we can live there together."

"Yes, we'll see. In fact, I'll meet you at school." He'd like that—he'd like the freedom of walking there. In the Carleton Park spring, with the evergreens coming into the light.

"Be there, be there," Jacob said, getting his things, including the lunch Galen had put in a pail. He'd been let down before.

Galen kissed him goodbye.

Christabel was looking suspicious. "Why wouldn't you go on living here? Was there something in Eugene's letter?"

"I'm not going to say anything," Galen answered, "until I get confirmation by a will that's supposed to be over at Eugene's mansion."

"A will?" Christabel was rigid.

"Just let me look," Galen insisted. "And one thing," he said to her, "the key, please."

"The key?" Christabel asked, looking threatened.

"To the Estate. Jacob and I need it if we are going over there today."

"Going through the back window should be good enough," Christabel said.

But Galen answered, "Not on your life. No sneaking around anymore. That was partly what they sent me to prison for. Certainly you've got a key somewhere."

"Look in the lion drawer, then," Christabel said—and there was a begrudging sound to her voice. "There's a whole raft of keys there. I think one of them's to the Estate. You may have to try them all."

And was gone before he could answer.

Taking his coffee into the sitting room, he could see Gregory out there in the courtyard bending down over the emerging hyacinths. Did that man ever sleep? Although there was the Estate to look after, and the enormous bills to pay, and possibly even reporters to see (he had scanned some of the return addresses of his mail), he didn't actually resist the idea of gardening for her, since maybe then he could talk to Gregory more. Christabel had hired on his landscaping business before.

The morning, while starting out gray, was breaking out into Rembrandt's *Bridge*, with gold in every window of the hotel. The evergreens on the distant hills were emerging sharp from the silver mist, along with a small footbridge in the courtyard, just over the water lilies that would bloom pink in summer. And with this sun, as though from the brush of a Master, he didn't mind going to the lion's drawer and not only drawing out two thick batches of keys, but also selecting out the one to his old work truck in the alley. Someone had kept air in the tires and driven it every now and then; his brother-in-law had seen to that.

It still ran, when he finally got into it. It only took an instant for him to put the truck in gear—and get launched toward his landscaping office to see if anyone had sent him mail there, too.

◆◆◆

Thomas Edison Elementary School seemed like a shimmering candle this afternoon, bright with the flickering of the children's movements, and rushed with the breeze of the teachers moving down the halls. Bells were sounding all over the place (maybe they were testing them), and the tight jonquils, rigid as military men, seemed just right in the beds bookending the entrance. Edison was old, brown and, plants and children aside, seemed done in a sepia photograph.

Not finding Jacob out in front, Galen searched the halls and then went down to what he knew was his son's homeroom. He felt rushed over by memories of Eugene and his own days in that old Roman brick school in Seattle. There was also that hovering janitor. Mrs. Daniels, Jacob's fifth grade home teacher, who was standing toward the front and facing rows of empty desks, looked up immediately and smiled, "Why, Galen, are you looking for Jacob? He just left."

"Gone again," Galen smiled. "He must be at his locker."

"And you," she said. "You're back, you're out, you've been released?"

"Yes," Galen answered. "My second day of freedom."

"You can be very proud of the way Jacob's been," she went on. "I'm going to put one of his drawings on the bulletin board—his version of a story we read from Frank Baum."

"Frank Baum's special to him," Galen said. He was looking in the direction of the boards.

"Maybe," she said, filing through some sheets, "he'll be the next Frank or illustrator of him."

She showed Galen a drawing. A magical garden, with ladies growing out of roses, with petals as waxy-looking as those in Technicolor.

"Yes," he said, "that's Jacob."

He had hung the "Get Out of Jail Free" up in his bedroom.

He heard, however, shouting outside in the hall, and in it Jacob's voice, so that both of them rushed out.

Jacob was being flung forward by two older kids, just as he was looking back over his shoulder and saying, "Fuck off!" as loud as he could. Seeing Galen and Mrs. Daniels, the bullies scurried away like spiders, and Jacob blushed deeply. "Sorry I was late, Dad."

Galen touched his hair. "What happened? Are you all right?"

"Yeah, it's just like Marston and Wills were giving me a hard time. It's all right now."

"Were they picking on you?" Mrs. Daniels asked.

"Yes," Jacob answered, looking down.

Mrs. Daniels got out her pencil. "I'll have a talk with their homeroom teacher."

But even after Mrs. Daniels left, Jacob was still cowering.

"What's going on?" Galen asked once more, patting his shoulder. "Doesn't look like you said everything. Are those the guys you were going to buy off with gum?"

"Yes, they were giving me a hard time."

"Hard time? What kind of hard time? Like before?"

Jacob squinted in the silence.

"They said we're both a couple of faggots."

Galen felt himself go beet red and ducked back into Mrs. Daniels' classroom, told her the rest, and she wrote that down too.

"We're not going to be preparing pupils for hate crimes around here," she said. "We'll look into this directly."

Galen wondered what would have happened, if anything, if they had been in the city of Mayfair.

"You let me know if they bother you again," Galen told him, as they went through the entrance.

As they headed toward the Estate, the four o'clock spring beds were dark with shadows. All seemed to be gathered into the facets of his uncle's many windows as they approached the house, and the outer walls still carried the sounds of the children at play on the field not two blocks from them. Galen hauled out the two loose strings of keys—ready to try them all. They glinted like a string of silver bait.

"Give me some. I'll try the back door," Jacob said.

Galen sent Jacob away with his half of the keys. He could hear Jacob jingling them, all the way around. He felt his anticipation rise. He began turning the keys noisily in the lock.

"Got it!" he heard Jacob say, and hurrying into the backyard, Galen went up the stairs and joined him, just as he was entering the kitchen through the back door. The place had a smell of coffee, tea, sandalwood, a smell that should have been stale, but it wasn't. Good, the electricity worked—was the next lamp going to disclose a ghost, who said, "Everything's going to be all right"?

The living room still remained over furnished. Jacob lit the Art Deco pole lamp, and it seemed to point them toward Eugene's library. He was now aware of the gallery of black and white photographs (Eugene's) following them as they moved along the scarlet hallway—The 1940 World's Fair in California (Treasure Island). There was the Pagoda of the Sun, the Court of Pacifica, and Rainbow Fountain. The pictures ended in a lithograph, an emblem for The Fair, which Galen now remembered Eugene had done on commission. It showed a bright sun breaking over the Golden Gate. The light from Eugene's works, photos and emblem alike, seemed to guide them toward a great bookcase.

As promised, there was Eugene's Almanac, obviously put together for Galen's benefit.

> February. Look for Horatian springs. When the flowerbeds seem metered in the most complex ways, borrowed from an earlier energy, the way Horace borrowed from the Greeks. Nevertheless, the emerging tulips make you think of other great creations—of athletes oiling their broad shoulders, as they do in Horace, or riding with steady hoof-beats toward a pastoral fountain. There is the story in Warner's translation, of a man after World War II, who, fresh out of a concentration camp and sent back home, rode out into the country the first day on a beautiful horse (called Horace), and shouted the Pyrrha poem in Latin.

There was an idol in one of the photographs back in the hallway, taken at the World's Fair at night, and the god just stood there in the shadows with light cascading like two streams down his shoulders. The way there was waning light in Eugene's backyard now. It was as though Eugene's prose created a new presence.

Going through the drawers, with Jacob eagerly watching him, he found journal after journal but nothing that looked legal. He had developed a sensitivity for it now, naturally. But, of course, everything had been in disarray those last months, so how could Galen expect something that would give them all a clear direction? Things were not at all as orderly as Eugene's letter had suggested. He remembered what Eugene had said about the energy required of him just to write that ghostly letter.

He and Jacob had reached the last shelf—of a closet. Taking out other lithographic work, newspaper clippings, and studio portraits of tuxedoed men who were perhaps Eugene's lovers, Galen discovered his own diaries.

"What in God's name?" he said aloud.

Jacob just lifted his brows in dismay.

Impossible that Eugene could have taken the diaries, because he'd never do anything like that, and, anyway, Galen had had them—he remembered— well after Eugene had died. Paging through, he saw, to his relief, that he had written bits and pieces (transferred over from scraps of paper in junior high) even while he had been staying with Eugene in Seattle, so even the 1950s weren't lost. But who—going back to his original question—would have tried to steal his life away by bringing these books clear over here?

He straightened his back.

"Dad," Jacob said, "did anyone ever call you a faggot before?"

"Yes," Galen answered.

"And what happened?"

"I looked to Uncle Eugene," he answered, pointing around the room. "He didn't make any apologies."

"So he didn't try to buy anyone off?"

"No," Galen replied with uncertainty.

He stood there, thinking, while Jacob ran off.

"Dad, I found a computer!" It wasn't long before the shout came from another room. And inside the den, Galen came upon Jacob, who in turning on the machine, was being met with a collage of pictures, even though computers from three years ago weren't supposed to be able to do that. "It must be some kind of Macintosh. Do you think Eugene would mind if I had a look?"

Galen almost answered, "Why don't you ask him?"—Eugene's presence was so strong. He felt he was aware of things in the attic now. Instead he said, "Looks like you're already looking. No, I don't think he'd mind. In fact, let me do a search for the will after I've gone upstairs."

"Good." Jacob's cheeks were already red with excitement.

With Jacob standing staring at the screen, Galen moved on up toward the attic stairs, as if following some signal. At the top of the landing, a small candle-flame-type light dimly disclosed Eugene's second library, which Galen already knew about. But he was surprised, however, to find a second desk. Why a second one? Clearly because, given its position, it was a refuge where a man as tall as Eugene could sit beneath the pitched roof without worry about bumping his head.

Galen, having seated himself in Eugene's place, suddenly had a slender volume of verse, *Pluto's Bounty* (Spenser and Company Publishers, Second Edition) catch his eye. It was in a dusty dust jacket which said it was the winner of the Jaspar Prize. It was by his mother.

There was an inscription. "To my dearest brother Eugene, with love from Christabel." A lifetime seemed to separate them, all of them, from that handwriting. He could scarcely visualize what it might have been like, back then in '46, when Christabel could have said such a loving thing to his uncle. Harder, even, to visualize Christabel writing a volume of verse—volumes, in fact, according to the blurb on the dust jacket and the clipping inside. And yet Galen could vaguely remember back to Seattle, when his uncle had been working for a can label company. One afternoon, after Galen had brought some of his own poems home from school, Eugene mentioned something about poetry running through the family's veins, sometimes in Christabel's and certainly the poet Vondel's, who was their direct ancestor. Galen had thought it odd at the time, but he hadn't pursued it. He knew she was artistic but not like this!

Armed now with the book, Galen was about to turn out the light and go back downstairs, when he saw a binder, marked with gilt lettering, *The World's Fair, 1939: A Memoir*, and paging through, he learned that his uncle had been hired on as a still photographer for the Exhibition, and for the movie, *Charlie Chan at Treasure Island*. Therefore the gallery downstairs. It was a sketchbook, full of just that—sketches—and tentative stills and commentary. Some of the photographs were hung on the walls.

From the sound of things, Jacob had seen something on the computer. As Galen came back down and entered the room, Jacob pointed to the screen, and Galen used the mouse. There a little folder led to another folder, to another, to another, like a sandalwood box in an Asian novelty store. This was Galen's Gift Shop.

Just then, a Victorian rosebud, an emblem over in the corner of the screen began to unfold before their eyes—it was opening into a magnificent yellow.

"Are you doing that?" Jacob asked.

"Yes," Galen answered. "This I didn't plan on,"

"You mean the flower?" Jacob asked.

"I mean all of it," Galen answered. "Why don't we print out both pages before we go back over."

This Jacob could do.

But before they could talk further, they came upon a third page which said, "Galen, please see to it that the Estate goes to AIDS House, as well as the Gay People's Alliance. The rest I leave to you to do as you see fit. By the Estate, I mean the house and property and furniture. Everything else, I would like you to be executor over. This statement cancels out all other wills. You will find a copy of this in the back of your Almanac. I've talked with your father about this."

He did find it—there it was. He had left the Almanac on the desk.

"What does it say?" Jacob asked, looking up at him.

"He wants his legacy—do you know what I mean by legacy?"

"No, not exactly," Jacob answered reluctantly.

"It means that what he's left behind, his gifts, he wants them to help gay people."

"Like you meant when you said he saved you from bullies?"

"Yes," Galen answered, feeling the presence of Eugene's ghost even more, "yes, yes."

◆◆◆

"Well, that," Ophelia said at dinner, "is that."

They were sitting in the family dining room. Everyone seemed, in fact, to be in a kind of post-Valentine's Day depression.

Galen was tired out by hours of trying to track down his daughter. He still couldn't come up with her number. He couldn't reach Yvonne, Teresa's mother, either. He had written constantly to Teresa in prison with no reply.

Christabel had hold of Eugene's note. "That is certainly *not* that. There's not an ounce of legality in this. You know, Galen, it will not hold up in court."

"I don't know that," he said. He was puzzling out his mother's face. The difference between the way she looked now and the way she did in her photo on her Jaspar Prize jacket. Not the age but the facial expression. Even so, certainly she could understand how he felt now.

"With your experience in the courts? You ought to know legalese backwards and forwards by now. This so-called note"—she held it between thumb and forefinger—"could have been written by anybody. There's no date, no signature."

"Then who put it there?" Jacob asked.

"How would I know?" Christabel asked. She stared straight in front of her, not at anybody at all. Piercing eyes. Blue.

"Well, Eugene's intention is clear. He wants his mansion to go to the gay community," Galen said. There was much up with him. Perhaps the barrier in trying to call Teresa was the start. He felt shame coming up, as if Christabel's obstructionist approach all along was something he was responsible for. Why should she have a gay son and a gay brother? He could have made things easier for her by being different, but he wasn't going to be different from who he was, not this time. His drinking all along had been pushing him into that bind.

Gregory came in, uninvited. From some point down the hall, he obviously had been listening.

"We need to raze that mansion to allow for parking," Christabel said. "The overflow lot we've always used before has been bought by an opportunist." She was slicing pound cake and handing it around. "We're in crisis."

"Every car," Ophelia said, despite what she had said earlier, "has to be gone to and gotten when the customer wants it."

"I don't mind valeting the cars," Gregory said, still standing. "And I know directly that giving the house away was Eugene's intention. He told me so. It was kind of an amends."

"Amends?" Ophelia asked. "What did Uncle Eugene ever do that was wrong?"

Galen had been so surprised by his father speaking up, he was silent. He assumed the same thing had happened to everybody else. But his mother was once again running away with the conversation. She didn't seem to understand that he meant to be in this argument, that he wasn't on the sidelines, and he felt fortified by his visit to the mansion. He had been in a luminous underworld, thank you.

"It's not for me to tell you that," Gregory answered. "I only know that Eugene wanted Galen to handle things and that AIDS house and the gay people were supposed to get the mansion."

"Eugene never was gay," Christabel said. Her blue eyes were turning on Galen.

"Wait a minute, wait a minute," Galen hastened to say. "If there is ever anything I know for sure, it's that. That's why his Memorial was such a sham."

Silence. Christabel was primping her silver hair, queen of this table. This room was an ornate one just in back of hotel's restaurant, perfect for private dining, with glittery golden enameling above, and tapers lit, and with the sound of the harp for the general clientele coming through the parted door. It could have had a sign hanging, "Christabel's Chamber."

Tamara, head of the hotel waitress staff, came in to clear. "I'm just so happy to see you back, Sir," she said to Galen in her Old World way. In fact, she was from the Old World. "I knew, reading the newspaper, they had done you an evil deed."

"Thank you, Tamara," Galen said. "I missed you."

She blushed, old as she was. "Thank you very much, Sir." She now stacked the dishes from the meal, which had been a wonderful prime rib.

"Mother, I can't tell you how spectacular everything was. This was the perfect welcome home," Galen said, trying to soften her up. "You knew prime rib and baked potatoes were my favorite." However, he wasn't going to relent. "You know, I just need to say, now that I've been to Eugene's mansion again, if I had been sober, if I hadn't been a drunk, I would have not only seen to the house two years ago, but would have given Eugene a proper Memorial Service. As it was, everything got glossed over."

"If you're going to be obstinate," she said, her blue eyes still rattling him, "I suppose there's nothing I can do. But answer me just one thing."

"Of course," he replied.

"What was wrong with Eugene's Memorial service?"

"Yes, I would like to know, too," Ophelia said, "because I supplied the flowers. I remember—they were carnations and roses."

"And I paid for them," Christabel said. "Paid for the whole program, as a matter of fact."

"There was not one word spoken about him being gay," Galen said. He pointed up.

"Because he wasn't gay," Christabel insisted again. She started clearing the table with Tamara. The Dutch teapot with the predictably blue pattern shook in her hands.

"And I tell you he was," Galen answered. "I grew up with him. I should know."

Hearing the raised voices, Jacob was beginning to cry. "How could he have protected Dad, if he wasn't?"

"I simply won't sit here and listen to this," Christabel said, ignoring her grandson. "First the Jaspar Prize dug up by the reporters and now this."

"Mother," Ophelia said. "You're going to spoil the dessert. Your delightful parfaits."

"Oh those," Christabel said. "Been on the menu for years." She shook her head over her tray of dirty dishes.

"How many times have I thought about those parfaits in prison," Galen said, still trying to sweeten her up. "Have waited for this moment when I could have one again."

Christabel looked skyward now, too. "Here we are talking about parfaits when our whole lives are at stake?"

"We found other treasure, Mother," Galen said, now that he had cleared the way. "My diaries. Do you know by the way how they got over there?"

"Not at all," she answered. "Impossible."

"Well, there they were." He couldn't resist, now, giving her a little nudge. "And then there was your book."

"Which book?" she asked. She was actually meeting his eyes.

"*Pluto's Bounty*," he answered.

She blanched a little. The title was like another clock striking through the house. In fact, the toll soon followed.

"From what I can see," Galen went on, "they look like beautiful poems—that one about orbiting around, as though satellite to another planet—"

"Enough of that, please," she said.

"And congratulations on the Jaspar Prize. I thought the reporters were wrong about that one," he added. "But the book exists."

"Mother," Ophelia said, her color heightening, "this calls for an all-rose occasion, now that you're admitting it. We must," she went on, standing up, "start talking about another celebration, a rediscovery party. One that my dear husband can come to."

"Keep your goddamn roses away from me," Christabel answered. "I don't want to be praised for something that happened forty-four years ago."

"Are they love poems?" Ophelia asked. "I'd love to see them."

"Some of them were addressed to me," Gregory told them. "I was still making some major discoveries about Pluto then." He was actually standing up through this reference to the past. Galen wanted to go over and pound him on the back.

"What major discoveries, Dad?" Ophelia asked. "I forget. I keep thinking you're just our bellman." She was still making notes in her datebook. It also had hearts on it.

"He has been just our bellman," Christabel insisted. "And now she's calling him 'Dad.'"

"That book may be worth a lot," Jacob said, getting wide-eyed again. "I can try to find out on my computer."

Gregory sat down at an empty seat at the table. "I found that there were some really odd objects going around old Pluto, which explained the deflection of motion."

"Could we please not have any more of this?" Christabel asked. And quite surprisingly, she wiped her eyes.

"Are you all right?" Ophelia asked. "I told you it was wrong to help carry all those flowers up to Galen's room last night. With your hay fever, it's madness. May I get you something?"

But Christabel completely ignored her as well. "Galen," she said, "you have to see that the whole Estate falls to me. I could have leveled that whole place to the ground if I had wanted to while you were gone. But out of deference to you and your delicate situation, I waited until you got out—"

"And I appreciate that," Galen told her. "But"—he put his hand up—"we have new instructions now. Eugene was gay, whether you think so or not. And"—he was ready to take command, take charge, especially now that Jacob was watching him—"you should not hide your light under a bushel any more than we should hide Uncle Eugene's. Gifts! Gifts!"

"Not gifts," she said. "You're just dredging up the past. Some thanks I get for waiting for you."

"That's what executors are supposed to do," Galen said. "Dredge up the past. "This is my dig"—he was looking at his son — "and I'm staking our claim."

"But you've got to understand," Christabel answered, "you're not his executor, I am. It's not your claim."

"We'll see about that," Galen said. "I'll go see Milton Williams, if necessary." He was going to make this a point of honor.

"There is no time for that," Christabel said. She was still wiping her eyes. "No time. The landscaping that we've paid you or your company to do has gone past ruin. We're wearing your own father out"—already she herself was slipping back to that name—"with all that work, I don't want you to spend time in Milton Williams' chambers. You have enough work for you as it is."

"I can handle any of that landscape work," Gregory said. "You know that, with Galen away for eighteen months."

"And possibly you don't know, Mother," Galen said, "the kind of energy it's possible to build up in prison. Do you have any idea how much you can store up while you're just sitting, staring at a few Dutch postcards? You've got enough energy to light up the whole city of New York."

"And what about me," Gregory put in. "Building up all that energy in that little room I have?"

Galen smiled over at him. His reach across Jacob was long enough to touch his father's hand.

"Rembrandt's *The Bridge*, is that not right, Galen?" Ophelia asked. "And *St. Peter's Denial?*" That's right, she had been up to his room, where he had transferred the postcards.

"Right," he answered.

"Magnificent. Inspirational," Ophelia said. "The tip of Western Civilization. Far greater than anything van Gogh ever did, poor dear."

"As I was saying," Galen went on, "I've got plenty of energy—enough for the landscaping, enough for Mr. Milton Williams of Williams, Smith, Johnson, and Randolph, enough for the Estate, and enough for Jacob and hopefully, Teresa. I mean to get back to it." He couldn't resist the tone and defying Christabel as though he were fifteen years old.

"Just don't dredge too far," Christabel said, blowing her nose. And was still crying. "You'll regret it."

Galen felt the pang. "Mother, I am sorry if I brought up something painful in the poetry. I won't mention *Pluto's Bounty* again if you don't want me to. But I am personally proud to have a mother who had such a brilliant literary career. Share the achievement."

"None of you have any idea what it's like to hear about your achievements when you haven't got it anymore."

"Oh yeah?" Gregory asked, then left, because he heard the bell, all the way out here.

◆◆◆

But what? What was it? There had been a light in the room.

And Galen, half-awake, was aware of a glow across the hotel courtyard. A guest had snapped a shade up suddenly. Darkness again. But then there was another light, coming from the Estate.

The Estate. Wait a minute, Galen heard himself say to himself in the hallway of sleep. The Estate—who could be in the Estate now? But as though a snooze button had been pushed, Galen, even with his ears perked up, took a little break and slept again. After he awoke with a start (how much later?), he reached the window just in time to see a light go out in the attic of his uncle's house.

Wait a minute, he thought, dropping into bed. Did I see that? Just then, a car went past on Holland Street, filling the room with partial light, the way the night traffic always did. Ah, hell's bells. And the clock downstairs was chiming—one, two, three, four. Four a.m. And Galen could not be sure if the light in the attic had been a dream or not. The night traffic or not. And it could have come on at the stroke of midnight at the witching hour, with the whole of the ghost of Eugene there, writing away on his new Baum-inspired book in the attic. And then gone out at 1 a.m., when Galen had finally roused himself. Or at 4 a.m., just a few seconds ago. What in the world is time when you're still asleep anyway?

The next morning there was a decided iciness to the room. The temperature had dropped dramatically during the night. Galen hurried into his clothes, got Jacob out of bed and ready for school.

"Remember," he said, "if those bullies give you any trouble—have Mrs. Daniels call me."

"Yes," Jacob said. Galen helped him on with his winter coat, taken from the closet. Handed him his lunchbox with the Teenage Mutant Ninja Turtles on the front.

In getting into his truck after breakfast and turning the key, he was reminded again (as he had been yesterday) that the motor was on its last legs, even though someone had kept it running, and he'd better start ransacking his memory for his old bicycle—ransack, even more, for that old rusty air pump, a holdover from the Seattle days and even Amsterdam, when he and Eugene had ridden throughout the cities together. Except this time it wasn't all that sweet and sentimental because he'd be hunting the old thing up because he was flat on his ass until some money came through. Waiting for the lawsuit to advance was like waiting for a win at Las Vegas or from Publisher's Clearing House.

The truck's engine turned over, and the whole thing advanced. Eventually he parked it in the downtown lot, right by the veiled lady statue near the town hall. With the weather in mid-valley Oregon being generally mild and the laws not so strict, Carleton Park had become a haven for the transient, the destitute. And here, in the lady's archway, people stayed warm, even overnight. Ironic, perhaps, that just one block down, was the town's major legal office building. The veiled lady was a refuge for all the cast-off people— not from the town, but from other places that would not have them—New York, California, and, of course, sister city Mayfair, across the river. As Galen approached it, the sanctuary's sunny shadow, the civic flowerpots, suspended from the lamp posts, seemed like the scales of Libra, for they occurred in doubles (crocuses all, a little frosty) on either side.

Milton Williams was his father's age and had a Rembrandt in his office (*Night Watch*) and spoke very British. He, as a matter of fact, looked like one of the aging self-portraits of Rembrandt himself. But he was British. He had spent many years in the Midlands before moving to America. He was extraordinarily urbane for an Oregon lawyer, and liked to joke before getting to the point, which usually nailed you upside down when it finally came. No surprise he was a star bridge player.

After hearing about the will and seeing the paper from the back of Eugene's Almanac, Milton Williams said nothing to the point for a while. He just went on and on about Galen's being Dutch, about Dam Square, Amsterdam, and then of Coventry Cathedral in England. And having been there during the bombing.

"Mighty disorienting that," he said at last. "Sort of like where you are right now with your uncle's will. Fact is, you haven't a leg to stand on. The roof has fallen in. Fallen in. Unless you have a document signed by three witnesses, there's nothing there that will hold up in court."

"Then," Galen began but stopped speaking and looked across at the painting. It was a mighty big reproduction of the *The Night Watch*. It was one of his uncle's favorites. "Then what do you suggest I do?"

"Reason with your mother. She's vulnerable right now. Especially about your daughter and that trust fund." Like Christabel last night, he was avoiding eye contact. He had his arms folded.

"My daughter? Trust fund?" Galen felt hit sideways.

"Yes, of course, she said she'd told you about the trust fund she'd set up for Teresa's education? While you were in prison, but, as I remember, even before. And her investments, of course, fell apart. All her ships miscarried.

She was our poor Merchant of Venice." He was still speaking into air, as though telling a story over the radio.

"Teresa is my responsibility," Galen said defensively. He was using his hands to show precision. "I'll take care of any college funds going her way myself. So don't worry about the ships miscarrying."

"That sounds fine, but you'll have to locate resources outside of Eugene's estate for that. Get a job better than the one you had before you went into prison. And by the way, welcome back to the living. I have to congratulate my colleagues for getting you out of that one." He was actually standing up and reaching across his desk to pat Galen on the shoulder.

At this moment, Milton reminded Galen a little of a white, friendly spider—or the old hermit crab in the play-and-read *Bozo Under the Sea*.

"It wasn't just your colleagues," Galen said. defensively. "It was mainly my family. Ophelia and Jacob and Andrew in particular."

"Good work, all. And so my advice is, sweet-talk your mother a little. Ask her for a little extra something for Teresa, since her other venture fell through. And a little money for yourself and AIDS House and the Gay People's Rehabilitation Group or whatever they call themselves. It's not at all as complicated or as contentious as it has to be, or most Oregonians might make it. I've seen whole families split up over something like this. Nip it in the bud." He settled back in his chair, like an orator who has just finished.

"But I don't just want a little money for AIDS House and the Gay People's Alliance," Galen said, standing up. He pointed to the note on Williams' desk. "Uncle wanted the whole house to go to them."

Williams laughed. "That's not possible. Unless, of course your mother agrees to it."

Galen threw up his hands. "How will she ever? She keeps saying Eugene was straight when really he was gay. There wasn't a true word spoken about him at his own memorial service."

"What do you mean?" Williams said again. "There were many words."

"But not about him," Galen told him. "Only what people thought. And being gay wasn't one of them."

"Just from where I sit," Williams replied, "it sounds like you've got a huge score to settle. I'd lay off in that direction." And started to sound American again. "Just be tactful with your mother. Sweeten her up."

Score? Maybe.

"You don't have to beg," Williams went on, after some consideration. "Just be reasonable. Just point out that your uncle was a good man. Just not completely tidy. If he'd consulted the law books or at least me, this wouldn't have happened. By the way, aren't you due for some excellent money soon?"

"Yes. Possibly," Galen answered. But he was making his voice tentative.

"A suit for your time in prison? Pain and suffering?" Williams asked.

"Yes for three-quarters of a million, on the face of it," Galen said. "If it had gone to federal court, it would have been for ten million. But they're probably going to settle outside."

"Excellent! Excellent! You'll get at least $250,000," Williams concluded.

"Who knows," Galen said, getting up and shaking hands in the glow of *The Night Watch*. "It may be for the best somehow. Everything else has."

Williams looked at him sideways. "Even prison?"

"Yes, I think so," Galen answered.

Double on the handshake. Back to British. "How intriguing."

Well, no time like the present. Christabel would be in her Sorceress Seamstress shop in the glorious hotel, and now that the early morning, just forenoon, was warming up and cooperating again, he'd just go see her and say that more unpaid nights in her house were impossible. Little did he know, until now (and his thoughts lasted him all the way back to Holland Avenue), that he was so afraid of becoming like Gregory, at least Gregory before his revitalization yesterday, that he felt he must do something. He could start by saying, "Look, Mother. This is how it is."

"Look, Mother," he actually said, arriving at last at the hotel. "This is how it is."

What he was about to say, of course, was going to be influenced by the striking of the clocks, and the constant sightings, through the glassed entrance, of his father, carrying luggage up and down. Check-out hour was imminent.

But his mother was in a different frame of mind than he had expected. She was sitting very contentedly, sewing in a blue upholstered armchair (French provincial), looking very pleased and serene, while the shop girls took care of all the customers, save himself. On the table beside her was a copy of *Pluto's Bounty*. The fabric she was working on (one stroke and then another) was the same color as her hair, and she seemed to form a single piece with the whole shop.

"Yes, then, let's hear," she said.

He explained that he must pay for his room-and-board (it was important to him) and also for Jacob's, that he would work on setting up a trust fund for Teresa, but in exchange, he must, simply, start asking for wages for any landscaping he did for the New Amsterdam—from here on out. And he was going to start looking for his own place.

"That sounds quite reasonable," she said—and she put a slight pause between "quite" and "reasonable," as if "quite" were the proper response to everything. It was in that missed beat that Galen remembered that this change in her should not at all be surprising—that she was always blissful when she was in her Sorceress Seamstress shop. Years ago, as a teenager, whenever he wanted to get something out of her, he would wait until she was here, working in the place which was the landing spot for the hotel's laundry and mending needs. Plus people from off the street could come in. And now he felt aware that the strokes of the needle must be the same as (or only a slight modification of) the strokes of the pen that had gone into *Pluto's Bounty*. That sweater (or whatever) was Jaspar Prize material. So to speak. And she must have been rereading her own work recently.

Feeling like a winner and just a little more grown-up, Galen then ventured to say, "And one other thing—"

"Yes?" She was regarding him.

"Please reconsider letting me be executor to Eugene's estate. And determine who gets what. You're right about your legal rights. In court, I haven't a leg to stand on. But the family, the fact of the matter is, knows perfectly well that he ultimately wanted me to look after him, living and dead." He knew he was using his supplicant look.

"I'll have to think about it," she said, with gold now going all through the shop—just as it had gone through the courtyard in Amsterdam. In Galen's mind's eye, the statue turned. "As they say in the plays, 'I'll bethink me.' And I'll say here and now, don't get your hopes up."

And it struck him, quite suddenly, that this was a poet he was looking at and that at some point, a long time ago, she had been moved to write of—

He remembered one of her poems. Not just the part about the planets and the satellites.

She had written of the god Pluto. Pluto as the patron saint of Amsterdam. And she had written about earth's riches and of a little landscaped courtyard. Maybe the very one he had taken refuge in, with the goddess statue. How all grew and unfolded under Pluto's shadow, which was, after all, not the shadow of death, but the shadow of Nature (transformed into She). And as he stood there and she looked back musingly, but with resistance, sewing slowly, she seemed to convey that, accept that. Through the window, his father was busy at his errands, carrying luggage across the courtyard, and Galen felt at equidistance from them, his father's hurrying, relentless, insect-like activity, and his mother's reflective repose.

"Well, at least that's settled," he said, and she nodded, and took up the next garment to be mended, looked over it at least, and then assigned it on. Behind her, the shop was very much alive with cloth and colors, spools of thread, and other, exquisite sought-after seamstresses moving about (it was the only such place in town, and Carleton Park believed in mending things, not throwing them away), and amidst all this hubbub, there was the copy of her book. It seemed to form a part of the gravitational pull.

"Yes," she replied at last. "It seems that some things will have to stay the way they are until I make up my mind." She waved him on, and he went out the door, back into the lobby, which was full of its own business, too—customers weaving in and out of a heavily carpeted place of expensive furniture and huge potted plants. It was as though the season of spring were waking everyone up, and he, feeling very vulnerable, was one of the targets.

Going into the gift shop, Galen got a newspaper. In the classifieds, there was a small rental house available not a block from the hotel. He couldn't buy anything just now, but at least this could be a start. The way things were, he couldn't stay at his mother's. He needed to be in a position of negotiation.

He left his truck off to be repaired—well, overhauled. Finally, he was getting into motion.

◆◆◆

He awoke from a nap, remembering the sonnet of Pieter Corneliszoon Hooft on time:

> *O speeding greybeard, who on swift wings haste your flight*
> *Still cutting through thin air, and never striking sail,*
> *Leave everyone behind, travel before the gale—*

In prison, Galen had most often thought of Amsterdam, the treasure house containing all the models for this hotel and this very room. Not this place, where so many things went wrong. The original Vondel Hotel just across from Amsterdam's Central Station was a locale very clear in Galen's mind's eye. He could enter the revolving door, cross under the stained-glass dome, and rest in the golden sitting room, taking in corridors and porticoes which went back three centuries, when it was an original *huis*. He and his uncle had gone to the hotel and researched its history—their family origins had given the momentum—and their sustained idyll and adventure, from Seattle to Amsterdam, had even included visits to the van Gogh exhibition, as well as to Rijkmuseum. The courtyard of that museum, now he remembered more clearly, graced the goddess who held the stone mirror above the maze of hedges, whose shadows made such even lines in the full sun. That's where he liked best to be when he imagined himself as golden dust, tracing out those long genealogical lines which took them back to Vondel himself. Galen could still sense the flickering's of that poet's light in Eugene's own writing. And he was reminded of Eugene's papers and the original old Vondel hotel every time he came here.

The phone rang. It was his daughter, Teresa.

"How would you be for Easter?" she asked.

"I'd like that," he said. "I have been trying and trying to reach you."

"I didn't want to be reached—not by you," she answered.

"Oh?"

"I've been to a counselor," she went on, "who's told me that I need to keep my distance—if my life was to improve."

"Has your life improved?" he asked.

"Not much," she answered flatly.

He had given a whole day of trying to reach this young woman, who was still talking about having nothing to do with him.

"Seems that it would, since you never came to see me in prison," he said with anger. "A whole year and a half—that's a long time to have a chance to improve."

He had had plans of speaking to her differently.

"No, I didn't come," she said defensively. "And I wouldn't have if I had to do it all over again."

"It's not going to happen all over again," Galen answered. "I was exonerated of all charges."

"I heard that. I read it in the papers," she told him. "My sorority sisters showed them to me."

It was obvious neither of them knew what else to say, but he kept grasping at that original sense of shame, that he had not been the father he had meant himself to be and that in some ways, she was right.

Galen tried again. "Could we meet, though," he said, "like you started out to say? I could drive up."

"You'd be willing to drive up?" she asked.

"Yes." Yes, yes, he would.

"You've forgotten before," she answered.

"I know, but this time I will remember," he said.

"How do I know you will?" she asked.

"Because this time I'm sober," he answered.

It came out, inevitably, that sobriety was now on his side. When he had been arguing with Christabel over the Estate, he had actually felt sobriety working against him, a little. It was like lifting the lid to a pot of steam and finding that he had been angry all along about that fucking lying memorial. But now he could say, straight, "I'll be there."

"Sober? You?" his daughter asked.

"Yes, didn't your mother tell you?" he asked back.

"No—it's hard to imagine," she said frankly.

"I know. But I will be there. I'll show." And he wanted to do this—he wanted to promise.

She agreed to Easter Sunday with some reluctance, even though originally it had been her idea in the first place. She gave him some odd directions about a spot just outside Forest Glade. Near a cemetery. Not at her sorority house. That was out of the question. He picked up from her tone that she was embarrassed. Ashamed, maybe. That she was trying to build a normal life for herself, too. As though she had had normal parents, a traditional upbringing. Therefore Easter, their Easter, was to be on her terms—on the sidelines.

"Two o'clock, then," he said, writing down the instructions about how to get there. Forest Glade was old hat to him—he'd even worked there—but this small, designated corner was unfamiliar. Her university was fifty miles to the north.

Hanging up the phone, he cried some, and when he looked up, he saw Jacob at the door, crying too.

"I thought we were going to have Easter together," Jacob said. Obviously, he had been listening in.

"Remember," Galen said, hugging him (if only it were this easy with Teresa!), "remember it'll be just a few hours."

"Yes, but then when you didn't hear from her, I thought"—Jacob wiped away some of his tears.

"I tell you what," Galen said. "You know there will be a lot of things going on here for Easter anyway. I'll be back by nine p.m. from Forest Glade, and we'll celebrate then."

"Promise?" That again.

"Absolutely," he answered. "I'll let you stay up. But only this once."

"You've forgotten before." Jacob still looked sheepish.

"But not this time," he said, with eyebrows raised.

And they shook on it.

Within an hour, he was working out in the hotel courtyard. Hands upon a shovel (turning the soil). Hands upon the pruning shears. Maybe this would sweeten his mother up, even if he did ask to be paid. Now the forsythia was bending to his hand, and as he shaped the umbrellas of boughs, they, budded and some beginning to bloom, became like chandeliers of gold. Just to have movement, now, these days out of prison, beyond bars, beyond scrutiny, a private moment again, like yesterday. To have a horizon. The dirt flew—up came the tufts of weeds from around the hyacinths. His father had only cleared away a bit. He could see the promises of pink, of blue, of white, and even a hint of perfume, as in, magnified, his St. Valentine's chamber. He was getting the hotel courtyard into shape. One sighting of a few bulbs in the soil took him in flight back to Holland, and the Haarlem tulip fields—an acreage of red, then yellow, and then motley stripe, in the springtime, when, as a child, he wanted to take a roll right on through. Then, now, down came the rusted stalks of hollyhocks, giving elbow room to the rose bushes, some of which were breaking out with spark-like points of red. A commotion in the sky would bring him to turn to the reflected cloud image in the huge plate glass window of the Estate across the street, then the cloud would be gone, leaving only what looked like a mammoth crack. But one more turmoil of wind, and it was clear—it was only the reflection of a branch, itself promising to bud. And here Teresa was, threatening to put him off again. Their finally getting together would never have happened, if it hadn't been for him. I'm the one who did the laundry when she was a baby. I washed and dried thousands of diapers. I'm the one who remembers how hot the snaps of her terries were when I took them out of the dryer. I'm the one who taught her how to swim; taught her how to drive. I'm the one who read *The Saturdays* to her at night—along with Eugene's first published storybook and *A Child's History of the World*. I'm the one who told her first about Leonardo da Vinci and how his disciples would quarrel just to paint a hand on his frescoes. I told her about Papageno in *The Magic Flute*. I'm entitled to a hearing because I'm her father!

In one corner he saw his father, smiling, watching, lifting his hand. "Thank you," his father called. And from within the hotel, Galen could hear the clock chime eleven. "This helps a lot. I can't do it all by myself anymore, even though I say I can."

Galen leaned on his shovel, smiled back—tried to show he was at leisure, but his father only disappeared back into the massive building before the chime was over.

Instinctively, Galen had been counting. And he surveyed his work.

"Mr. Melville?"

"Yes," Galen answered.

And he saw there an elfin man, one he recognized from the days of the trial. Somehow, too, he remembered him being in drag at one time. Yes—a cross-dressing elf? In any case, he knew he had seen him before. Now the man was wearing a white dress shirt and a paisley vest, which accented his puff of prematurely white hair.

"I'm Patrick of the *Daily*. I just heard you got out of prison." The short man looked at him closely, as if to puzzle him out.

"Yes, that's right." Galen put down his shovel.

"Your family told us you were refusing to speak to reporters, but I thought I'd try anyway," the man said.

"I'm not refusing to speak to reporters. When did they tell you that?" Galen asked.

"Yesterday."

"Well, they can learn to speak for themselves," Galen answered.

The man gestured. "Everyone's curious. And so let me ask—just what plans do you have for the future?"

"I expect Mayfair to pay damages," Galen said. "Several witnesses have come back to testify they were coerced by the police to say I was the one they saw go into the Midnight Mart. I don't hold any grudges, but I also think justice ought to be served. We were going to go to federal court."

"To say the least," Patrick answered. "Pardon my saying so—but I think you got screwed." He had written a few things down on a little Rainbow pad—pink. He did, in fact, have red dwarf's cheeks. The pink camellia bushes were in back of him, in bloom. Anyway, it seemed as though he had come today just to hear his own opinion rather than ask Galen his.

"Hey," Galen said, "I think I know you from somewhere."

"Yes, I'm from the Royal Court," Patrick said.

"The Royal Court?" Galen asked.

"Yes. You probably have seen me, just not dressed the way I am now. And by the way, the Royal Court is going to see that justice is done on your behalf, too." Patrick pointed a finger.

"Really?" Galen asked.

"Yes," Patrick said, "a demonstration of sorts. Drag Queen Daws is archdeacon of the First Episcopal Church, so it's about time he got embarrassed. You know that every Sunday afternoon after service, he's out there cavorting with his boyfriends. Meanwhile he pushes his law cases against us in court."

"That Daws. D.A. Daws. Boy, did he go after me. What are you going to do?" Galen asked, eyebrows up.

"One of these Sundays, the drag brothers and sisters are going to stage a sit-in in the front pew. Daws's brother is the minister, and he's archdeacon. We'll be embarrassing the whole family. We won't say a word, but we may have a film crew. Everyone will get the verified rumor that D.A. Daws is one of us."

"Well, if the justice is on my account," Galen answered, "I'm much obliged."

Patrick became all business again. "Well, somewhat. Anything else you want to add?"

"Only that—until the suit is settled, I'm glad to be restored to my normal life," Galen said.

"You mean to your family here?" Patrick asked.

"Yes. And to my son and daughter." But Galen felt nervous even referring to Teresa.

"And what plans have been made on the Estate?" Patrick added. "It's been understood by the community that Mr. Eugene intended it to go to AIDS House and to a prospective community center for us queers."

So Uncle Eugene had let it be known to others. At least underground.

"From what I can gather from my family," Galen said, "his papers have yet to be completely sorted through, so we can't be clear." He waited. He wondered if he should add something, so Christabel would feel cornered. Would recognize that word had gotten around about Eugene's intentions. It was a calculated risk Galen was suddenly willing to take. "Yes," he resumed, "a letter arrived—three years after my uncle died. And then we found a will as a result."

"From your uncle?" Patrick's impish face was all questions.

"Yes."

"Eureka! What conclusions can you draw from this letter from the dead?" Patrick asked.

"Only that I think the Estate should go to gay people, too," Galen answered, going for broke.

"So it isn't clear, after all, that the Estate goes squarely to the family?" Patrick said, dazzled.

"Not at all," Galen said, and said so with some heat.

"Well I am," Patrick said, holding out a pink hand, "much obliged to you. I had written to you anyway and got no reply, so I'm certainly glad I decided just to drop in."

"I've hardly had time to open my mail," Galen smiled. "Next thing I've got to do is the bills."

"Of course, of course, of course, but here's my card. Once you get through your uncle's relics, do let me know of any more late-breaking news. As it is, this is front-page stuff already." The man seemed to have a fire inside of him, just lit.

He disappeared very suddenly—as Galen bent to pick up the shovel. It was as though the man had been a belated valentine, falling from heaven and was returning back up, with the wind machine running in reverse. Galen just stood there like the post-prison Rip Van Winkle he still thought he was, with only the camellias and forsythia as company. His spilling the beans would have repercussions.

Standing there in the courtyard, looking out at the starts of hyacinths and flowering quince, he held Patrick's card and looked at the reflection of the tree, like a crack in the window.

◆◆◆

The next morning—in fact, on moving day out of his family's house—Christabel was just plain not speaking to him. For once, Galen wished that Ophelia and Andrew shared breakfast and dinner at the family homestead instead of just dinner, since they (he realized now) provided such shelter and balance. It was just cereal this morning, and Jacob was about to leave for school.

"What's wrong?" Galen asked at last.

Christabel gave him a glance. She shoved a copy of *The Carleton Park Daily* his way.

"Homeward-returning citizen gets voice from the grave," the front-page article read. It had been a while in arriving. Patrick had said it was headline material—and it hadn't gotten that limelight—but still, here the story was, still, and on the first page.

Galen glanced through. The whole article was very true to the interview. They had used an old picture from the trial. Galen, pre-recovery. And to Galen's thinking, his look was light-years away from what the mirror showed now. Bearded, shaggy, back then, eyes at half-mast. Other than that, the story offered nothing to be embarrassed about.

"So?" Galen asked, just as Jacob had come in.

"Hey, Dad, cool," Jacob said, looking over his shoulder.

Christabel still stood in silence.

"Don't you understand," Christabel said, "this means AIDS House and the whole gay and lesbian community will be knocking at our door any minute? Feeling they deserve the Estate?"

"What else could I have told Patrick?" Galen asked, trying for a smile.

"Anything but this," his mother said, squaring off her words.

"Milton Williams told me to be tactful," Galen said. "And I can't be. Eugene's the one who put me in a Superman suit years ago. Don't you remember?"

"Superman suit? What Superman suit?" Christabel asked.

"The one I wore when we protested—1970. One of the major protests—"

"No," Christabel said, sighing, cutting him off. "Of course I don't remember anything of the kind. And as long as you're in this house, you're not entitled to talk about your uncle that way."

At that moment, Gregory came to the door, just as Jacob went out, reluctantly, for school. Andrew followed Gregory, sweating. His wife Ophelia was nowhere to be seen. It was unseasonably warm out.

"I just saw the U-Haul," Gregory said, coming in. "I just had to take time off to come in and say to Galen, don't move. I hope it's not too late."

"Dad, I told you this was on the horizon," Galen answered. "If it wasn't going to be this rental, it would be something else."

"This is just the end of me," Gregory said.

"Leaving?" Christabel asked. "What do you mean leaving?" She seemed even to regret what she had just said.

Andrew went up and put his muscular arm around Gregory. "Hey, Dad, we're just moving Galen and Jacob down the block."

"I know," Gregory answered. "But it's like I can't just look out and see you, Galen. Not just you alone, but both you and Jacob will be gone."

"Why are you leaving?" Christabel asked. "I've never understood that."

"It's time I grew up," Galen said. "I have to get out. It's time I started pulling my own weight."

Through all of this, however, he could tell that Gregory was drunk. It made his own heart into a small wooden figurine. Stunted. Dwarfish. On some theme of childhood. He recognized that wooden feeling instantly.

Andrew, beautiful and muscular, said, of course, "Hey, Greg and Christabel, Ophelia and I will be living just across the street from Galen and Jacob. So you can come over anytime and also check in with Galen and Jacob. We always told you we have an open door."

"I've got a room," Gregory said gloomily. "Already. And I don't like changes."

Galen was standing, now, in the full sun. "Dad, Mom—Andrew and I have to go. We've only got the U-Haul for so long."

"When you didn't show right away," Andrew told him, "I took the key and carried some of the stuff out of your room myself. Just the things that weren't personal. We can start on the mattress now."

"There's nothing personal about that, either," Galen said, laughing. "At least not lately."

"Dad, you can help us if you want to," Andrew said, patting him again. "Or like I said, watch us."

"I will not," Gregory said petulantly. "You're going against everything I ask."

"I'm not going to argue with you about it," Galen answered. "I know I'm going to get a cash settlement from Mayfair, and Jacob needs to have his own place. I'm just a postscript on the second floor here. If possible, this is going to be rent with option to buy."

Christabel was furious. "Postscript!"

It was two o'clock by the time they got upstairs for the big move. The hall clock sounded, and Galen reflected that he would miss it. And the heat bothered him. Still, he felt grateful Andrew had a knack for moving things along in good order. To add to all that, he was a skilled singer and acrobat, and his mechanical acumen had transformed the hotel. A genius in some aspects in making things work. He also ran an antique store, was a fisherman's guide, and had a hand in publishing. He considered himself a loser, but he was the ultimate Renaissance man, a total success, even though he didn't know it.

The bureau with the mirror was the hardest piece to move down the stairs, and, since they didn't detach the mirror, Galen was at first pretty sure everything would go to smash by the time they hit the landing. All views of the old house—now growing warmer—shook in reflection as they took it one step at a time, but somehow everything stayed in balance, under Andrew's direction.

Galen's complete set of diaries (boxed) constituted the final piece that went into the truck. When he checked out his room just to be sure they'd gotten everything, he had the feeling of a traveler who has just looked at his previous stopover—that this resting place would soon be available for some other wayfarer, a place like all the others he had stayed in during his life. Christabel could soon rent this out again. For even in the years with his wife Yvonne, he had known, somehow, while living in the family home with her, that his days were numbered. He would soon be back on the temporary circuit again, if not on the street itself.

So he shut the door on this old life, left the key in the lion drawer.

He swung the screen door and was out. The door whisked behind him. Ahead was the rental, a plain two-bedroom cottage in the modern style, a little skimpy in places because, perhaps, it had been built during the War and materials had been somewhat scarce.

They hadn't been there two minutes when Anton, Andrew's friend, showed up. He was striking and tall, with a very defined physique. He reflected Andrew's well-built ease, and had obviously been asked, at least in part, because of his strength.

Anton gave a hand to getting the furniture off thick and fast, putting his whole sinewy body into it. On the hardwoods of the living room—which had the cathedral ceiling—Galen realized that this hearthside affair was quickly becoming gay. The very prints on the wall said so. What a far cry from his prison cell where the toilet and the bars dictated everything. Through the picture window, the birdbath and statue were a small Rijkmuseum courtyard. There was also a tangle of pink flowering quince, bright as confetti, set in ivy.

Outside, the hot world of Carleton Park was an oasis of lawn and sprinklers, with spring briefly masquerading as summer. Inside, Galen felt that the three of them looked like a sweaty chain gang of brawny men who had just taken off their shirts. It was a hot day, Galen thought, when I finally got into that Superman suit and stepped out into the middle of that San Francisco auditorium. There was no going back, then, either. The look we got from those staid, hypocritical psychiatrists was like the look of a line of frogs on a swamp log in the Ozarks. Low-growling, disgruntled, but ready to hop whenever hopping was necessary to save their little green asses.

The shadows turned darker and cooler in the living room. Anton and Andrew, like two synchronized brothers, even helped take the utensils out of the boxes. They put the beds back together, set up Jacob's computer in the back bedroom. And in the little side nook—too small to house a bed—they were to put some of Eugene's effects, which were still at the mansion and were marked out for Galen in the will.

"I forgot," Galen said, "we'd better get them now."

They all three made a tight, sweaty fit on the front seat of the U-Haul. As they headed along the final block, Galen saw a figure darting behind the window curtains of the Estate. First floor.

"I saw that, too," Anton said.

Galen had brought the truck to a halt.

They jumped out, and headed non-stop toward the shadow, but inside the Estate, it eluded them.

"I've got another idea," Galen said.

He led them down some stairs and into the cellar. Then, grabbing a flashlight from his uncle's worktable, Galen found the door, opening to a subterranean hallway with pictures hanging on the walls, too—of Holland tulip fields, a diagram of the planet Pluto, a photo of the Vondel Hotel on Damrak in Amsterdam. He'd remembered it suddenly.

At the other end, he could see someone retreating, and they ran down the passageway, up some stairs, and smack into the basement of the hotel. They got up into the kitchen just to hear the door bang, and see a scared Tamara, who was just coming in with a heavy tray of dishes and who said they shouldn't be coming in here with all that dust and sweat on them.

"Did you see anybody leave here in a hurry?" Galen asked.

"No," she answered, putting down her tray and looking imposed upon.

"Well, I'll be damned," Anton said. "What is it we're after? What we saw in the window?"

"Someone breaking into my uncle's. I thought I saw it the other night. But we don't seem to be any better than ghost chasers."

There wasn't anything else to do but go back for what they had come for at the Estate. But somehow, Galen knew that he would get to the bottom of this before long. Maybe the fugitive had left something behind that would give him away.

But in looking through the remainder of the house, they found nothing else disturbed. So they piled the photos and pictures of Treasure Island, also the framed can labels Eugene had helped design, and all the children's books, published and unpublished, into the U-Haul and created a full-blown Uncle niche in a corner of the rental. The fleeing stranger be damned. On the wall, the light of the World Fair's cascaded down the shoulders of the idol. It seemed as though the life of this new home was springing from this corner.

They had Pepsi in the living room and toweled off.

"That was some underground we were in," Anton said. "My grandmother had something like that—a memoir gallery—but she kept it in a room she had set aside. Like for trophies."

"I remember my mother talking about a secret passageway," Galen answered. "It belonged to the history of the hotel. And then I think my uncle showed it to me."

Andrew had put his tank top back on. The red, white, and blue. "Ophelia's mentioned it, too. She may have picked it up from Eugene."

Outside, it seemed as though there were many mirages.

"Maybe Ophelia's the one," Anton said. "She might have had the key and was looking for something."

"Ophelia was not in that flash of white we saw," Galen answered. "She always wears colors. Besides, I've never known her to run from anything. Or hide anything, except once."

"That is the truth," Andrew said, "but did you see a flash of white?"

"I thought it was red," Anton answered.

"I thought it was green," Andrew said.

"God," Galen said, "you guys are a big help."

"Besides," Andrew said, "Ophelia would not keep something like that from me."

Jacob came in, red and puffy. "Grandma said you'd be here."

"Go and in and see what your room looks like," Galen told him.

A cheer came from the back.

"Dad?" Jacob called.

"Yes."

"Do I still have to stay with my new paper route if we get three-quarters of a million dollars?" The voice was loud coming from the room.

"We'll talk about that then," Galen said. "We don't have three-quarters of a million dollars yet."

"That's what I thought," Jacob said, re-emerging, a little crestfallen.

Anton was putting his shirt back on. A pity, because he looked so good. Broad-shouldered, like a giant in the earth.

◆◆◆

"You're quite a celebrity," Anton said, when they were at Ophelia's that night for dinner. They had been asked to help set up the room. "It's time I got filled in on the facts." This man's warmth went straight through to Galen. It was then Galen was aware of the gold in the red of Anton's hair. It was going to be a more private than usual conversation, since Jacob was away, staying the night with a friend.

"As I remember," Galen answered, "so are you. Didn't we talk once? Weren't you in some magazine or on television?"

"That's my twin, Scott," Anton said. "He's a model. I merely work at the family nursery."

"You and Galen have so much in common," Ophelia said, coming into the dining room from the kitchen. "We thought it would be a mistake never to introduce you."

"I knew your uncle," Anton said. "Always admired him. I'm glad to meet the man who's going to be his executor. Who's guided by his ghost, as our *Daily* puts it." He was smiling with strong, decided lines to his jaw.

"Well, thanks to that, since I feel I'm in hot water because of it," Galen told him. "My family's not sure yet what's going to happen to things."

As he had spoken, Galen was aware of the heat of Ophelia's usually cold dining room. Also, he was aware of Anton slouching because of his height. He should talk—he had his own stoop, had had it since prison.

"Let us help you get the flowers on the table," Anton said. "The two of us know something about them. I grow and Galen plants."

"Well," Ophelia said—she was in purple satin—"I thought it would be a shame to let them go to waste." And so carnations went on the table in rings that were fit for *A Midsummer Night's Dream*, once Anton and Galen set to work.

Galen was aware of Anton's extraordinary energy beside him, as everything was decked across the linen. The man bustled in his knit yellow polo shirt, as if showing just the tip of his strength, although in this case, his body also said "heat." The man was dark-skinned, both naturally and from the sun, and seemed to hint, although having a Mediterranean hue, that he might also have come from somewhere in Scandinavia as well. While young-looking, he was probably just Galen's age. Now for the sixty-four-dollar question again—gay? Surely Andrew and Ophelia would not throw him an unknown quantity or closet case.

"Are you a Carleton Park man?" Galen asked him. They went outside since they had finished setting up.

"It's Mayfair where I'm at," Anton answered, "although it's a little in the outlying area, toward the Coburg Hills."

"The Coburg Hills," Galen said. "Every time I come back to Carleton, they're the first thing I notice." He strained to see them from here. You could see a tip. He had to look over the laurel bush in the window. "They're like old friends."

Anton appeared as if he didn't know exactly what to say, but added, "But I've lived here a very long time. In one way or another, all my life. I grew up in Mayfair. Or Coburg, if you will. My father owned the nursery before I took over."

"And all this time we never ran into each other," Galen said. "When we have, as Ophelia says, so much in common."

Anton smiled, and if he hadn't been so shy, Galen was sure he would have looked directly at him. "When my father ran the nursery, which was up until last year, I hung out in the back beds. It's only lately I've been working the front. But I've seen you," Anton said with emphasis. "I've kept an eye on you." And for some reason, he reminded Galen of Patrick. As if the man might want to get more information. Anton was scrutinizing the trunk of a coral bark maple.

"I hope you haven't been disappointed," Galen answered. "I don't feel lately there's been much to watch."

"Actually, we were at the same workout center a few years back," Anton admitted. Something prompted him to say, "I've seen you in the shower."

Galen flushed, felt naked, very suddenly. Like the nude white lilies, rouged with pink, planted at the base of the coral bark tree. He hadn't felt drawn like this since Leo. And it was different from Leo, too, because his ex was by night. Anton was more a man by day, Galen could be sure.

"I wish I'd remembered you in the shower," Galen answered. Through the French doors to the kitchen, Andrew and a coaxed Gregory were now bringing in the Chinese food which Ophelia herself had made, while, all the while, no doubt, dealing with customers and phoning them to remind them about Easter FTDs.

Anton looked at him sidelong, obviously jinxed to silence. It was almost as if they could hear the showers running in the hotel in the next block. Other presences were there. Galen saw Darren, his first lover, in memory—for

Anton's shirt was yellow, like one Darren used to wear, forming a rather stunning accent, slow arriving, to his red hair and beard, also closely cropped.

They stepped inside the house again. Gregory was waiting patiently by the kitchen door. "Is there anything else I can do?" he humbly asked.

Ophelia kissed him loudly. "No, Father, Dear. You're OK with my calling you that?"

Gregory had turned beet red. "Yes."

"And you must stay here for dinner since you brought it in. You can sit beside me, and I can tell you all about my plans for Easter. What I'm going to do for my Easter window. I'm working on it now" (smiling, with Gregory kind of hunched there, dismayed) "and how you can help me with the deliveries the way Galen did with the valentine flowers, if you've got the time."

"I've always got the time," he said. "Just ask. But I won't stay to dinner. We have a full house tonight. They're going to need me every minute to get that luggage up to the rooms and the cars back into the lot way down the street."

"Well, suit yourself, but I'll make you take some food with you. You *do* have a refrigerator in that little room of yours still going, don't you?" She had an arm around his shoulder.

"Yes," Gregory smiled, "half a refrigerator."

Christabel's step was in the kitchen. Gregory always took someone in the kitchen as his cue to leave. He looked at Galen wistfully. "And don't you be a stranger," he said.

"Never have been," Galen said. "Except when they threw me in prison. And I'm going to be by to see you. I want to know more about what Eugene said to you."

Gregory had to think a minute. "Yes, yes."

With the kitchen door open, Ophelia went out with their father, guiding him, her hand still on his shoulder at first, then gathering food and flowers for him as she went.

For all his recollections of showers and lovers, Galen again felt a pang seeing him leave and shouted out, saying, "Just remember—I'm just down the street."

His father turned. It was obvious his father felt completely strange being so conspicuous. "Yes, but I still don't like that move. You don't be a stranger."

The dinner they sat down to was luxurious, and Christabel, once she came in, looked nonplussed to be the one to be served. And she still seemed furious with Galen's moving out, and spilling the beans to Patrick.

When there was a break in the family conversation, Galen said to Anton, "I can't imagine living here your whole life, it's really overwhelming. Especially in Mayfair."

Anton looked chastened. "It is. Hard to think anyone would want to, right? Or could survive?"

"I didn't mean that," Galen said, looking at him intently. "I mean overwhelmed in a good way."

"Miraculous I would say," Anton answered, "and maybe even a little silly."

"Silly?" Galen asked.

"Silly," Anton repeated. "Just consider—living in and around Mayfair all that time. The city that tried to nail you for as much prison time as it could."

"I really try not to see it that way," Galen answered. "Not the whole city at least. Maybe just the government."

"But that's just what we live with constantly. Nevertheless, I was very much moved by the way you wrangled with them," Anton said, returning his intentness. "That you just didn't stand back and take it, and now you've got this lawsuit filed."

"Funny"—and Galen tried to put his finger on it. "That's really out of synch with the way I've been seeing things."

And why? Maybe because the scenery had been so stark, so despairing, almost—when he had been hauled out of the county jail and into the prison van (all secured with other jailbirds for company), and all was in a powdery August haze, with the sun going down and Galen feeling that this was it, all over. And he was still carrying some of the shame with him.

"Well, consider it like this," Anton said. "That it's from the perspective of a man who's been in Mayfair like a closet. And then there's this man who's telling them they have no right to put him down."

"Do you mean the closet closet?" Galen asked.

"Yes," Anton said.

Christabel caught the word, of course, from across the table. It was clear she had something to add.

"Well that, of course," Galen said, "is good news." Instinctively, he got up, ostensibly to help Ophelia slice up the cake. Anton followed. They stood in the kitchen, really not helping at all but momentarily confidential.

"Being gay hasn't been an attraction for me until recently," Anton answered. "It's been more or less a burden. Especially being that I'm one of those people who can't seem to leave Mayfair. But because I now own the family business, and have been here all my born days, and because I've been pretty well rooted, I have had the money to travel, and I've been able to see it doesn't have to be like this everywhere."

"It's not like this even here. Carleton Park is far better than Mayfair," Galen said. "If we're talking acceptance." He made a broadening gesture with his hands and pointed to a horizon through the window.

"And that's what we are talking," Anton said, looking away. "You should see—I fly down to San Francisco, and they'll say, oh you're from Oregon, that homophobia state. Did you hear about that man's trial—Galen Melville's?"

Galen puffed up a little. A gilt-framed mirror hung conveniently above the sideboard. He looked at himself as they started back to the table. "They actually said that about *me*?"

"Absolutely." Anton folded his arms.

"My, my," Galen said. "So did you like San Francisco?"

"Yes, but while it's relatively low on the homophobia, it's not all that livable," Anton said.

"That's what I found, too," Galen answered. "And Uncle did as well, I believe."

"You were down there?" Anton asked.

"Yes, I lived with Eugene down in California for a number of years. Living with Uncle had been one of the great goals of my life." Galen was stopped by the melancholy of the memory for a moment. They went back to the dining table.

"I know what you mean," Anton answered. "I have a father who gave us a lot. He wasn't one of those who slave-drive their kids into a family business. He just was so naturally generous, we all wanted to work for him. Even donating our time."

"That doesn't sound very American," Galen said. "Or at least not like my family here."

"He wasn't American," Anton said.

Galen then heard that Anton's father was Dutch-Danish. And when Anton's own mother had died, his grandmother had come and kept house for them. She had originally lived in Denmark. Her name was Gertrude, and she liked to be called "Gertrude of Denmark." Anton had been to the old country, and to Holland, too, to visit shirt-tail relatives. He got to see the tulip fields there—every color of the rainbow. Also, St. Bavo's church, where he heard the organ that the young Mozart had played on.

When Anton was saying this, Galen's memory slyly presented him with Anton in the shower. He had the smooth muscles of a gymnast.

Christabel and Ophelia brought in the sliced cake.

"Yes," Galen said, "I heard it. That organ. I listened to it in prison. On tape."

"Then you know what the Toccata and Fugue must have sounded like," Anton replied. "Do you know"—he put a hand up. "I heard that exact same Toccata and Fugue years later in a cave in Arkansas, where they had built a pipe organ for tourists. Strange, isn't it, how we can travel that much distance? And then everything comes up as a reminder."

"Nothing like Toccata and Fugue," Andrew said. "The apex of civilization as we know it."

Galen wanted to hear more from Anton, but he could see that dessert was over.

Ophelia was stacking the dishes. "Anton, you must come and see us again."

"Yes," Galen added, "I want more of your travels. More about that cave. Much better than prison. Where I heard that music."

"Won't you be with busy with everything—the gardening, the executor work, and Jacob's school?" Anton asked, looking shy again.

"Not that busy," Galen said. "Give me your phone number. We'll be having another dinner soon and celebrating something. We celebrate something here all the time—or at least Ophelia does"—she smiled, looking over "We're always looking for an excuse. Possibly celebrating the rediscovery"—he couldn't resist saying it loudly—"of Christabel's collection of poems. Or you could come here for Palm Sunday brunch."

Christabel looked over, too, as if to say, "Who asked him?"

"You go to church?" Anton asked.

"This Palm Sunday I will be. The rest of the family goes four times a year, and this is one of the times. I hear there might be a demonstration there. In protest against Drag Queen Daws, who's archdeacon of the First Episcopal and hounded my tail at the trial." Galen was wondering if this was enough to scare Anton off.

"I don't know"—more of Anton's muscles were showing as he started stacking dishes from his chair—"if I'd go or not." He seemed held by the Hills, his Hills, visible through the window. That's where he worked, to the north. It actually seemed as though he carried these gentle rises of land on his shoulders. Atlas. Yes. Or maybe his shoulders merged with the hills behind him. Meanwhile, the March weather couldn't make up its mind about anything. Nothing. A few sprinkles of rain, with the evening star still emerging. And Galen certainly didn't mind waiting for Anton's answer. He just stood there, filling his lungs with the smell of the earth coming through another French door. And therefore the smell of Anton.

"The family's depending on me to show up to their church service," Anton said at last. "But I think I could swing it. An opportunity with—you—doesn't come around every day."

"Well," Galen said, smiling, "meet me at the house on Sunday, then, 10 a.m. Palm Sunday breakfast. My mother always does it. Maybe I can get Ophelia and Andrew to come with us, since they're your friends, too."

"Just like family," Anton said.

"Absolutely."

Anton gave Galen his card. It had a green trellis on it.

◆◆◆

Galen and Anton and Jacob were sitting in church together, after breakfast. Christabel had refused to sit in the same area and had found a place at the back. Just in front of them, the Drag Queen Squad was filing in, ready to sabotage District Attorney and Archdeacon Daws, by filling up the front row. The congregation could be felt adjusting itself, uncomfortable. Still, Galen was aware of Christ smiling down on them and throwing a green light everywhere from his landscaped background. Only a few days ago, after coffee, Anton had taken Galen out to Brandsmark Gardens, his family's nursery. They were growers, specializing in rhododendrons. Being in Mayfair, the place had never gotten Galen's business, but he had often heard good things.

The spring which appeared in the windows below the stained glass fluttered suddenly in its leaves, energized, silvered, and the winds, pressing through the street, as though guided by a spirit, took his gaze up to the top again. If you were allowed to see ghosts on Palm Sunday, the way you were on Halloween or Christmas, Galen thought he might see Eugene and a whole legion of celestial associates at his back, while the unlit moon in the sky rolled forward, in the clarion blue, as if it would allow just a wink from the planet Pluto to be visible to the naked, sun-glanced eye.

The processional was starting on the organ, and all were rising, including the drag queens in the front row. One of them wore fishnet stockings, but they weren't stockings at all, but poster paint in black crisscrosses. Another had a pink feather boa that could have been thrown over Ann-Margaret's bedspread.

A complete rumble was going through the church, as the sheet-white Drag Queen Daws, still looking the Deacon and District Attorney in his black business suit, mounted the podium for the offertory Biblical lesson. His brother, the soul of patience and magnanimity and dressed in a purple robe, stepped off to one side, and tried to be above the presence of the drag ladies. "After all, it *is* Palm Sunday," his glance seemed to say.

Anton said at last, "If that film crew outside catches me on film, goodbye family. They're going to savor that for their pre-Easter dinner on the six o'clock news."

"Is there a film crew outside?"

Anton nodded. "I just heard the person next to me."

"I only heard they might be here," Galen answered.

"A film crew, Dad," Jacob said on the other side of him. "Cool."

Through the tense service, Galen smiled but was worried for Anton. Staring at the profoundly ruffled Daws brothers, representing both Church and State as though they were a set of Scales, he tried to sit very still as he remembered again his uncle helping him into a Superman suit at the San Francisco Hilton. He had then flown into the giant meeting room and then later dancing a dance in one of the most important social actions known to the gay world as far as he, Galen, was concerned. "Torture!" "Murder!" his compatriots had shouted at the psychiatrists, there at the American Psychiatric Association Convention in 1970, psychiatrists who had used electroshock therapy to "correct" Nature and gayness.

Galen remembered his uncle's hands, patting him, giving him courage to go out there and give them hell. Return hellfire with hellfire. "What do we want?" "Freedom." "When do we want it?" "Now." And not only were his uncle's hands there; his uncle himself—all of him—was there right behind him in the 1970 Board Room when Galen ran in. "What do we want?" "Freedom." "When do we want it?" "Now." And he remembered another time he had been caught in a costume, this time a dress,—as a child. How close had he been to suicide then?

With the Postlude, a chant came up, "Give them hell, Drag Queen Daws. Give them hell, Drag Queen Daws."

With a roll, everyone was rolling out of the sanctuary like a loosened rock, and they were all left on the church steps with the clouds running northward in the sky and the bells ringing. Not so surprisingly, the new month of April had decided to focus much of itself on their retinue, for a special glow seemed to surround them as they stood there, with his mother, newly emerging from the church, as the center of attention. The camera crew gathered again. Also friends. It was vernal chaos.

"Congratulations, Mrs. Melville," a reporter said. "Wonderful article on you. Can't wait to read your book when it comes out again."

"Lovely verses in the paper," another said. "Had no idea you could write like that. Good seamstresses make good poets, I always say. But how long have you known that Mr. Daws was a drag queen?

"Mr. Daws a drag queen?" Christabel asked, dismayed.

"The District Attorney who prosecuted me," Galen said, stepping in front. "The one who dug up evidence which wasn't there. The archdeacon up in front today reading the lesson."

"I have no idea," Christabel said. "I did notice those strange-looking women in their Easter best, if that's what you mean."

And soon they were joined by the drag queens. "Did you feel supported, Galen?" one of them asked. She was quite large, with a Popeye-anchor tattoo on her forearm.

"Supported in what?" Galen asked. They were all stopped on the church steps.

"In being the victim of closet-Queenism," she answered.

"What is closet-Queenism?" Christabel asked.

A young, swish reporter in a suit answered her in a quick and efficient way as possible.

"We're just here to remind Daws who he is," another drag queen said.

"And it's clear"—an apparent tough who wore a scarf like his grandmother's—"we did just that. We got him, we got him. In a gentle sort of way."

"The gentle sort of way is the only way," reporter Patrick said, joining them, dressed in a skirt.

Things were still in chaos, but this time in front of the church. Well-wishers of his mother—and Galen himself—still flocked past ("So good to

61

see you out of prison again" Again?), while meanwhile the camera crew, which had been waiting outside, recorded everything.

"Well, we are interested in getting your reaction," the reporter said. And he was looking at Galen. Where was Anton? Galen strained to see and to get away. He was holding on to Jacob's hand.

Oh God, this young man (eighteen years?) *was* all slicked back and suited up, dressed for success like Deacon Daws, and completely glib. He also served to remind Galen that much had changed over the years and even in the last one and a half.

"I am very much touched," he said at last, "that these gentlemen— gentlewomen, ladies—would all turn out to register protest, but I'm not altogether sure the embarrassment of D.A. Daws would have been my first priority."

Finally, Galen saw that Anton had drifted down Holland Avenue, trying to sneak away. Having freed his hand, Jacob was going, a little, in his direction. He certainly couldn't blame Anton—who would want fallout like this?

"But it is our understanding, Mr. Melville, that not only did you win a recent victory over the courts by being released from prison and restored to your normal life, but that you are, in actuality, a famous pioneer in gay activism. You actually staged a protest in a Superman suit yourself in San Francisco in 1970. You are, in fact, the Man in the Superman Suit."

"Yes," Galen answered.

There was a hushed gasp.

"The Man in the Superman Suit."

"The Man in the Superman Suit."

"So it seems," the reporter said, "that what happened today was in complete accord with your background."

"Well, my heavens, Galen," Christabel said. "So that's what you and Eugene were up to. Protest."

"Now who's Eugene?" the reporter asked.

"The man from whom these kind folks heard the voice from the grave," Patrick said, crowding in and trying to sound smooth but ending up rather awkward. He had been standing by. "The one the *Carleton Park Daily* wrote the *exclusive* copyrighted article about."

"Dad, you're famous again," Jacob observed, having drifted back. "Now all you have to do is get rich. And that's soon."

Downwind of all this, Anton stood at the curb. The chimes were going off, and a second flight of pigeons were flying up with rainbows on their necks. Old fall leaves were spiraling upwards, and a fresh cool wind came down and blew across the tulips.

At last, the whole group seemed to disburse like confetti, and Anton soon joined him again, walking humbly and eventually hanging his head. Jacob was walking with Christabel.

"Completely afraid of those cameras, Galen," Anton confessed. "Should have been there to support you."

"Oh, hell," Galen answered.

"Hell?" Anton asked.

"Yeah. I mean," Galen said, "even though it's Palm Sunday, let's not look for anything earth-shattering. That Rockettes line of drag queens was being nice by coming into the front pew, but I don't think history was made."

"But I've been waiting for something like this to happen," Anton said. "I can't tell you what I suffered for missing Stonewall. And I was in New York at the time, too."

But before Anton could add anything else, Gregory up the street—on the steps of the great church—had D.A. Daws pushed up against a stone column and was pointing a finger directly in his face, and then ultimately turning back down the sidewalk. The church chimes gave another peal for the quarter of the hour. Their family quartet had made a good pre-Easter parade—down Holland Avenue, of course, of course—and then back. Galen was reminded of the scenes from his uncle's photographs—Treasure Island—with the sunlight so delicate, so fanned with shadows in the timid warmth, it seemed imported in, like Anton's rhododendrons, in pots.

He opened the door of the hotel for his friend while the rest of the family hurried up the street to the house—Jacob was talking about their Easter plans with Christabel.

Inside. Discreet Dutch gods and goddesses perched and floated in the lobby, and the pole lamps were all silver in the sun. Galen, guiding him, was suddenly aware of the plushness of the carpet—and, in fact, the whole room.

They went back to the Board Room and just sat. *The Bridge* was on the wall. But also Anne Frank House. And a photo of some canal boats, full color. Perhaps also done by his uncle. Every picture radiated for a moment, and Galen's arm went along the top of the old divan, brushing Anton's shoulders. Definitely, they were back in Amsterdam, in the courtyard of the Rijkmuseum. It seemed natural, inevitable; Galen turned and patted him. Anton responded.

"Do you believe in ghosts?" Galen asked

"What a question, "Anton said, making his arm tighter. "I suppose so, why?"

"Well, lately, I've been getting flashes that maybe Uncle Eugene is walking around the Estate at night. Like that apparition we saw last week."

"Have you been getting a full view of him?" Anton asked. "There certainly wasn't anything like back then when we thought we saw him."

"Well," Galen said, "I do get lights going on in the middle of the night—I think—when nobody's supposed to be over there. As if Uncle's working on a new book. Or something. Or as if he's discontent with my handling of his Estate." Galen's expression went into a puzzle.

Anton flexed a little. "I don't know, my friend, what to say. Except that maybe you could try talking to your uncle. In spirit, I mean. That could ease things along."

"Really? That's why I was thinking about going to church. Maybe to have a spell of meditation while I was waiting for Reverend Daws, the brother, to speak. Or even during."

"During the music," Anton said. "That's best. It's great. Like that Bach music I heard on an organ in a cave. Or in the grotto of St. Bavo's. Dank as hell there, but beautiful. Glistening, almost. Music. I talked to my grandmother, then. I was beside myself with grief and pain at the time. So I talked to her. Or her spirit. My dear grandmother, who I used to visit every day up to Evergreen Nursing Care when I went to school. She used to wait for me every afternoon at four p.m."

"You visited her every day you were in college?" Galen asked.

"Childish, isn't it?" Anton said.

"No, just different," Galen replied.

"I loved it—because I felt homesick," Anton answered. "I've talked with her ghost after she died about my being gay."

"You talked to your grandmother about being gay?" Galen was squinting. The room was filling with light.

"Not her, but like I said, her ghost."

The door opened, and they were interrupted.

"Saw the demonstration in the street," a young man in a beret said. "Any decision made on the Melville estate?'

He introduced himself as Michael, officer to AIDS House. The Gay Alliance had enlisted him to ask the same question.

"No decision yet," Galen told him.

"Let us know. Keep in touch."

The man disappeared. Galen turned to embrace Anton again, but then Gregory opened the door, drunk. "Boy, did I give that Daws a piece of my mind! Stupid shit!"

Galen wanted to hustle him out. The breakup of the mood was intolerable.

"What about?" Anton asked, looking frightened and withdrawing his arm.

"About trying to prosecute my boy and then not apologizing. Not Apologizing. 'At least have the manhood to say when you are wrong,' I told him."

"You didn't need to do that," Galen said. He went up to his father. The uniform looked slept in. "Let me take you back to your room," he said reluctantly. And with that, Gregory began to droop. Between the two of them, Galen and Anton, they walked him down the block.

◆ ◆ ◆

Easter at last. He even checked to see if maybe Jacob might like to spend time with Yvonne, his mother, but nothing doing. The prospect of Easter followed him as he got some of the yards ready for outdoor parties, with tulips all in a row, carefully mulched, marshaled, even, as his uncle had mentioned in his journals. The yellow petals, striped with red, were so perfect they seemed touched with a watercolor brush. While his mother was busy giving an interview with reporters about why Eugene's estate legally belonged to the family and how her lawyers were working on the inheritance—she was adamant, right now, about not giving it up—he had his truck filled with gas, and he bought Easter presents and cards. The Easter basket he awkwardly put together (Ophelia helped him with a few things) could become like a peace offering to Teresa. He hoped this wouldn't backfire like his exposure of his uncle's letter. Far from being cornered into generosity and handing the Estate over to the Gay Alliance and AIDS house, Christabel was clinging tighter, even as her estimate of herself as a poet rose, and she was inviting reporters to an upcoming reading.

Carleton Park kept gaining color as they neared Easter week. It was like the tulips; its rows of hedges and trees became orchards, miraculously free of rain. The sun came out the way it did when he had moved. At one customer's, he trimmed the last of the dead roses and planted pansies in the empty places, and it seemed as if artesian wells came bubbling up, turning purple. Especially in the stone urns where their splashed magenta and vermilion and yellows seemed to spill over.

The drift of the week settled him at last, gave him a resting point, finally, in the dining room of the New Amsterdam, Easter morning, one hour ahead of opening time. It was a tradition always to let the staff in ahead of the customers—to sit and have a cup of coffee. So he just sat, getting ready for his journey to Forest Glade, watching Tamara put orchids at each of the tables, while Gregory brought in the Easter lilies for the banquet centerpiece at the middle of the room. The lobby clock sounded. But Christabel had not come in yet. Jacob was at Andrew and Ophelia's. But he was soon to join his grandmother.

Tamara came over with a cup and a small pot for a refill. She seemed to be answering the clock. There was a kind of hush of "Easter morn," as if all the nineteenth-century poets in the bookcases the next room over were allowed to speak all at once, but in a whisper.

"See, Tamara," he said, "I'm going to get this fund set up."

His father was listening, but also standing by a distant table, ready to hear the bell.

"Yes," she answered. She had forgiven him for coming into the dining room so dirty a few weeks back.

"And I'm going to call it the College Fund. It's going to be for my daughter," Galen said.

"Yes." She nodded approval.

"Dad, you can join," Galen said. His father was hanging back after carrying in the flowers. Now standing near the clock.

"No, no," his father said. He had been sheepish since his outburst with D.A. Daws last Sunday. His outburst and his collapse. But he still stood there.

"And I'm going to feel really grand and important writing checks on this account," Galen went on, "because I'm going to have them printed with 'college fund' up in the corner," His father was following his every word. "It's funny, because I'm going to see myself, I think, as big as the Chase Manhattan Bank." He smiled.

Tamara was listening closely too, as she always did, but also she had to go on with her Easter work. She was pulling orchids from one of Ophelia's boxes and putting them, very carefully, into the fluted, rose-tinted vases, for not all the tables had been taken care of

"I wish," she said, "there had been something like that for me. Your daughter, I'm sure, is very proud of you."

"I can't see," his father put in, "I can't see how they could arrest you like that and throw you into prison when you were this good father all along."

Galen and Tamara just looked at each other.

"I don't think," Galen said, answering Tamara, "that my daughter is very proud of me."

"But I would be," Tamara told him. "When I was in Amsterdam, I used to take the tram all the way to the University of Amsterdam. I loved standing there—for very often there wasn't a seat—and just looking at all the shop windows and the canals; it was like a whole new world, all going past at once."

"And then what happened?" Galen asked.

"Well, you see—no college fund for me. My parents could not afford to help. My father had a stand of tulip bulbs right on Damark, and we just, the three of us, made ends meet. So with the expenses getting away from us, I worked in a—what is the word?—*standbeeld?*—shop near the *Universiteit.*" His mother had come in, looking at Gregory suspiciously. "Mrs. Melville," Tamara said, "what would you call a *standbeeld* shop?"

"*Standbeeld?*" Christabel asked. "Oh, you mean the icon store that you worked in on *Slijstraat* before you came to us at the Hotel?"

Tamara seemed pleased. "Yes, the icon store. That was what I was trying to say, Mr. Galen." She hurried her cart away.

"So are you nearly gone?" his mother asked him. "On your way to Forest Glade?"

"He's going to see Teresa," his father said. "And he's got a fund all set up for her."

"Yes, I was telling Tamara about the college fund I want to set up for Teresa. I don't think I can go up to Forest Glade empty-handed. I need to have something which says, 'this time I won't bail.'" He felt vulnerable saying this, afraid she might think he was trying to set an example of generosity. Of a sneaky sort. Maybe he was.

"I wanted to do that myself," Christabel said. "The fund, I mean. Milton Williams must have told you. I had some investments specifically set aside in my mind, but they all failed. I tried to rally them, but the hotel's been in such chaos lately, it would have been too risky. Like you, I wanted to carry through on what I promised."

"Chaos?" Gregory asked. "Chaos—is that what I do, what I contribute to?"

It was hard to see chaos. The dining room was beautifully lit up with the morning, with the gilt on the ceiling, and with the orchid-accented linen. What else could she hope for?

"Money for her wasn't your job," Galen said. "It was mine. It's one of the first things I need to do now that I'm out. You did enough."

"Tell me," she said, in a tone strikingly personal for her, "does Teresa want to see you? Has she reconciled?"

"No," Galen said, "not from the sound of things. Although, of course, I'm going."

"She's kept herself away from me, too," she said. "It's hard not seeing your own granddaughter. Yvonne—well, she's independent. But I loved knowing Teresa. The way I love knowing Jacob. Well, you must endure your heartbreak the best way you can."

"I'm trying," Galen said, finishing his coffee.

Gregory was undergoing some old-man tears.

"So many things," she went on, "didn't turn out the way we'd planned. If I have anything to say to you, it's take her on her own terms."

"Yes, yes," Gregory said, as a departing. "That's the only way."

"I'll try," Galen told them.

She had made a move as though she were about to take his hand but then stopped.

"Thanks, Mother," he said, getting up and finishing his coffee. And then, on the spur of the moment, he bent down and kissed her cheek. She colored, and almost knocked over her orchid.

"Happy Easter."

"Happy Easter."

He would have backed up and said something else, but she had already turned her attention to Tamara. She was talking about details of the hotel brunch, and with relief. He made a move to say some soothing things to his father, but he was gone. And there had been no bell that had sent him off. Family, still, to Galen, seemed like a mirage.

◆◆◆

The freeway seemed almost silent this early on the holiday. Let's go north. The roadside meadows were full of wildflowers—English daisies and dandelions, punctuated by clusters of daffodils. About fifty miles up, the farm fields leveled out into orchards of flowering cherry and ornamental plum, as if the clouds had lowered themselves in a pink sunrise and were upheld by one branch after another. He thought of Tamara and her odysseys by tram. How vulnerable she must have felt as a young, poor girl, traveling the city to

school. He imagined her studying—what would it have been? Vondel? Grotius? Poets that were more contemporary? Or maybe she had studied English, which served her so well now. He had seen her handwriting often. That he remembered, too. Because he used to work the mailroom in the hotel. She would send letters out in Dutch in a perfect, rounded hand, from a fountain pen he had seen her carry with her, and she would get letters back with exotic stamps attached—windmills, roses, tulips, and grand-looking men and women with intellectual faces, as though in a gallery. Sometimes she would save the stamps for him and he would mount them in his collection. He had a whole page from her. That had been back in the days when he had been imagining where his father might be. And now that he was here, he wanted to get him sobered up. And stay sobered up.

The driving instructions (it was time to look at them) were characteristically complicated, hard to follow. Like Teresa herself. As he turned off the freeway in the general direction of Oregon's Forest Glade (didn't every state have one?), he hoped he would not get lost, that he would stay lucid and be not one minute late for this Easter appointment. One back route led into another. As best as he could figure, he was to meet her near some field in the hills near the back of her sorority, and he wondered if all this turning and swerving were all that necessary.

For the first time—in how long?—he felt that he was on his own. For the first time since prison, he'd ventured out, driving on the open highway. There had been so many things to do, he'd scarcely thought he'd been sheltering himself, but actually, he'd stayed within a two- or three-mile radius of the New Amsterdam almost the whole time. It was a way of keeping so much from coming at him all at once. And now he could feel the gravitational pull of the prison, which was not all that far from here. No wonder he'd stuck close to his room.

Just when he felt most vulnerable—that was the time to pull over. A wild, white Tartarian cherry tree spread over everything—the last remains of what had been a cemetery garden, maybe. Although he could not see beyond the next hill, he could sense that Forest Glade and its small university were there. That this place was the kind that Teresa used to find as a child, a pocket of silence, full of birds and greenery, where she could play and have him watch her, on her own, delighted, but safe as well.

She was coming up over the hill to meet him. She was all in white, as if they might be going to church together. The apparently still clouds above her seemed to match the rhythm of her shadow on the grass, and for an instant, it seemed impossible that the family could have ever split, that she would have ever known anything like bitterness. But there was a point to how perfect her hair was, and there was an edge to the way she viewed him, once he could see her gaze.

"Happy Easter," he said.

"Happy Easter."

She hugged him, but he sensed the distance.

"You've chosen quite a spot," he said cheerfully. "It reminds me of one the places we used to visit when you were small."

"Yes," she said, smiling. "Maybe I was thinking of that."

"God, we used to do this when you were young every other week. You were four, five, six. During all those years."

"Yes," she said, now adopting a counselor's tone, "but you have to realize that I'm much older now. No longer a child."

"Did I say you were a child?" Galen asked.

"No."

And he wanted to cower again, slink under the grass. Should they just pack up and drive back to the sorority now—leave her off? A memory came of "Meet the Easter Bunny" when he'd taken her to a shopping mall south of Mayfair on an afternoon he'd wrenched free from house painting. He'd gone there in his spotted overalls. The Easter Bunny was just like Santa Claus at Christmas but had looked bored in the photograph. But he had gotten her there. She owed him something.

"I just don't want you to go off into memories," she said, as though in entreaty and as if she could follow his line of thinking.

He leaned against the truck—as before, when he used to visit in the pre-prison days, he had no idea how much time she'd want to spend with him. How long any of this was going to last. She was dressed as if she was going to attend class, although that was impossible. She was wearing a lengthy white shirt, stylish jeans and a loose denim blazer. Her blonde hair was long, and she had a touch of lipstick. She seemed so much older than when he had last seen her. However, her brown eyes were open and vulnerable—there was no hardened look—and she still had an elfin cast to her face. Thank goodness that had not been lost.

"What would you like to do right here right now?" he asked her.

She looked at him with a toss of her head. "I don't know. I just had this idea about Easter, even though my counselor wasn't in favor of it. She was sure you wouldn't show."

Nettled—and there were many nettles in sight, in this sunlit, bird-sung acre—he opened the truck door and handed her the Easter basket. "I brought this for you. If this is all that happens today, that will be fine with me."

She took it, and her look softened. "Thank you." She fidgeted with the plastic grass.

"Now tell me where you'd like to go from here." They just couldn't stay standing.

"Right over that hill," she said, pointing. "There's a little cafe at the bottom. We can have breakfast there." She smiled.

Galen never expected she'd suggest anything like this. He began to rush around in his head, thinking maybe there was some help for this after all. He got his light jacket from the truck, and together, they climbed the old grave-stoned hill.

"Do you come here often?" he asked, smiling.

"When I want to get away from the sorority—yes." It seemed hard for her to admit this.

"I'm still not sure where the town is, in relation to this place," Galen said, looking back and forth.

"We're on the outskirts. When I'm walking from the sorority, I have to do a lot of switching back and forth on back trails to get to this place." She was looking reflectively, almost bemused, at him.

"You should be careful," he said. "Especially when you are alone."

"You forget—I've learned how to take care of myself." She moved slightly away.

"No—just expressing a concern. As your father," he answered, following her up the hill.

The little cafe came ten minutes later. Mostly ten minutes of silence. Teresa put her basket on the table, and they ordered. They had a matronly waitress, who'd obviously waited on Teresa many times. Finally, Teresa introduced him as her father.

"May I ask," Galen began, "why we had to walk here? I could have picked you up at the sorority."

"I didn't want my friends to see," she answered frankly. "Your story's been around. Most recently, what happened on Palm Sunday."

"The paper didn't say much on that score. Only that I wanted to keep Uncle's estate for"—he held out on "gay."

"For your friends,' she said.

They were brought eggs sunny side up. Bacon. And Easter rabbit napkins. Watching his daughter eat, Galen at first wanted to rush out with, "So you're ashamed of me!" but caught himself up long enough to realize this was only partly true, that to some extent she had created another life for herself with this cafe and the graveyard, and he had been invited in. Nevertheless, it was just as he suspected.

"Tell me," he said, "what else do you do when you come to this part of town?"

The question so surprised her, she stopped eating. "I write in a journal a little, I sketch."

"That must be something very important to you," he said.

"Yes," she answered.

"When I was in prison," he said, referring to it at last, "it was for me, too."

In her elliptical manner—alive since they'd met at the base of the hill— she went on and said, "I'm very sorry, Dad, I didn't come to see you. I wish I could have, but Mom wouldn't let me."

"It doesn't matter," he said. "It's all right." It surprised him that he could say that. He never thought he could.

"Are you sure you mean it?" she said, speaking with relief.

"Yes—couldn't be more sure," he answered. "But your mother—she seems determined to keep you from me."

"I can't hear any words against her," she told him flatly. "If it hadn't been for her, I would have fallen through the cracks."

"Yeah, well, that's the way you see it. I think she wants to get even, because Jacob wants to stay with me."

They stared each other down. "What Jacob does has nothing to do with me. You know I think he's a total weirdo. And that's a cheap shot about Mom."

"Yeah, you're right," he admitted.

She went on eating. It was time, now, to pull out the checkbook idea.

"Teresa," he said, calling her suddenly by name, "I'd like you to accept these checks I want to send you. I've called it a college fund. I want you to have help while you're in school. From me. It's not a lot. I expect more money later. But I hope you will take it."

"How can I take it when I don't want to be seen with you?" She still wasn't looking at him.

"You're OK with seeing me here, aren't you?" he observed.

She looked around. "Yes, sort of."

"Well, that's good enough," he told her, and felt relief himself.

"I can't be seen with you," she said, "because you're known all around the county as gay. Your trial did that. And then people got the *Carleton Park Daily* when they ran that story about you getting out. And then again the demonstration last week. I heard all about it."

Galen felt the anger coming up. "At home? Is that where it came from?"

She hesitated.

"From home," he concluded.

Nevertheless, some of his humor was back. "So an ex-con is not the problem—it's being gay?"

She smiled at his laughter. "It's both."

"Well," he said, "you still haven't told me whether you will take my money."

"OK," she said, "I'll take it."

"Great," he answered. "It will do me a world of good."

The cafe window provided a view of the hill they had come across. For the first time, he was aware of Eugene's presence in a lonely landscape—as if nature were not as cold and indifferent as it seemed sometimes. In the past few nights, the lights had been on in the Estate. However, he'd rushed over so many times lately that he had given up trying to track the ghost down. Always, always, the lights were out by the time he got there. But now, he found a kind of radiance in the landscape. Years ago, in that chaos and tension of Christabel's boarding house, he'd sometimes, as a child, go down to the goldfish pond down in the park and think that some saving ghost was not far off. His father, perhaps, if he was dead. He felt, now, that the Tartarian cherry tree was like that pond. Knowing that it was there, out of sight, on the other side, was a comfort. Like the time when, also as a child, he had been at the insane Stop-the-Bully camp for picked-on boys out on Bainbridge Island. Every night, he'd walk to the edge and stare out over the expanse to the edge of the cityscape, where he could see the water tower that identified his neighborhood. Little did he know that soon Uncle Eugene would be touching down in that vicinity as though from a flying saucer or a ladder from God.

"So I need your address," he said at last. "Somewhere where I can send the check. I'd rather not go through your mother. Especially because of all the news she's been giving you."

"You can send it care of the sorority," she said. "Here, I'll write it out for you."

An even greater sense of relief.

Once she tore the sheet off from a small notebook in her purse, she made a move to go.

He took out his wallet to pay the bill.

"No," she insisted. "It was my idea. It's my Easter. But I do have to go. I have to get back to the sorority."

He was engulfed again. Abandoned, somewhat terrified. "Is this all the time we have?" he asked.

"Yes."

He didn't say anything more, but thought, as she paid at the counter, that they would at least have the return walk.

But that wasn't going to happen either. "I'll go back to the sorority from here," she told him. She hugged him quickly. "See you soon, OK?"

"Yes," he answered. "I'll put a check in the mail tomorrow."

Thank God for that folded piece of paper. Her address.

"Goodbye," she said.

"Goodbye."

But he still stood islanded.

He headed down the street into the vacant lot (he'd hardly noticed it before) that led back to the trail. Thank God, he'd remembered the way he had come. Maybe if he had seen a phone in the diner, he would have called a friend in A.A., but he was hesitant (his defect) to try to reach anyone on Easter. There were small blue flowers, called creeping Veronica, on either side of him, small enough to form shadows in the grass, and straight ahead over the top of the knoll, were arcs and arcs of English daisies, accented by dandelions and gravestones. He was literally walking hill and dale, over the hills and far away. A child's tune from a piano book called *Jack and the Beanstalk: A Story with Music* came back to him. Somehow the notes, fitfully played in his memory ("Climbing the Beanstalk"), were like the pioneer roses that held out their valiant leaves to the new sun. The bells sounded from Teresa's campus far away. He checked his watch. Could it really be that late?

They had had breakfast and yes it was a late breakfast, but he could hardly believe that time had gone by like that.

Strange, but at the top of the hill, he could see the outer edge of the town, the diner, the tower that was tolling, and even Teresa (her white figure). And she had stopped and was talking to someone, a young man. She might have a boyfriend by now. Someone gifted? Intelligent? Maybe she had made plans for the future that she would never tell him about.

He went down the hill, glad to see his truck. To him, it was waiting patiently. Funny, but he had worried about someone trying to break in, on a country road like this. But, of course, it was so old and beat up, who in the world would want to steal it? Gratefully, he got out the key. And just sat there, looking out at the Easter hill, warming and flowering in the sun, as though it were no graveyard at all.

Well, what is it I'm trying to get back to? he thought. What escaped me?

He sat with memories of Teresa for he didn't know how long when the face of a young woman appeared in the driver's window beside him. It was a young woman in running shorts. About Teresa's age.

Galen rolled down the glass.

"I'm sorry," she said, "but I'm lost. I went down this road following some directions from some friends, and I got turned around. I seem to be going in circles. We were out doing one of those runs where the leader invents the route as we go along. I got behind. Could you tell me how to get out?"

"Where do you want to go?" he asked.

"Back to campus," she said, her face still in worry. "I'm not from around here."

"I would be happy to drive you," he said, "but if you want to go on running, you just go up over that hill." He pointed. "That will put you right back on the edge of Forest Glade."

"Is there a path?" she asked, still looking shy.

"Yes," he answered. "I'll show you."

Getting out and walking her to the spot, he saw that she had some rainbow jewelry around her neck. She was wearing a long-sleeved white runner's top, with her hair tied back. During their walk, she also had been looking at him closely. "You're Galen Melville, aren't you?" she asked.

"Yes," he answered. He liked standing with her at the base of the hill like this.

"I've appreciated what you've done for us," she said, her face relaxed now. "I read about you in the papers. I'm glad you're out of prison."

"I'm glad to be out, too," he said.

She smiled. "Well, thanks." And headed up the road, which had now become apparent. With an easy gait, she ran up to the top, where she paused and waved to him. She was quite thin. He could tell she was thrilled to find the town on the other side. As he stood, in the full sun now, she disappeared.

He returned to his truck and turned the ignition. He couldn't go straight to the hotel and pick Jacob up. He needed to stop in at Andrew and Ophelia's just to decompress. And so he drove through the spring landscape, which was waning and would soon be Easter night.

He found Andrew and Ophelia just hanging out in their living room—which adjoined the flower shop. Andrew was sitting on the floor, with his back against the sofa. He was wearing his red-white-and-blue tank top again and was sewing on a catcher's mitt. Ophelia, with gold hair down, was working on something on a clipboard.

"How did it go?" they asked.

"Hard," Galen said, trooping in, "but it was OK."

"She'll come round," Andrew said. "Give her time. I did, with my father."

"She was on her guard," Galen confessed, "and we still had all this mysterious stuff about how we would meet and where we would meet. I had to go through it."

"It runs in the family," Ophelia said.

"What runs in the family?" Galen asked.

"Uncle Eugene was pretty mysterious, too, sometimes," Ophelia answered. "Especially in those last days. First he was in the closet, and then he wasn't. Then we were open about it and then we weren't." Her complete candor on this subject was surprising. "And then there's of course Father, who's one big walking mystery."

Andrew's arm made all kinds of muscles while he was sewing. "Well, I don't know about myself. I mean, if I had been born later, I probably would be gay. It was just that I was too late."

"You?" Galen asked.

"Yes," Ophelia answered, "Andrew's always said that." Her face was bright beneath the mane of blonde, almost white hair.

"I probably would have been much happier," Andrew said, "as a gay man. I mean Ophelia's perfect for me"—Ophelia smiled back adoringly—"but I'm

76

probably wired to be gay. I feel that all the time. Just when I'm looking at things, especially in the circus. And it's probably why I'm always looking for a hug. Can't get enough. Of course, I was never hugged by my father, who was a drunk."

"Andrew's always liked the physical side of people," Ophelia said. "Especially in men. Especially in the circus, and then he grew up on a dairy."

"A dairy?" Galen asked. "A dairy's cows. You never told me this."

"Milkmen," Andrew said. "They used to come in, and I loved being around them."

There was silence. Then— "That's how I got to know Anton," Andrew went on. "His family's nursery was just down the road. When I grew up, I found I liked the men working at the nursery as much as I liked the men at the dairy."

"You mean you were boyfriends?" Galen asked. "You and Anton?"

Galen and Ophelia both laughed. "No, no," Andrew said, "I just thought he was a great guy. And then he kind of disappeared into the back of his father's business. I had to go in search of him recently."

Ophelia got up to find some more papers for her clipboard and then came back. "Listen, want us to help you plant a garden? There's never been much of one there at that rental. We could get some things for you at Anton's wholesale." She settled down again. "We want you to be happy with that, so you won't leave. We were talking with Jacob about it today when he was over here."

"My bungalow?" Galen asked.

"Yes, already I've got hundreds of bulbs," Ophelia said, taking out a list from under the clipboard.

"I'll see," Galen answered. "But I'm not going to leave. Don't worry."

But, really, he didn't feel very garden-centered at this moment. And he had felt vulnerable talking about Anton. The heartbreak of the morning—not heartbreak, exactly, but the strain of being with Teresa—and then the surprise visit of the girl runner, so mysterious and somehow important, too. But beyond that, he was just sitting here tonight, at his brother- and sister-in-law's, seeing two people who'd been together for over twenty years and were loving and at peace. The tackle of envy was so strong, even getting up out of his chair and holding steady was a major feat.

"Another idea"—Andrew began, turning his mitt.

"Andrew," Ophelia interrupted, "why don't you throw that away? You've had it for over a millennium. He used to play major league at one time, and that mitt's his holdover."

"Major league?" Galen asked. "Major league?"

"Just for a short while," Andrew confessed. "It's not worth talking about, really. The San Diego Padres."

"But you—"

"Anyway, what I was going to say," Andrew went on, "is that whole Mayflower Theatre block is going to come available, too."

"The block?" Galen asked.

"Yes, just the next street over," Andrew said. "The Mayflower was originally a church, and it got converted into a little theatre and offices, and now the Movies 12 down at the mall has eaten up all the business, and so the theatre's closed, and the block's up for grabs. You might think about moving your landscaping office there."

The bell from the church sounded—the one further down the block.

"His vision of a family," Ophelia said.

"Just a thought," Andrew added, still caressing and sewing his mitt.

"Oh my God," Galen said suddenly. "What time is it?"

Andrew looked at his watch. "Eight-forty-five."

"Saved by the bell," Galen said. "Literally. Speaking of family. I almost forgot I have to meet Jacob back at the hotel for Easter, and I forgot to get him something. I better get my ass out of here and see if there is a—open." And he almost said it—Midnight Mart. Thank God, he didn't. Not on Easter night!

"Just hold on there," Ophelia said, getting up. "Look, Dear," she said, turning back to Andrew for a moment and holding out the clipboard, "it looks like we're going to clear our taxes."

"Great," Andrew said, grinning back.

"Anyway," Ophelia said, "we'll just make up another basket like I did with the other for Teresa. I've got ten thousand things here we can put in it."

Ten thousand things it was. Eggs, of course, jelly beans, but also a tiny toy drum, a magic scarf, a porcelain rabbit, and an Easter egg that you could see into as well. Daffodils had to top it. The ceramic ribbon that surrounded it was purple, interwoven with yellow.

Galen tucked the basket under his arm.

"Hey, Galen," Andrew said, "don't rush off."

"He's got to go see Jacob," Ophelia retorted. "If he gets there late, he'll have to take even more things to make up for it."

He kissed Ophelia.

And Andrew.

This was new for both of them.

"Hey, this guy's no shrinking violet," Andrew said, blushing with pleasure. "That's it. That's it. Contact."

"My, Galen," Ophelia said. "This was a *pleasant* surprise."

They both stood at the door attending him.

"You never come often enough," Ophelia said. "You used to come all the time."

"I delivered those flowers for you when I first got out," he said.

"You know what I mean," Ophelia answered. "I mean really come over."

"Prison held me up for a while," Galen said. "Prison has a way of doing that. But I'll be back. I'll bring Father, too. Maybe we can all sober him up."

He went away from the darkened florist shop and house. Ophelia switched her sign off. He would have liked it on. But, still, up ahead on this great Holland Avenue was the New Amsterdam, lit as though it were the city's answer to Chicago's Buckingham Fountain. There was a great rush of light.

At the family house, Jacob met him at the door, looking sad. "I thought you had forgotten."

"Not on your life," Galen answered. They sat in the living room, which Christabel had abandoned. Jacob was already staring at the Easter basket. Looking into the egg while holding up to the light and looking in. "Hey, Dad, cool. Carleton Park is in there."

"That's just like Ophelia," Galen answered. "And Andrew. Tell me, how did Easter go?"

"Fine. We all went to church again," he answered.

"How was the sermon?"

"I don't remember. A lot of people." He started eating his candy. "I almost forgot. Anton called."

They told Christabel goodbye. She was in her room. When Jacob was finally in bed back at the house, the presence that had been building during the day and perhaps since the previous week was entirely upon him. Eugene was as much there as he had been the day Galen had gotten out of prison and he had come in here with the letter. Through the window, which looked out at the Hotel, he could see the flickering colors of someone's TV and even the shape of a face on the screen. Christabel's. Really? Maybe from one of those dozen interviews she had been given?

A thought struck him suddenly and he went to the other window. Yes, the Estate was all ablaze with light. It seemed a matter of course.

"Dad, Dad"—Jacob was in the hall. "Did you see—?"

"Yes."

Jacob was running outside, even in his pajamas, but by the time they were at the window again, the lights were out.

Still, they headed out into the street, and Galen drew out the key, and they went in through the front door. Utter dark in the vestibule.

The living room was draped with shadow. On came the lights—nothing. Upstairs, the desk which Galen had sat in. But no one was at it.

"Not again," Jacob said.

"Sooner or later, we'll get to the bottom of this," Galen said, putting a hand on the back of Jacob's head. "Let's go back."

With dragging feet, Jacob obeyed.

Returning to the house and with Jacob bedded down once more, he undressed and sat on the one chair in his room. He'd love to call Anton now, but it had gotten too late. With a sudden thought, he went into the living room and picked up the phone. To see if Christabel was still up.

"Yes," she answered.

He imagined her sitting up in bed, her hair down like Ophelia's, but hers was that primary silver and blonde. "Just wanted to see how you were," he told her. "I didn't get a chance to ask."

"Are you calling about your trip, Galen? How was Teresa?"

"Distant," Galen answered. "But not beyond all hope."

"Of course not, of course," she said.

There was silence.

"I have a hunch about something," he said. "I've got the feeling that whoever's got the lights going in that Estate when we're not there is coming over from the hotel."

"I thought we agreed it was a ghost," she answered. For he had told her his theory.

"I'm sure in some respects, it is. But another part of me is thinking it actually may be someone. Someone in the flesh." He was going to gamble again. "I think it's someone who is discontent with the way Eugene's will is being carried out."

"Are the lights on now?" she asked.

"They just were," he said.

"Go to bed for now," she told him. "It sounds like you've had a hard day."

"I just want to know," he said, "if you're considering letting up at that estate?"

"I told you 'no,'" she insisted. "I told you no. It needs to become a parking lot. Now go to sleep."

He went back into his room, defeated, and there it was—on his desk. "Everything's going to be all right," on a piece of paper, just below the unlit lamp.

But he didn't even question it. He couldn't afford to quibble over what he needed right now. He'd take it where he could find it. He could see his own night garden through the window. Pluto's garden. The statue and the hedges like the perfect ones in Amsterdam. Except they always had a square of sun. He wondered now—and it hadn't struck him until this moment—if the young woman who had run by, lost, this afternoon had waited until she had recognized his face before approaching the window. After all, it was a fairly risky thing she had done. Approaching a man way out in nowhere. If so, if she had first reassured herself, then all his coming out, all his struggle with the courts, with D. A. Daws, with prison, and the newspapers had been for something. The way Anton had said. She had trusted him. That had to be enough for right now.

Part Two
Constructive Minds

Early summer. He was on his bike; his truck was in the shop again. He was down to his last dregs financially, especially after the checks he had been sending to Teresa. Also, the cost of living on his own with Jacob in the rental had finally caught up with him. No more Christabel as patron, only as babysitter.

Still, it was unseasonably hot and beautiful on this ride at eleven a.m.; a secretary had called that morning and told him to get over by noon. The City of Mayfair had come up with a settlement. He asked, of course, if it was five dollars or 750,000, but she could not tell him anything; he would have to come into the office. She gave him the address of the City Chambers, which he had known so well during the trial, but it was a different room, naturally.

Anton had said he would drive him, and sit it out with him, until they were called in and got the news. It was surprising, because lately Anton had been so distant—his family had seen him on TV in the aftermath of the drag queen sit-in and was not happy. Nor was Anton.

"No," Galen said. "There's no reason why you have to break your day up." Besides, he wanted the time to himself, just to settle.

The day was clear, robin's egg blue, with heat like a fine golden smoke rising through the dome. It was so easy to drive to Mayfair on your bike— and especially in simple and spellbound weather like this. All of you have to do is go up Holland Avenue to the Church and then turn down an alleyway to the bike path and go straight to the river. Head east, moving past fence after fence hung with purple clematis, with the sun clustered in its leaves. The river dipped into shadows, past the sight of a best-kept local secret, a heron's rookery, with bills pointing up out of cone-shaped nests.

In another moment, Galen was skidding into Mayfair. He was not to find a town square here, reserved for the weary. No hanging baskets. No lady statue presiding over all. Instead, he must have passed five Midnight Marts before he got to the City Chambers. It was a seventies construction, crisscrossed by many gray catwalks. In the courtyard, many, many people were waiting on benches for their sentences or decisions on their petitions. From his perspective near the bicycle rack, he could see the town laid out in front of him, in one strip mall after the next, Bi-Mart, Walmart, Total-Mart, Cost-Mart, with little desert spaces in between. He headed straight for an office whose name and number he had had to write down—"Risk Investigation"—and there found a secretary who handed him a letter of settlement for $500,000.

"Do you want to talk to someone about this?" she asked. She looked almost frightened, as though she had just given a potion to Dr. Jekyll.

"Yes," Galen answered, shaken by the sight of the sum. "Seeing that I haven't talked to anybody here since getting out of the pen."

He was shown into a conference room, where a man shortly appeared— he was also short—and said his name was Siems and that he was from Portland. "I'm one of the several attorneys," he said, "who negotiated your suit through the firm you chose. I'd strongly advise you take what they offer. It was a balance struck between Mayfair and their insurance companies. I don't think you will ever get any more, even if we take it to the federal level."

"I'm content with $500,000," Galen said, "especially since I don't think, now at least, any time was lost."

"I don't know what you mean," Siems answered—who reflected Milton Williams—"but if I were you, I wouldn't let anybody quote me on that." He was hard-driven, genie-like, and moved like a dervish. Galen thought of the men he saw at classical concerts, dragged there by their wives and who stood in the lobby until the very last minute, waiting for the bell.

"I don't know why not," Galen said. "It's true—and what are they going to do—renege?"

"No," Siems said. "But I'd try, if I were you, to say instead that Mayfair was the one who is being generous. Save Mayfair some embarrassment. Tell the world how great they're being. This whole thing has branded them as the worst homophobic town this side of the Mississippi. And they're not saying they did anything wrong."

"It wasn't the town—I made that plain—it was the investigating officers themselves. They forced those poor witnesses. By the way, what about that pathetic thug who eventually fessed up?" Galen asked.

"He's out on parole already," Siems said.

Galen felt a pang of fury, but said, "Well, what a relief. No perfect Marlon Brando look-alike should ever have to suffer the evils of prison. They might have put him in some prison version of *A Streetcar Named Desire*. Imagine what Stella would look like. A jailbird in drag?"

Siems did not find this witty or maybe even comprehensible. His looks reminded Galen again instead of a portrait he had seen of Rembrandt—in the last phase. With Milton Williams there had been some ambiguity. Also, as opposed to the former office, there was nothing else in this Walmart-style conference room to bring this association on. Instead, just some obligatory van Gogh cherry trees on the south wall. Still, Siems said, "I'm glad to see you're taking it in your stride. There's an infinity of paperwork you'll have to process if you're going to go along with the $500,000, so your humor will be useful." He handed him a sheaf of papers. "Please sign all these and get them back within the week. There's a self-addressed stamped envelope enclosed."

"And the check?" Galen asked.

"Forthcoming from us in three weeks," Siems told him.

"Excellent," Galen said. "It'll get my truck out of hock."

"I assume"—Siems smiled at last—"there will be something left after you do that."

"Probably. But I don't know what I'll do with all of it. I haven't thought about a post-windfall time. I thought the litigation would take much longer." Galen was scratching his head.

"Better be ready with some idea. The press will be at your door as soon as this becomes a part of public record." Siems was looking at him in warning.

"That I'm used to," Galen said. "My whole family over in Carleton Park has become a matter of public record."

"It's interesting that while your mother's getting airtime on her poems, you'll be getting it on your lawsuit," Siems observed, giving his second smile of the day.

Galen put the letter of settlement in with the rest of the red tape in his folder. "I want to thank you and your firm. I wasn't at all sure who was working at this—they kept it such a big secret—but I appreciate what's been done."

"We're being paid, too, you know," Siems said, returning to the blasé. "And don't expect a check for the full $500,000. There will be at least a quarter missing."

"Yes." Although Galen was disappointed. He had assumed their cut had been taken already.

In the outer office, Galen could feel that he was being seen as an altogether different man, as the staff took him in once more. They smiled. Yet how often had he come into rooms like this before and during the trial and been tagged, with sidelong glances, as the world's worst recreant?

"Goodbye," he said to them.

"Oh, Goodbye, Mr. Melville, and congratulations," the secretary said, now at liberty.

Yes, congratulations. Congratulations? Contrary to the time when he had been first sent up, the idea of being paid for months, days, minutes, seconds seemed odd. And certainly the idea of being exonerated did. Or at least exonerated by money.

He reached his bike—put the legal sheath into his saddle bag, and got on, with one last look at the Mayfair creatures still waiting on their outdoor benches. Having a few cigarettes. He felt almost guilty with his money—of being maybe the only one getting good news today. He rode off thinking, if I could buy off their time with what I've got, I would.

The river path received him again, and he wondered if anything in his life would change, now that Fortune was within his reach. Still, there was the great stretch of the Astor Street bike path ahead, along a main thoroughfare in Carleton Park, rich with pink hawthorn, now dimming with the hotter weather. And Holland Avenue was coming up, with the reassuring hotel.

But in the lobby, every reporter in the county was waiting.

"Do you not feel vindicated?" Patrick asked. "That Mayfair has admitted to being homophobic?"

"Nothing like that has been said," Galen answered. "It was an out-of-court settlement. In fact, they're not admitting anything." He had scarcely gotten past the revolving door.

"How about the earlier spring protest—at the church—from the Drag Queen Squad? Don't you think they helped?" Patrick asked. He should have said "we," but was being cagey with the news.

Somewhere in the midst of all this, Galen was sure he was being asked if he would like to be on a talk show. Christabel had been on several already. Giving vent, on and on, to her memory, which was proving vast. The reissue of *Pluto's Bounty* had been a hit. Aged Jaspar-Prize-winning seamstress and hotel owner makes good. It had even reached the *New York Times*.

"What do you plan to do with the money?" Patrick asked.

Now the camera men's lights were on, and Galen was being put on videotape.

"Well, I hope to be a partner in a health club," Galen answered. In the past few months, he had been talking with Andrew.

"What about your uncle's estate?"

"AIDS House and the Gay People's Alliance are supposed to take over, but my family still opposes it," Galen answered, still undaunted by the prospect of Christabel.

"Will you maybe make a contribution instead if they have the Estate demolished?" Patrick asked.

"I don't know," Galen said. "I haven't given up on getting them to donate it."

Through all of this—it hit Galen very suddenly—he had the strongest desire to lie down naked in a field with Anton.

"What about your uncle?" Patrick went on. "Do you still get voice messages from him?"

This was a little backhanded, but Galen thought about the note that had last appeared on his desk.

"Do you have any bitterness remaining concerning that time you lost being in prison?" another reporter asked before Galen could try to answer Patrick. Here was the young blood from Palm Sunday.

"I don't think so," Galen answered.

"Why not?"

"A lot of good things came out of it," Galen said.

"What good things?" The young man was giving signals to roll more videotape. He seemed as surprised as Siems had.

"Standing up for myself for one," Galen answered. "Stopping drinking for another. I also read a lot, and if you want to be free of distractions, prison's best."

This brought laughter.

However, in answering this last question, he was aware there was something off-key about the hotel. Some of the staff, including Tamara, were watching from the sidelines, but they seemed very upset, as if caught in the middle of something else. Where was Gregory?

"It would be very good," Galen went on, "if my mother Christabel were here. I'm reluctant to take over her lobby like this."

Just then, Gregory did walk in—clearly the cause of the staff worry—putting down a customer's luggage. The customer was not in sight.

Patrick knew who he was.

He brought the microphone up to the uniformed man, who could have been in a 1940s movie. The kind seen in a hotel in *Charlie Chan*.

"How do you feel about your son being absolved of his crime and awarded half a million dollars?"

"Me?" For a moment, Gregory didn't seem to know where he was. Then he came up and put his arm around Galen. "I didn't know until just now—about the money. But I knew all along he was innocent. And I gave Drag Queen Daws a tongue-lashing for what he did. I did it on Palm Sunday. I wish I had had a palm branch to whip his ass."

Once again, Galen felt embarrassed. "That's all you need to say, Father. They get it."

"Wait a minute," Patrick said. "Wait a minute. Did you say Drag Queen Daws?" The cameras were on again.

"That's what I said."

"What's your comment, then, on the fact that you see our District Attorney as a drag queen."

"That he is a f-" Gregory stopped himself. And Galen was surprised that he didn't seem to be drunk. "That he is unconscionable hypocrite, and I told him so."

He then patted Galen on the shoulder, as though he really had been his father all these years.

Patrick was delighted with what he had gotten him to say.

◆◆◆

The June sky, so blue it seemed to be lowering itself toward the earth, was clear of rain for another moment. It was specked with white clouds and sent out warm eddies, lighting up the Coburg Hills enough to show Anton up there on the distant path, herding some potted rhododendrons into a truck. Some were still in flower—the extraordinary red of Taurus, the magnificent orange of Piccadilly—and yet, quite separate from the colors, from all this festival, so silent in the leaves, was the movement of his body, not far from cloud. Galen got out of his truck, and the slam of his door caused Anton to stop and look in his direction. He waved.

The little motored garden cart scurried down, as though to welcome Galen home.

"I didn't think I'd see you today," Anton said, getting out. "So what's the verdict? Did they give you anything?"

"$500,000," Galen answered.

Anton looked grave. "That's a lot of money. And you're still going to stay in Carleton Park?"

"Why not? It won't take me long to figure out where everything goes," Galen answered.

"I just assumed you'd shoot for something higher and out of town," Anton said.

"I've had the thought," Galen said, "of going in with Andrew on the health club. In the Mayflower Building."

"Is that what you're going to do for sure?" Anton asked.

"We'll wait and see," Galen answered. "Anyway, I'll take two of those Tauruses."

"What—you're still doing your landscaping?" Anton stooped to pick one of the rhododendrons up—"you're still going to want to hang out with the likes of me?"

"Why not?" Galen asked, smiling.

"I don't know—you're not going to find a lot of us that are rich and handsome," Anton replied. "That's my brother's department." Galen felt he was hearing Anton making preparations to cut and run, get away fast. Galen's windfall was not helping any.

"Well, you know, Anton, I have these flashes from my Uncle Eugene."

Anton lifted and squared the plants in the truck Galen had borrowed from Andrew. His was still in the shop. "Yeah, of course I know that."

"Well, I don't think he would tell me to go to Hollywood and look for the most glamorous people I could find. He was full of Hollywood disillusion himself. He was screwed there. Literally and figuratively."

"Was he what you thought we were chasing when we were moving you— Uncle Eugene," Anton said.

"Yes. Does it make sense now?"

Anton stretched his back. "I don't know, my friend. I can certainly understand why you would want to believe that. In fact, I wish I had me an Uncle Eugene."

"I thought you had your grandmother," Galen answered. "I mean, as a guiding light."

Meanwhile, the June weather shifted. It sprinkled rain and sun on the two of them. In the family house, just off the nursery, he was aware of someone coming to the window and parting the lace just as the light struck. His mother, maybe.

"The family's depending on me to stay in the closet," Anton said at last, clearly aware of the lace. "And I realized how 'not out' I am. Much of the balance of life for them depends on my being hidden."

"I thought you said you were forty, and it was time to change," Galen said, instantly regretting "catching" him like this. And, clearly, his winning the lawsuit made it worse for Anton. He seemed cowed not only by "gay" but "gay success." And someone—unless Galen was completely off base—he, Anton, was attracted to.

"Yes, well, that's what I thought." Anton folded his arms, defensive. Galen recognized his smell now, earthy, but with a few drops of cologne or a scrub of Irish Spring. "But it's not the way it turned out. I mean, if we're talking about the inside of me."

They were standing close to the truck. The red shadows of the Taurus rhododendrons were upon them, their sleeves, their jeans.

Galen felt like taking a gamble. His winnings had made him bold. "I'd like to lie together with you sometime. In bed, naked."

Anton looked frightened. He was silent some time. "I'm sorry, Galen," he answered. "Being in bed with you is a long ways away, as much as I might enjoy it."

"I don't mean," Galen said, "we have to actually—unite—I just mean lie together."

"I heard you," Anton answered, now trying to catch up. "It's something I'd like, but I can't just now."

"Well," Galen said, smiling, "let me know when you'd like to get together. I'd be happy to see you anytime and under any circumstances."

"Just with family, too?" Anton asked.

"Absolutely," Galen answered. "And with family. We don't have to be in bed to have a good time. We know that already." However, he wasn't sure he meant it.

"Good luck following what Uncle Eugene wants," Anton said, obviously relieved Galen would be leaving.

"Thanks. I'm sure I'll be looking for his guidance sometime today. Lately, it seems to happen hourly."

"Maybe," Anton said, "just maybe I'll stop being so fucked up and cowed and I can join you on this. I'd love to." He looked away.

"Sure," Galen answered. And remembered his own shame of just a few months ago. He left with his flowers. The man kept waving—his whole arm still—until the truck was almost a half-mile down the road. And someone was again parting the curtains of the window of the distant building.

And so, ahead, Galen kept his eye on the spot of the hills—the New Amsterdam was forming its white peak, and then he felt a full revisit of the shame, this time of having been so forward with such a shy man. The rhododendrons rattled in back. But the smell of the earth possessed him. And he thought of the tight gray sweatshirt on Anton, accentuating his muscles, and then the red reflected from the rhododendrons on the man's sleeves and the gold in his red hair—

The Estate was visible, and, sure enough, the light on the second story was on. Galen's heart leapt as he pushed on the gas and headed straight home, even though returning to Mrs. Madison's was next on the agenda. But as he approached the house, the light went out—like a rainbow, like a mirage. The closer you got, the more it went to vapor.

He had given up on trying to catch anybody or anything. It was true there was plenty of time, whenever he arrived at the place, for someone to have escaped out the backdoor or through the underground passage. Some culprit, posing as his uncle. He had to allow for that. He got out of his truck leisurely and let the Estate just stand there and while he breathed in the month of June, breathed in early summer. The laurel still sent out its sharp scent, and the gold lilies still clustered and bloomed, like a wreath of sunrise. The old wood of the 1890s snapped for a moment—crackled—in the sun, brief but intent on the white paint. Standing there with his backdoor key out, Galen thought that if he could solve this mystery, he would have the answer to such things like, well, whether there was a heaven or whether the world would go on. But, most importantly, whether he was doing right by his children. Just imagine that the house held not a wreath of lilies, but a full-fledged Wraith.

All right, let's open the door. Galen, stepping in for the first time since he had seen the lightshows, allowed himself to notice that there was a slight alteration to things. A sofa cushion (the one with the ploughing peasant on the case) was a bit out of position—he was pretty sure. And what about Uncle's journals? One year was out of sequence—hadn't that come from someone else? And upstairs, the pens were in disarray. All right, all right, this was proof positive. He had seen the light on in broad daylight, and now this. Should they put in a burglar alarm until this all got settled? Or should he just sit here in Uncle's chair and talk with him?

"Uncle," he suddenly heard himself saying to himself—and aloud, "if you're here, give me a sign. Just one sign. The subtlest imaginable. Because I've gotten all too delayed on carrying out your orders."

And as he stood there, he felt arms holding him suddenly. Not tangibly, exactly. But distinct. They were the way he imagined Anton's would be. Hold on, then, Uncle, he thought, don't let go. Then the June light, having hidden itself for a moment, came straight through the upper window, struck straight through a piece of suspended spectral glass Galen had not noticed before and cast a rainbow on the desk.

There was a photograph—a snapshot—framed just beside the blotter. It was of himself, at fourteen, with a man in bib overalls and a shaggy beard. For the first time, Galen actually stared at the picture. The snapshot was blurry—he couldn't make out the man.

The glow filled the house, and in that moment, the spirit not of Eugene but of Anton revisited him. And all the rich goings-on, in dreams, of the night before. Pluto's wand was over him again, and somewhere in the bedroom he saw in his mind's eye, himself and Anton take their places in the naked sheets. In the reverie, Anton was lifting himself so they could meet, and from behind, Galen pressed again and again, in perfect composition with the tanned back, the arched chest, the tense biceps. They were a bridal couple in a house whose owner blessed them, made room for them, protected them from shame, in "everything is going to be all right." A giant wished to be open to him for a moment. They were like cave-dwellers, no, rather, sculptures carved from rock, a union of lovers as though in a frieze, struck from stone, for all the world to see, but natural, not unsightly, just two masses lying together, a part of earth's architecture. Or if Anton's sign was Taurus, this man was a bull Galen took by the horns, and together they revolved in dance, Aquarius and Taurus, a blend of stars shielding the rock face which reflected their celestial meeting point in earth tones, like a harmony caught in the embodiment of a composer's notes. A scrutable line, meant for humans. Earth's scrutiny— that's what he wanted.

The moment passed.

In his mind, the two of them sunk down into each other's arms.

He stared at the photograph again. This was taken back at Catherine Blaine Junior High. Something remarkable. He'd been piling things into his locker after school (ninth grader), thinking about Klaatu the interplanetary traveler in the film *The Day the Earth Stood Still*, and suddenly he was aware of spring crocuses (saffron) out in the courtyard, which was surrounded by windows on all four sides, and which centered the fifties school. They always kept the place locked. It was only for viewing, and it could be seen from almost everywhere: a rectangle of perfect lawn, as though kept under glass, bordered by laurel and rhododendrons, and, of course, these crocuses now. The only one who was allowed in was Mr. Biggs, the janitor and gardener, and Galen could see him, tending to the borders. This was the man in the photograph.

It was a simultaneous moment, Galen thought. For Mr. Biggs stared over just as I was slamming my locker and turning. The tall, angular slender man was looking at me. I realized then that every day after school, he'd been staring at me like that, a face above the laurels, kindly and fixed, just as the 3:30 bell was going off. He signaled to me that day, and with my books and paper route bag in tow, I hauled myself over there. I thought he would put me to work. But instead, he just shook my hand and said, "That-a-boy."

"That-a-boy what?" I had asked.

"That-a-boy for doing your homework," Mr. Biggs had answered. "Doing your paper route."

His hand held on to mine for what seemed like minutes. The dirt showed on my palms afterwards. He was not pulling me into anything mean, but his face was so strained and hurt and earnest looking.

"Thank you, Mr. Biggs, but I have to go," Galen had told him.

"Of course you do. You work hard. Like me. But I know you work hard," he had said. "Your teachers all tell me you do. I've asked around."

I had been at such a loss—at all this praise. There were hundreds and hundreds of children, adolescents there. I felt honored and frightened, but I wanted my hand back. But you see now I think that my man might have been Gregory. The face—the photograph is blurry and he did have that beard— could be the one which popped up four years later when I was sent back here to Carleton Park to finish out high school—when I found out that Gregory the gardener was my father (the god who had been lost over Burma)—and he'd never been to Burma and never been totally lost, at least in terms of that War. And he certainly wasn't a god. And if Gregory had been Mr. Biggs, maybe he had taken the job to spy on me—better, watch over me—and maybe even Uncle Eugene knew, because when I told him about Mr. Biggs, he had not worried over what had happened, the way many, many parents might, just told me to let the incident pass—Mr. Biggs was a good man—just probably lonely.

But all that day, after that, when I delivered my newspapers, I remember now that the houses seemed different to me. The little ships in some of the fancy, stained glass windows floated differently; the Tiffany irises had had a greater blue tinct. The arbors that were just getting their starts of leaf parted their ways more easily for me. Maybe on some level I knew I had two fathers—three, four, including Klaatu and Augustus, Mom's second husband.

Galen went home and checked his diary—the one he had kept in junior high from the transferred scraps of paper. There was no year listed. But for May 25, it said, "He was there again. Waiting for me after school. He said, 'That-a-boy.'"

◆◆◆

The next night, Galen found his father's door ajar. There was June evening light through the hotel. An enclosed hotel. Not bustling at this hour, not particularly fashionable. Just the grandest thing in town. Overblown and quiet. The grandfather clock sounded from the lobby, beating out the meter of her poetry. Plutonic love, Plutonic love, it said again, what do we know of Plutonic love? Something so far out of reach, one of his mother's poems had said, something so far removed we set our sights on it.

Through the door, his father was on his stationary bicycle, slowly treadling, one little man, his face refined to muscle and bone, alert, taut; he looked like a hamster in a wheel, with nothing else to do in the cage. This was what he had in the world—what he was supposed to be doing, just a man in a bellman's shirt and slacks taking a few minutes out, instinctively, because it was the only thing available behind bars, the best thing going.

"Oh, why, Galen," he said, coming to attention and getting off. "Come in, come in." He snapped up newspapers, magazines to make his room presentable.

Galen still stood.

"Sit down," Gregory said, still looking nonplussed.

They took seats opposite each other in the tiny room. A few artifacts from England, Holland. Christabel's Holland. And now Gregory sat fixed. His face plain, naked, craggy. Had the man been a tree, Galen could have planted him. Replanted. That's the way he looked. Like some old but slender cedar, who's never been allowed to find full soil. Clutching the cliff.

"I just want to repeat," Galen said. "You're welcome at our place. Anytime." And then it passed through his mind that Gregory might come and live with them. Escape the hotel. And Christabel. Have his own life. And a real bicycle. And could walk Jacob to school, and Gregory could come and live with them. At last be replanted. He held that thought.

His father didn't know how to answer. Maybe he had just been nipping at the bottle. No, it was because he, Galen, wasn't saying anything further. His father was waiting for him to go on.

"Father," Galen said, "I have something else to tell you—or at least ask."

"Yes?" Gregory asked.

"Can you think way back to about 1959?" Galen asked.

That caused something of a shock. Gregory had to hold on to his desk, sitting down. "Why 1959?"

"Because that was when I was in Seattle with Uncle Eugene. You know when I lived with him for several years?" Galen asked.

"Of course I know," Gregory answered.

"It was when I thought you were dead in the War."

Gregory didn't say anything.

"Anyway," Galen went on, "I used to go to Catherine Blaine Junior High, and I had this locker close to the courtyard—"

Gregory was on the edge of his chair—uneasy. Ready to fly off, having just sat down. "Courtyard, yes?"

"And there was this janitor there who went by the name of Biggs. He used to keep watch over me, even though I wouldn't have called it that at that time. I remember his face, and I wondered if that man wasn't you," Galen concluded at last.

Gregory stood up and went to a drawer—his smaller version of the lion's ring compartment and desk that Galen had transferred from the hotel to his home. He pulled out the same small black-and-white photograph. It wasn't as blurry as the one in the Estate. "There we are," he said, "you and 'Mr. Biggs.' 'Mr. Big' couldn't never be your father in those days, and so he decided to do the back road. He did exactly what you said he did. He moved there to keep watch. When you returned to Carleton Park and this hotel and the house, I followed you back. But when you later asked me about everything, you didn't make any connection between me and Mr. Biggs."

"Of course I didn't," Galen said. "I had started drinking by then. Just enough to be slightly fogged. All the time."

"Tell me about it. Of course I should have told you I was your father. From the start. But I was too ashamed," his father said. "Your mother liked the family the way it was. When I came back to her, as you know, she didn't want things disturbed and she had that short second marriage. I might have gone on forever keeping quiet if you hadn't put two and two together your senior year or whenever it was. Of course, Ophelia already knew."

"Did Uncle know you had followed me to Seattle?" Galen asked.

"No," Gregory answered.

"Then he really did believe you were just a nice man looking after me back then—and you were, you were," Galen said.

"I was not a nice man," his father told him. "I was a coward who wanted to be near you. I didn't say anything because I felt I had lost too much already. How could I ever make up to you all those years you were alone, from birth to your teens, when I hadn't been around? Ophelia I could leave to your mother, but with you—it was too late already"—and Gregory had gone into a shout—"I had run out of time by the time I had gotten to Catherine Blaine."

"But you still had this picture taken?" Galen asked.

"Why not?" his father said. "I asked the art teacher. She thought it was a little strange my asking her, but she did it."

"Of course I understand," Galen said, scratching his head. "Of course—it's just that I don't remember it."

"It came after that big group graduation picture from Catherine Blaine. That's why you're wearing a white dress shirt. Oh"—his head went back, a little melodramatically—"the pain of regret."

"I don't see why," Galen answered, still holding the picture—which was good of the both of them. "Seems like you accomplished what you set out to. I came through in one piece, did all right in high school—tell me, did you stay on in Seattle for my part of high school there, too?"

"Yes," Gregory said. "I used to do drive-bys of your house, yours and Eugene's. Walk through Queen Anne High. See you now and then. First on your paper route after school. Later at the record store where you worked. But this time more at a distance. I had another janitor's job by then."

"But what about your job—your profession?" Galen asked.

"Teacher of Astronomy once," Gregory said. "I was rather young and brilliant. But then came the War, and I saw too many frightening things. So I just dropped out. I've sort of been drinking ever since."

"You don't have to," Galen said.

"Drink? You found a way out?" his father asked.

"Yes."

"I guess I've kind of known it. From the moment you got out of prison, I noticed." He smiled, despite his pain. "You see, I've been watching you a long time."

Galen handed him back his photograph. "I'd like to make a copy when you feel you could spare it."

"Keep it," Gregory said. "I have another. Many others. Xeroxes."

"Yes," Galen said. "I've seen one over at the Estate. How did it get over there?"

"I gave Eugene copies before he died," Gregory told him. "I explained."

Galen was close to asking his father about the mysterious appearances and disappearances in the Estate but decided to wait. Anyway, this mystery was settled. "I'll come again?" he inquired, getting up.

"Of course. I say this to both you and Ophelia. Just say it, and I'm there. Or here," his father said.

"I ask because I think maybe I asked too much tonight," Galen said.

Gregory looked pensive. Still, his face reminded Galen of something carved out of a tree. "No, it was bound to come up sooner or later." This time, he held out his hand to be shaken—no hug. "Just promise me you won't move out of town."

"I have no plans to move out of town," Galen said. He made a move toward hugging him, but already his father was getting back on his bicycle.

◆◆◆

But that night, he went down into the cool basement of an old church and started to feel unburdened the moment he began helping with the folding chairs. French doors let in green shadows from a small square used as a park and for church school. Galen just sat there and allowed himself to settle. He was still sweaty from helping Jacob with his paper route. The Steps and Traditions of the A.A. meeting were read, and the circle filled out to about twenty. Galen let the ghost of his uncle take wing, and as he did, he looked over and saw his father sitting in one of the chairs, introducing himself as a newcomer who had drunk that day. Galen remembered the expression on Mr. Biggs' face—it was the same.

"I don't have anything left," Gregory said to the circle. "Nothing. I kept holding on to my son, my daughter and grandson, hoping that watching them grow would be enough. But my son and grandson left weeks ago from the house where I've been living. And my granddaughter is already gone. And now I know if they had stayed, it still wouldn't have been enough. Not even that. I would have found an excuse to drink again. I have all my life. I'm seventy years old."

Galen had not taken his eyes off his father.

"I have a son," Gregory went on, "who's here tonight. I've been seeing him come to this meeting. And I want to be just like him—sober. I've deceived a lot of people, I've let down a lot of people, but maybe it isn't too late."

As his father ended, Galen tried to speak but couldn't. Many of the people in the meeting were crying, and he noticed now that included himself. Everyone knew who the father and the son were. But, then again, what was so odd? It had been coming a long time. He had told his father about this meeting since getting out of prison, but he had never expected him to come.

Afterwards, he went up and gripped him, but again Gregory slipped away. He wasn't steady on his feet with the new sobriety and could be pushed over at any time. For the first time, his chocolate uniform had wrinkles at the cuffs.

"Please, Galen," he said. "Please wait until I'm really sober. It's too much right now, still off the bottle just a few hours."

Many came over, welcomed him, said to come back. Gregory nodded.

"That's all you've got to do, Dad," Galen said. "Stay off the bottle. Bit by bit."

"Yes, yes, I know," Gregory answered. "I've tried this before. I know."

"Can I help you?" Galen asked. "Can I do anything?"

"No," his father told him, "just let me come back. And don't give me any advice. You're good at that."

"Will you tell me," Galen asked quickly, "were you the one who sent me those notes, kept turning all those lights on in the Estate, who used the underground passage?"

"Yes, yes," Gregory said, his eyes looking a little wild and frightened, "but I'm too done in right now to explain. I'll tell you later when I'm sober."

Galen had to let him go. He had to stand there in the church basement with his arms empty again.

When he got back to his house and said good night to Ophelia, who had been watching Jacob, he wished he could see his ghost in the darkness. For mystery and belief had imbued these past months, like a guardian spirit. Now it was too easily solved, a set of phenomena all laid out. Inwardly, he cowered, thinking of Gregory, night after night, going over there and setting things up, doing whatever. Maybe it was then, beneath Uncle's lamp, he had printed out those supposedly reassuring messages, when all along his hand had probably shaken with alcohol. It was no wonder they had never been signed; he most likely would have been incapable of writing his own name. Or maybe he had been thinking of what messages to write while he had been on that hamster seat of his bicycle in that little nook? For some reason, it reminded him of a joke he had heard, prophetically, back in the 1950s, about a group of scientists who had designed the perfect computer, one big enough to answer any question. Of course, the moment the last bolt was fastened, they got together before an assembled world to ask, "Is there or is there not a God?" and so in the card went, and the lights flashed, and the "gears" clicked and suddenly another card dropped down—"Question: Is there or is there not a God? Answer: There is one now."

Nevertheless, his heart ached with the desire to salvage all these past months; he refused to strip them of their meaning. He could not believe that his being misled was enough to cancel this steady motion to things—straight from St. Valentine's Day to this entry into his own home.

In the morning, he awoke to another oasis day. It was all he could do to keep from running at a full gallop down to the hotel to see if his father had made it through the night sober. But he had gotten the distinct message to leave him alone.

He got breakfast ready for Jacob. Andrew and Ophelia were coming right over.

"We were just waiting for those beautiful green curtains to open," she said. "Now we know you're up."

It must have been seventy degrees outside already. Andrew was wearing a Hawaiian shirt—red lotuses. Ophelia had her hair up and was carrying in vase after vase of gladiolas. She was wearing her heavenly blue sundress.

"Anyway," she went on, "I just wanted us to celebrate the money you received. *The Carleton Park Daily* is full of it"—a newspaper was handed across. At last the reporters had put together the story. "Mayfair Beaten in Court Dispute," the headline read. And below, "Son of Jaspar Prize Winner Vindicated of all Homophobic Charges." Galen could see that Patrick had been at work, of course, and that the story was copyrighted. Homophobic charges. His father's label of "hypocrite"—as applied to Daws was there, too. A string of denials followed.

"I tried to talk Ophelia into waiting," Andrew said, "but she wanted to be one of the first to congratulate you."

"What about Father?" Galen asked, trying to conceal his tone. "Have you seen him today?"

"Just out carrying luggage like before," Andrew answered. "The whole hotel is jumping. And then the Handel Festival is on the horizon. We're booked to the eyebrows."

Somehow Galen felt comforted by the thought of his father still going up and down stairs and parking cars. Maybe there was no better way to get through the alcoholic shakes. However, if his father did not show at the meeting tonight, he'd track him down.

"I was going to say I could drive you over to get your truck, if today is the day," Andrew said.

"It is," Galen smiled. "But why don't you two have some breakfast with us first?"

"Can't, can't," Ophelia said. "Too much to do. I suppose you heard there were some shootings over in Mayfair again, and I decided to deliver flowers to the patients."

"No, I didn't. Was anybody killed?" Galen asked.

"No, but a few flowers never hurt anybody," Ophelia observed.

Andrew just looked at Galen and shrugged. "At least she's not asking anybody else to deliver them. At least she's doing it herself."

"Unless, of course, it gets too hectic," Ophelia answered.

"If I were you," Andrew said, "I'd get my rig and get to work as soon as I could, $500,000 or no $500,000. Otherwise, you're a sitting duck for Ophelia asking you to FTD. And you and I can now definitely talk about the health club."

"Finding something to do won't be hard," Galen said, "because I've got a job over in the Oasis district that I've been putting off for weeks. Mayfair money or no Mayfair money. And, yes, I'm looking into that health club."

But now that Jacob's breakfast was all ready, he couldn't help but want to tell them all about the disappearance of the Ghost, and the explanation of the notes and lights. Anything to stop being this clueless Rip Van Winkle, whose only line seemed to be, "Oh, really? Well, that's news to me." But on some level, he was waiting for that familiar iridescence to appear in the windows at some point or—to give him some direction, once he suspended that spectral piece, transferred from the Estate, from their own chandelier. A Ouija-type message in this bungalow.

Jacob came in and sat down next to him.

"Come, Jacob," Ophelia said, "when you're done, let's you and I do a little delivery today. Then, after, we can arrange the whole storefront window any way you want it, and I'll make you a big lunch?"

"Good deal," Jacob said. "Dad, when are we going to spend all of your money? I have the most friends I've ever had."

"When we get the money," Galen said.

It took only minutes for Andrew to drive him to "Adam's Truck Repair," and then Galen was free to go over to the Oasis district, and feel extremely vulnerable. He had not been there in a long time, and he was spooked by all the memories that went with it. For close by was the Oasis Hotel, near the river, whose dance lounge had been his gay haunt for years. The place was a 1950s relic, modeled on a gay hotel in Honolulu, and the whole spirit that radiated from the district was one of a hot equator. When you went into the lounge, it seemed that you were diving into an aquarium, with all kinds of odd fish swimming about. The river and the gay nude beach were close by, and not far from there was the Mayflower block, which, while stolid and gardened and full of daytime downtown businesses, still had a certain hue— the promise of rejuvenation. And his cousin Keystone's Casablanca Tapes was there, too. And Dr. Dick's Hollywood Sports Clinic. Along with the Mayflower Theatre.

He stopped at the Oasis Hotel first and asked if they still wanted him— he was so late in following up on his work orders.

"Of course, we want you," the desk clerk said. And winked. "A celebrity like you."

The place was a reconstructed Holiday Inn, with only five stories to speak for itself. Carrying his garden tools up the back stairs, Galen had the distinct feeling of being in a birdcage. He came out on a pretty sunroof, with a central fountain of aquamarine water. The lawn furniture was spindly, with the woven patterns coming undone in places. But the gorgeous dirt beds he liked to work—and he wondered why he had procrastinated so long in coming up. He started clipping the roses (yellow Blaze variety), and trimmed the clematis, trying not to disturb the sunbathers, who looked particularly trim and beautiful. Actually, there was a private health club on this fifth floor, and the members were allowed to use the roof as a semi-nudist spot in summer. There were several out this early afternoon.

Even from these few stories up, he could see most of Carleton Park in perspective, which was now like a floating island of rough magic, so glimmering and ethereal, one forgot that such things as a city like Mayfair or an official like Daws could exist. It was a city such as his uncle, had he really been a ghost after all, would have given him. In fact, it was like the L.A. his uncle had lived in when Galen had paid his visit in 1965.

The bamboo had gotten greatly out of hand, and as he whacked it down, all the parrots, set imperiously out in their green cages, protested and cussed him out. "Don't give me any of your lip," he said.

"Fuck you," the parrot told him.

"You don't seem to be having a lot of luck over there," one of the nearly naked sunbathers called.

"No," he answered flatly, not looking over, "but I'll survive."

It seemed that wherever you went, there was always a wiseass or a parrot around. Same difference.

The birds went on squawking in their cages, protesting the pruning. He staked up the gladiolas, which were red and opening to white centers. The white climber rose had virtually fallen from its lattice, and Galen tried to guide it back in without getting the briars.

"Here, let me help you," the sunbather called again, getting up and coming over. Full standing, he had a well-cut quarterback's body. He was in nothing but Rayon shorts. Galen recognized him from the Sports Section of the *Daily* as a former decathloner. He also recognized him from his days back in the bar. With Leo. Like Leo, this man was gay but not out.

"Thanks," Galen said, "but you're in greater danger of getting stuck. I've at least got a shirt on."

"I'm tough," the man said a little mock-heroically. "And I think I know you. You're the one who got awarded all the money. You're pretty famous. Along with your fabulous family."

Fabulous?

The man held the lattice taut, shoved its points more firmly into the soil.

"I suppose so," Galen answered.

They wove the rose bush back into position. Just two more briars through the lattice, and it would be fine.

"I appreciate your help," Galen added.

For some reason—probably all the preoccupying thoughts about his father—he wanted to be left alone this morning, or noon, or whatever hour was, despite this man's beauty. He just wanted to catch up on his projects. Perfected, the fabric of blossoms now stood before them.

He and the stranger were getting mild, ironic applause from the other sunbathers.

"What a pretty display," one of them called.

"You two look like a store window," another commentator observed.

"Yeah—Ophelia's—the Scrupulous Florist," the first said.

"That's fitting. She's his sister."

"I would think," the decathloner went on to Galen, "that you wouldn't need to be doing this anymore."

"You mean getting all this shit?"

"No, I mean working at all," the athlete answered.

"I haven't got the money yet," Galen told him. And in the instant, it struck him that if he were to take care of all the people in his life—Teresa, Jacob, Christabel, Gregory—there wouldn't be much left. Gone in a breath.

"If you have any extra," the man went on, "just let me know. I know a lot of good charities it could go to. By the way, let me introduce myself—Brent."

They shook hands. The hand was oily—sunscreen. Galen could now catch his scent, even apart from the roses. It was like salt, of the ocean.

"I've had a lot of offers already," Galen said. "But I'll keep you in mind. You know, we've met before."

"Yes," Brent answered. "I know your brother-in-law, Andrew. He's helped me with the promotion of my work."

Galen, who had been picking up his shears again, nearly let his jaw drop. "You actually work?"

"Of course I *actually* work," Brent answered defensively. "Why wouldn't I?"

"You can't work," Galen went on, taking in his body. "It's impossible you could have a profession. Nobody like you actually *works*."

Brent's brow came down, nearly in a thundercloud. "Well, thanks a lot."

Galen knew his statement was utterly tactless, and he didn't want to end up apologizing to this man—who was starting to get on his nerves as it was.

The plain truth was—these mirages never had jobs. Never. They were always just passing through. In their late twenties, they were candidates for being kept by an older man. This Brent was perfect houseboy material, and he actually worked.

Galen tried to cover himself. "I thought you were a professional athlete. Weren't you on the cover of *Men's Exercise?*"

"Yes," Brent answered. "But that was a long time ago. I work at Doc Hollywood's now."

Galen started cutting down some of the hibiscus, which had also overgrown. "Physical therapy and such are businesses I'd like to know more about."

"Are you thinking about going into them?" Brent asked, excited. With his quarterback's build, he had lit up like a summer mirage, out in a midnight hayfield.

"Possibly. I'm thinking of buying a health club. But I would have to get training to do anything in it." He stood there, aware of how vague he must have seemed. He was a ragamuffin, newly into money, thin, and blackened by the sun. He, Galen, should have been occupying his extra summer time with an amateur production of Shakespeare or Gilbert and Sullivan. Looking poised.

Brent was following him from plant to plant as he continued working. "Would you call me if you want to find out more? Would you let me know? I'd be happy to give it."

"Sure. I will," Galen answered.

The glimmering, tanned figure was striding over to his backpack and then returning. Why should a physical therapist work so hard at walking? "I'm going to go down to the beach in a few minutes, but here's my number. Give me a call."

He seemed to be waiting for Galen to return the favor, but Galen just said, "Thanks," pocketed the card and started in on the nasturtiums. He could well imagine the sensation known as "Brent" would cause down at the nude beach.

Brent was waving goodbye and ambling toward the door. With that much mass, Brent seemed capable of causing the spindly chaises to shake. And everything else. He was Godzilla clearing a Tokyo street. And yet he wasn't a giant at all. Just beautifully formed.

In getting ready to go, Galen found copies of *The Daily* littered about, and he picked these up as well, while the rest of the sunburnt group talked among themselves, obviously having connected him, finally, with the front page. One woman in particular looked as though she was covered by no more than one or two of Ophelia's lanceolate gladiola leaves. On a very, very dark suntan. Galen wondered if she ever left this place.

Passing him on his drive back, the Estate, deprived of its ghost only stood there, its white front glimmering. How different from his own bungalow up ahead, with its bushes ranging from blue to pink. He and Jacob now thought they would call it Hydrangea House.

Now home, he found a note from Jacob saying that he would be at Christabel's until dinner—working on some play he was writing—he walked to the dresser and took out the piece of prism glass, very carefully wrapped, and suspended it from the chandelier. The very heat of the shadowed living room seemed to send light through, patterning the walls, the ceiling. He looked for his uncle from every conceivable angle, someone to comfort him while he was waiting to meet up with his father. The iridescence passed across the panels, the nook, over the photographs of Treasure Island. Galen took out the Almanac from the same drawer and read—

July is to lie beside the brook, let it meander; to lie pensively and be reminded that men have taken their ease this way for millennia. Remember how Horace talked about it in his odes, in that rustic retreat, safe from sirens like Pyrrha, letting the world flash by in a watery reflection. That ease, that stance, that lying at leisure was no doubt imitated after something in the Hellenistic poets, and then at this Roman juncture, imitated later in the 18th century, in the English country churchyard, which also had a brook running through, with the stained-glass window just in the distance and the single stream of cloud arching over the little cathedral, like a skywriter streak or smoke issuing from a chimney. Let me just lie in the floating mirage of July, and feel like I'm bridging whole millennia.

Then when he was least suspecting it, he felt lust for Brent firing up. He hadn't even known it was there.

◆◆◆

They had been at a morning A.A. meeting. When it was over, Galen walked his father back to the hotel. He could pick Jacob up there. As they went down the avenue, he had the curious feeling of being out in Forest Glade again and moving across hill and dale to see Teresa and meet up with her double in the form of the runner.

Standing in the hotel's grand entrance, Galen could see Jacob and Christabel in the Sorceress Seamstress shop looking over the top of the half-door and appearing dismayed. And behind them, he could see Yvonne.

"Will I see you at the meeting tomorrow?" Galen asked before going in. "Will you call me if you need to?"

"Yes, yes, of course," his father answered. And before Galen could pass through, Gregory grabbed and hugged him.

"Thanks, Dad," he said. "Looks like I'm going to need that."

Coming into the shop, Galen was struck by how elegant both of them looked, Yvonne and his mother. But also, a huge current seemed to run between them. The energy lit up the whole place, which appeared filled with costumes, with Jacob cowering over in the corner. He visibly brightened when he saw Galen come in and instantly went over and took his hand.

"What's going on?" Galen asked.

"I've come to take Jacob back," Yvonne said. "Obviously, there's too much ruckus going on around here for him to stay on."

Her braided hair and her subdued red lipstick suggested a sense of command.

"What's wrong?" he asked.

"Clearly too much chaos," she said with a sense of concern. "Whether you've settled for half a million or nothing at all. You can't have reporters and solicitors for your money going through that revolving door every hour on the hour and have a sense of normalcy for Jacob."

She was actually still quite pretty. Her body had stayed slim and athletic. A successful pediatrician with a style that fit family medicine.

"I have never agreed with you about normalcy," Galen said. "You know that."

"Maybe not," she answered, "but we need to agree on what's best for Jacob."

"And Jacob's opinion is," Jacob said, "he wants to stay here. You know what will happen anyway." He jumped off the window seat, letting go, temporarily, Galen's hand. "You'll send me off to tai chi and ignore me most of the time anyway. That's what happened just a few days ago."

"That's not the case now," Yvonne answered, taking a pencil from her purse. "Boris and I have a whole set of plans we're going to follow when you get home. Starting with picnics." She wrote items down on a rainbow pad as if she were going to give Galen a timetable.

"I'm sorry," Jacob said. "But I want to do my play."

"And probably to the detriment of your good health and exercise program," his mother told him. "Why do you want to write a play anyway?"

"Exercise program?" Jacob said. "What exercise program?"

"That's what I mean," she went on. "I'm concerned about his weight," she said, looking at Galen and Christabel.

"Oh, stop it," Christabel said, "there's nothing wrong with Jacob's weight."

Yvonne gave her a glance.

"I want to know," Galen said, "who Boris is."

"Boris is my new sweetheart. We're nearly engaged," she said.

"She spent a good part of her time trying to sell us on Boris," Christabel said. "Just before you came in. He's a lawyer."

"If Jacob is going to have a new father," she said, "he needs to get to know him."

"New father!" Jacob said. "New father!"

"Listen, Yvonne, what do you say to Jacob coming up for a week?" Galen asked. "Once his play is done."

"'Play is done'?" she asked. "You make him sound like a young Eugene O'Neill."

"He may very well be," Christabel said defensively. "You forget that on our side of the family at least, there's talent. Joost Vondel, the Shakespeare of Holland, is in a direct line to—"

"You don't have to go on and on about your lineage, Christabel," Yvonne said. "I've heard about it."

"I don't want to go," Jacob said.

"You could tolerate it for a week," Galen said.

Yvonne got her purse. "Well, I'll consider it. But this hubbub I hear about in the papers has got to stop."

"Let's be in touch, then," Galen said, standing up and realizing that this was one of their first non-apocalyptic goodbyes in many years. "And we can decide when the week might be. And Jacob and I can talk about it on the side before then. And we can work out visitation again."

While Galen had been in prison, Yvonne had left the matter of parenting up to Christabel, because she, Yvonne, was venturing into her new medical practice and obviously a new boyfriend. Whatever motherly attention she had, she directed toward Teresa. Now she wanted to come back into Jacob's life; Galen could identify with that.

"I can tell you now," Jacob said. "No, no. Let her have Teresa full-time. She's happy with them. She's the right girl for it. A regular Sally Sorority."

"I never see Teresa," Yvonne said, looking sad suddenly. "Hardly. She's at school. She wants to be on her own."

Noise in the lobby. He could see through the glass in the door that once again, on a sunny and sereny evening, the couches being taken up by reporters hot for facts.

"You have to realize, too," Galen said, "that things are rarely like this here. And Jacob and I have moved to our own home down the street. Give us the benefit of the doubt."

"I'll try," Yvonne said. And finally left.

There was silence.

"My God," Christabel said. "That woman is the ultimate limit. Seeing her, I'm almost glad you're gay."

"Ditto," Jacob said. "And not almost."

Galen looked over at him. "How do you feel? Does all this bother you?"

Jacob looked up. "No. But there is something I want to talk about. In private."

Christabel got her purse. "I'll go out there and deal with the reporters as best as I know how—although I don't seem to be doing too well in that area lately. Maybe they'll want to hear about my trip to Amsterdam."

"Trip to Amsterdam?" Jacob asked.

"Yes. I'll tell you two more about it later," Christabel answered, going through the door.

Watching her leave, he saw the lobby become settled again.

Galen sat down amidst all the threads and needles, the bolts of cloth, and the hanging clothes. He still felt like he was in a nymph's chamber. Maybe under the sea.

"Well, friend?" he asked.

"Dad," Jacob said, "that guy named Boris Voxman was out in the car the whole time she was here."

"Oh? Why didn't he come in?" Galen asked.

"I don't know," Jacob answered. "But she started in by telling me that if ever I have problems, I should call him. If ever I need guidance on growing up, call him. Don't talk to you. He's got all the answers. She wants him to be my father."

"Oh yeah?" Galen felt his heart drop to the bottom of him.

"Yeah. And it's so stupid, too," Jacob said. "I don't want to go up there and sit around and wait for her to come home from work. Or be put into some Judo class because she thinks I might get bored or gain too much weight while she's away. Shit."

"Well, you don't need to take all of this on," Galen said, recovering himself at last. "You let me handle it. You can't be brainwashed in one week."

"Can I go now?" Jacob asked. "I've got a new lead on something for my play."

"Yes," Galen said, smiling.

Jacob went off. Galen stepped out into the lobby. Christabel had led the reporters off somewhere. Galen had had too much for one day. He sat down on a vacated couch and looked at the summer hues down the avenue. All the aspen trees were in mint condition, and there was an endless blue light that formed a hallway toward the horizon. Here on the walls, the Vermeers and Rembrandts hung stalwart, with small hills and dales in the background and shining through. He wondered how much progress he had made on forming a family. Maybe it was over in Amsterdam that he could find it. Christabel seemed to be looking there, too.

◆◆◆

August days. The white butterflies fly above the sprinklers. The days narrow to a candle on the horizon in the morning and widen to broad expanses of stars at night. At midnight, it's still possible to swim naked in the river, or at five in the morning, still possible to jog across town in just shorts, following one silvered tree after the next.

The white butterflies flutter through the courtyard of the hotel, where time seems to be even slower now, and where Galen finds himself measuring the passing of time by his father's sobriety, and Andrew's designing of a new health club. On these long oasis days, Brent begins opening doors for him into the world of health—what is it?—care? Concern? Brent takes Galen to Doc Hollywood's on a Saturday and shows him the entire floor.

The famous Doc was gone the day they went in—Galen learned that he was off on a sabbatical in Europe—with the whole unit left in charge of a Dutch physical therapist, Pieter. The place, as Galen passed through it, offered striking similarities to something he had seen in Holland over twenty years ago.

"Many of the methods we use here are Dutch," Brent said. "They come from an institute in Amsterdam. Brilliantly gifted people both here and there."

"What would it be like to have talent like that?" Galen asked. "Like the talent you have in your hands? But maybe I can imagine it. My mother, she's Dutch, and she writes. And my son Jacob—it looks like he might write, too."

"Well, you have your gardening," Brent smiled. "Isn't that a gift? I mean—just think about the way that rooftop garden looks, or your own backyard, or the New Amsterdam court. Or the space just outside the Mayflower Building. That's all distinctly you."

108

"I've never thought of it that way," Galen said as they moved down to the next therapy room. "Never. That I might have a certain signature."

"Those garden spots look a little like Seattle," Brent said. "And a little like L.A. Actually, they remind me of one of your uncle's children's books, like what you showed me—the painted backdrop, if you know what I mean."

"Yes, I do."

Even in this short time, Galen was realizing how much he liked Brent. Had staked in him. And Brent was becoming tender because they were becoming a couple. The retreat of Anton, along with Uncle Eugene's ghost, had much to do with it. Anton had taken himself out of the picture after Galen's windfall. It was also connected to the struggle Anton was having with his family. And there was no magic left in the Estate. It had become so barren, Galen sometimes thought of even letting his mother sell it without a fight. And then he had to consider Teresa—he kept calling her asking to see her again, but she kept putting him off. She was getting used to the idea of another visit from him, she said.

So he took up with Brent, and they had their first swim together at Brent's mother's condominium (Brent did "trick" dives, he called them, for Galen's benefit), and later that day, they made love. The disappearance of the ghost was only tolerable now with the constant contact with Brent's smooth skin—and with the doorways he was opening for him. Galen wondered what this month would have been like if Brent hadn't happened along.

But there were moments when Brent gave him some pause, just the same. They were at Brent's mother's gated community one afternoon, and for some reason, meeting her was still not part of the plan. They were not even going to go into her apartment to change. All of it was to be in the clubhouse dressing room instead. There the windows were screened by the bamboo outside, and a slanted orange light came through on the lockers suggesting, or assuring, secrecy. Brent removed an expensive gold chain from his wrist and one from around his neck and stood naked before him. Galen had the sense that this dance was something that had been done often before and for a lot of other admirers. Sometimes Brent seemed to move in a series of *Playgirl* flashers. Brent pulled the yellow tank suit on very slowly—long after Galen had pulled on his baggy red trunks.

Dowsed with hormones and heady with the light in the room—the mute hallways of lockers making him think back on Catherine Blaine Junior High and all its corridors—Galen said, as answer to his blood, "How about a hug?" and opened his arms.

To his surprise, Brent said, "Well, not just now."

"You mean I'm just going to have to stand here holding air?" Galen asked, attempting to smile.

"Yeah, well, Galen"—significantly Brent put the cooler between them, a large white contraption that he had been very particular about bringing. He wanted to be sure they had exactly the right soda pop. "Yeah, well, Galen, what if somebody came in here and saw us? What would they think?"

"I imagine," Galen said, "they would think, 'Here's an old guy latching on to a young guy.'"

Obviously, Brent had not been listening fully. "Lech? You're no lech."

"That's not what I said. I said 'latch.'" Galen folded his arms pedantically, and given his baggy shorts, knew he must look ridiculous.

"Yeah, well," Brent went on, still absorbed, "don't be so hard on yourself." He shut the locker door on the glitter of his jewelry on the hook inside. In prison, one of Galen's cellmates had taught him the difference between the real stuff and Woolworth's. This was real stuff. "I don't know why," Brent went on, "you guys always have to be that way."

"What way? Who's 'you guys'?" Galen asked.

"Never mind," Brent answered and hulked away.

Nevertheless, outdoors, beside the kidney-shaped pool, which they had to themselves, even the private little fence was a sunny aquamarine. Just as when he had gotten his own room back—which had led to the new house—Galen was dazzled by the privacy. And his spirits, which had been dashed a little back at the locker, heated him up again. Brent moved two chaises so that he and Galen could look at each other sideways, sort of like two cop cars when the officers wanted to talk from their driver's seats. Brent had also made a nice arrangement of pop on one of the glassed tables.

"You've gone to a lot of work," Galen said. "I appreciate it." And he again was about to touch Brent—it would have been easy given the way their chaises were positioned—but the body signals still said all bets were off. So Galen just sat and tried to let the sun take him. Of course, it did just what it was supposed to do and heated him up more. Beyond the fence, the evergreens of the nearby hills seemed to form yet another fence. Exasperating because if ever the two of them should feel safe, it should be now.

Brent went over to the diving board, turned his back on Galen and flipped, like an arcing bird, straight into the water. He hauled his huge back out again, and then slowly formed himself for another dive, this time taking longer to draw his arms out from his sides. It seemed, again, as if this were a routine that had been done many times before. In another series of calendar shots, Brent folded into the water and then got back out again.

He dried off, lying flat, so that his head was almost beside Galen's.

Galen, surveying, put his hand over his and said, "Is it so hard now to do this? Isn't it OK? Can't I touch you?"

"Galen, Galen," Brent said, "you know I don't mind. It's just what if somebody sees?" He still didn't move his hand, as if he did need to soak something up before going into retreat. "I do need the contact, Man. I do. But my mother, she—"

"What about your mother?" Galen asked.

"She'd really be upset if she came in here and saw us," Brent answered.

"But I had no idea she even knew we were here," Galen said.

"Well, she doesn't. She just knows that I bring men here from time to time. I mean friends." Brent was hesitating.

"Why can't you tell her about us—or tell her about yourself, for that matter?" Galen asked.

"It's just part of the agreement. Galen, don't ask me anymore." And he turned on his stomach, away from Galen's hand. But it couldn't have been a few seconds more when he was flipping back over and beckoning him to come and get on top of him.

"Brent, what's up with you, anyway?" But Galen was so stirred he was hardly going to argue any longer. He lowered his whole body over Brent— which was what Brent had preferred in bed—and, yes, the whole spindly piece of lawn furniture gave up the ghost and came crashing down on the cement.

"Needed that, though," Brent said, getting up like the cat in the cartoon who never gets a scratch from the falling piano. He stooped over the tangled chaises and started to bend the pieces straight. "Needed that a lot."

Galen didn't feel a thing, except his hormones.

Brent liked to take him cruising around in a red Mercedes, or white Lexus, whose headlights flipped up. Still, the summer oasis-hopping that they did was merely a backdrop for what Galen was learning about the world of massage. It was as if the curvature of the basic human skeleton—and flesh— were within his reach now. An idea was forming about how pain might be set right by having tendons, muscles, viscera hanging at ease upon the bones. As he envisioned it—and he envisioned it every time Brent would allow him to hold him—he realized how many days he had spent waiting for Eugene's ghost to appear, for the light to go on in the windows of the Estate. Since prison, he had given almost every particle of his energy to intangibles, and now he had crash-landed into his own feet, his own fingertips, his own lungs. And on top of Brent.

The blue pool of Brent's mother's gated community became their mainstay, their home base. He got back into running again, into swimming—consistently. He was brought back to memories of the time in the penitentiary when his only solace had been the Dutch postcards, the A.A. meetings, and his time in the exercise yard, or the one run he was allowed in town, under guard, as a part of minimum security. The prison had actually had an officer run with them, along with people of the community, over the hills, past the shaded ponds, and the little cottages, where people, miraculously, lived at liberty. Those few moments when the body wasn't punished.

Well, now, the freedom increased, in August, the most idyllic month of the year. He attended to his obligations. He saw to the money when it arrived. Finally. He laid aside $20,000 for Teresa's college fund—and the same amount for Jacob. He mentally reserved a space for another $20,000 for Andrew when the Mayflower deal came through. He put the rest away for safekeeping; until his mind cleared. He actually began to think about buying Christabel off, so she would release the Estate to the Gay Alliance and AIDS House. Yes, so he would put that money away, and besides, he had not gotten $500,000—the lawyers had taken over a quarter, just as Siems the Short had said.

It was clear, as he had probably known all along, that the settlement would not settle him for life—he'd better follow up on these new doors that were opening. A disappointment, certainly, since his uncle's letter had told him he deserved all of his legacy, and he had thought that eventually, Fate would reward him anyway. Good luck. No, the biggest change in Carleton Park was that everybody thought he was rich, and so they were ready to give him money and position at the raise of an eyebrow. And also ask for cash back for themselves. $500,000 didn't go as far these days as it used to.

In Brent's bed, Brent would hold him and tell him about how he himself had discovered his profession. How high school and college football had given him respect for how the body moved and operated, eventually leading him into the need to take away people's pain, particularly men's. He had seen so much wreckage on the field. Maybe this was where the recklessness and the reserve both came from.

"I would love to have that for myself," Galen said. "The ambition. Or better than that. The—sense of mission. To help people. Especially now. When I got out of prison, I was guided. Led. Now it's gotten all hazy. I want something else. A direction."

"You think I can give you that?" Brent rested his head against the headboard, the veins in his neck standing out. Galen was reminded of the photograph of the idol in his uncle's den. The rivulets of light spreading down its shoulders.

"I suppose," Galen said. Galen was so aware of himself physically, now, it was almost crushing. His toenails scraped against the sheet. He was conscious of his brownness, as if he could not shower away all the earth he had worked with—he brought a dust storm with him to bed. And all the scents. Of pine, spruce, arborvitae. Rose. Myrtle. In fact, together he and Brent seemed a tangle underneath the lattice of Brent's morning-gloried bedspread.

"You suppose? You're not sure?" Brent asked.

"I was thinking," Galen answered, "if my uncle's theory is right, it could be you, or it could be someone else, anyone else. Maybe even Jacob. Or Anton. Anyone could give me direction. And that's what I want."

"What's your uncle's theory?" Brent asked.

"It's called 're-embodiment,'" Galen answered. Among his papers, he had found a pamphlet his uncle had written. "People come back in different forms. Nothing is ever lost. Maybe you're a form of my uncle. Or Jacob is. Or Anton."

"I don't want to hear about Anton," Brent said and turned over in bed. On his stomach again. Once more, Galen was reminded of their talk in the chaises. "It just seems to me," Brent went on, "that you're being pretty demanding. I mean, why do you need to ask for more? You not only have a job, and money, and me, but also the bonanza of your family. What's this about some divine direction? You were just being superstitious about your uncle."

Galen felt even more burdened by the earth. The pastels (surprisingly chosen) of Brent's bedroom accentuated this. The curtains were gauzy pink, with sashes. Galen now imagined himself as a lanky brown troll who'd snuck into the boudoir of some royal page or the kept "minion" of the king. Which king? Who?

"A bonanza?" Galen asked. "You want to call it a bonanza?"

"I do," Brent answered, twisting his hands. "You have no idea what it's like not to belong."

"If you want to be more included, just say the word," Galen said. "We could have some family outings together anytime."

That was it for now, and they slept on through, their own togetherness being enough for the moment. But later, Brent did say the word. So Galen proposed that on their next swim, they bring Jacob along. It would be just like two fathers and a son, as in the book, *Daddy's Roommate*, which had caused such a stir at the Mayfair library. The whole city was up in arms about getting it off the shelf, along with *Heather Has Two Mommies*. Brent at least thought it was a wonderful proposal. As for Jacob—he was skeptical. But then, when Galen said he wouldn't have to swim at all but could just sit by the pool and write his play—and in sunglasses—he became more agreeable. It could seem like Hollywood. He could be his great uncle. Scenarios in L.A. As the time drew closer, Brent, however, became nervous. Jacob's presence might lure out Brent's mysterious mother.

So on this particular Saturday, they had to show up once more for the locker room in the clubhouse. To Galen's surprise, Brent refused to stand naked in front of either one of them this time; when he drew off his Bermudas, there his swimming suit was. This particular bit of prudery caused Galen to tighten up. Jacob got into his striped suit, which Andrew had given him on his birthday, his extra weight hanging on his hips like the folds of a small accordion. They went out to the poolside, and the heat was voluminous.

"Want anything to drink, Buddy?" Brent asked Jacob.

"Coke, thanks," Jacob said. And looked a little like one of the Andy Hardy kids playing poolside director. He opened his notebook and started printing, very carefully, with a pencil.

A young mother and her grade-school daughter had stationed themselves at the north end. The sight of Brent made them nod an approving hello, as if he were a lifeguard. Like Jacob, they had suits accented with red, white, and blue.

Brent began his dives again. The young mother and daughter looked at each other and applauded enthusiastically. They cupped their hands against the sun as if witnessing the landing of some divine aircraft.

"Dad," Jacob said, "what do you think if I have my play take place in San Francisco?"

"Sounds like a good setting," Galen answered.

"I was thinking the St. Francis Hotel," Jacob said. Jacob was not even looking at Brent emerging from the pool. He had been writing as he had been speaking.

"Hey, Jake," Brent called, "why don't you come in?"

Galen knew Jacob hated that name.

"Not right now," Jacob answered. "I'm talking with Dad."

"Don't you want to go in?" Galen asked him. "As long as we're here? Save drinking that coke until after you've had your swim."

"No, no—I want to ask you about this," Jacob insisted. "Besides, you said I didn't have to go in the water."

Galen tried to settle in and listen. He didn't want to turn into Christabel—urging good hardy male-oriented play for red-blooded boys. Nevertheless, he wanted Brent included.

"Well," Galen began, "I don't think there is any St. Francis Hotel. There's the Sir Francis Drake—that's been a big one for years."

"No, no. See"—Jacob, at last, looked up. ("Good dive," he said, as an afterthought.) "See, St. Francis is the name of the hotel in *Charlie Chan at Treasure Island*. I thought it would make things a lot more mysterious if I used a fictitious name. Also, St. Francis is dead, and that's fitting for the séance I'm going to have in the back room."

"Sir Francis is dead, too," Galen said irrelevantly. "And then you want to be sure that old hotels have back rooms where séances can happen."

"We have a back room—the Board Room at the New Amsterdam," Jacob observed.

But before Galen could answer, Brent came over. "Hey, I don't like having to listen on the side." When Galen automatically reached for his hand, he eluded him. Things were beginning to slide.

"You're going to regret not getting in," Brent said to Jacob. "You can write your play anytime."

"I'll get in when I get a minute," Jacob said huffily. "I'm just about done with the first act. And I can't write my play anytime. I have to go with the inspiration."

"Who's going to be in the séance?" Galen asked.

"Well, Charlie, and his number one son and a magician and a lady," Jacob said, resuming enthusiasm. "They're going to call a couple of people up from the grave. That's in this latest Frank Baum book I've found."

"You mean that one that Uncle actually wrote?" Galen asked.

"Yeah," Jacob answered.

"Who are they going to call up from the grave?" Brent asked.

"Well, Frank Baum and then this favorite uncle." Jacob smiled.

"Sounds familiar," Brent answered. He had taken a nearby chaise and was lying back, with his hand over his eyes. "It'd sure be nice, though, to call anyone up from the grave that you wanted to. Anyway, I've seen that happen in a lot of movies."

Jacob looked defensive. "Well, yeah, but it will have some new things, too."

"I wasn't saying it wasn't original," Brent answered back. "But to be honest with you, it does sound like you're picking up on your Dad's superstitions."

Galen felt the pinch, but to smooth things over, he got in the water and urged the other two to follow. Naturally, Brent did; naturally, Jacob did not. The pool was large enough for short laps, so the two of them started in. Galen, although feeling apprehensive, felt as though he were swimming in the center of a sapphire. His blood slowly heated again, and when the rest weren't looking, he grabbed Brent's hand underwater. Brent's brows came together, and he shook his head, water going everywhere, and got his hand free.

"Maybe," he could hear Jacob saying from behind his sunglasses. "Maybe I should set this play in a dime store or on a fairgrounds."

"You see," Brent said, "your brains are frying out. Come in, come in."

"No, no," Jacob answered.

The woman and her daughter, now highlighted by silver sun, were still waiting, obviously for more trick dives from Brent.

◆◆◆

Through this month of mirages, Galen kept making phone calls to Anton, who would only put him off and say he was going through something yet again with his family. He might have to move out and even give up Brandsmark Gardens. Although Galen had stopped hounding, Anton continued to have a gravitational pull on him, still. He suspected it was the windfall money still that was driving Anton off. Things were just too good for Galen in order for Anton to join in.

Nevertheless, Galen could not deny how much he liked him, and Jacob made it worse by plainly saying that Brent was a jerk, compared to Anton. On his side, Brent said he would prefer it if they didn't try any more family outings. Andrew, who had known both Anton and Brent before Galen had, expressed surprise, in his mild way, that Anton was out and Brent was in. On the other hand, Ophelia just told Galen he was way off-center.

Meanwhile, Galen helped out at the hotel. His mother was to leave for Amsterdam to do an international reading in October, and she had a local one coming up here in Carleton Park in just a few weeks. Gregory worked like a trooper to stay sober and do his job at the hotel. Still, it was clear he felt awkward and almost inoperative without booze.

Galen was out trimming in the courtyard when his father crept up with two suitcases.

"You're not leaving, Dad?" Galen asked.

"No, no." His father stood there in the full sun, his iron fingers still tight against the handles. Galen put down his shovel.

"What's up, Dad?" Galen asked.

"This is going to sound strange, but if you wanted to carry baggage without falling down, what would you do?" His father looked hangdog again, apologetic.

The question did not sound at all strange. His own sense of balance had been shot to hell for months after he had gotten sober. He remembered being grateful in one respect for prison—for having such a narrow track to walk on—to go out into the great world would have made him seasick, especially with the blinding light. He seemed to be in a constantly rocking boat.

"Here"—he went up right behind his father and grasped his wrists—"just look straight in front of you, making sure that the bags you do carry are in balance. Now let's try it." And together, as one man, they went down the narrow-paved path of the courtyard. "How is that? Does that seem steady?"

"Yes, I think so," his father said, blushing. He took a moment to try it on his own. "All these years. I've never even thought about it. Never even thought about it! Could carry anything. But when I got sober, I started thinking about it. Like the guy on the tightrope who looks down all of a sudden."

"And when you set the bags down or pick them up," Galen said, "be sure to bend your knees, to save your back."

"Like this?" His father lowered himself gracefully. After all, he had not been a bellman all these years for nothing.

"Yes, just exactly," Galen said, patting him on his strong shoulder.

The church tower tolled, and Galen was aware, in the silence, of the stone maiden splashing water over in the fountain.

"How long has this been going on?" he asked. "This equilibrium problem?"

"For a while," his father answered. "I asked a doctor about it, and he said it's just something to put up with."

"Well, that was me, too," Galen said. "Is me, too, except that I have Rip Van Winkle's Syndrome. Still waking up."

His father just went on standing there, as if something else was supposed to happen. "Well, I guess I'd best get these bags down to the parking lot," he said at last. "I'll see you at the meeting tonight. I have a month sober."

"My God. You've never been sober that long," Galen said, patting him again.

"Never. I wish I could describe it to you," his father said.

"You don't have to," Galen answered.

"I'll tell you what it's like," his father went on. "It's like I've been under an empty goldfish bowl, and they've just taken it away. I can breathe so deeply, can see so clearly, it makes me light-headed, and I have a hard time standing on my own two feet, carrying luggage, doing chores."

"That's me," Galen answered. "All around. While being forgetful."

"But all this business"—his father dropped his suitcases again—"about being so awkward, like you're just learning to walk."

"Yes," Galen said. "Things I could do loaded—and do so easily—I have to learn all over again."

"Like what?" his father asked.

"Talking to people, figuring out what I say after I say hello. Managing finances—eating, working. I wish I had a nickel for every time I've felt like an amnesiac since getting out of prison." Galen picked up his shovel, leaned on it.

His father laughed. Resumed with the luggage. "Now that's me. Rip the Bellman."

Galen put one arm around him while still holding the shovel, encircled his shoulders. "See you tonight."

The sun was so strong by this point that, had he not touched his father, he might have thought it all a mirage. A few days ago, he had cut down an old hawthorn, and so now he had to replant the hydrangeas that had been protected by its shade. But, for a moment, he was caught by the idea that although his father was a new man, there seemed in him some of the old qualities, too. Like the loyalty Galen had remembered a few weeks ago and the willingness not to be the center of attention, even when asking for help.

He dug holes for the hydrangeas, poured in fertilizer. It was still early enough in the morning that the transplanting would not shock the plants which had been placed in so sunny a spot. In spading around the flowers, he allowed their iridescence to take him over; they glimmered and formed arcs of blue, purple, pink, and red, like limited rainbows, and he thought again of his uncle and the time he had flown to L.A. in '65.

Hadn't that been his way of asking for help, too? But for what?

Galen returned the shovel and the rake to the little shed, just off the courtyard. The white butterflies were visiting the fountain. It was impossible not to believe that they held little bits of spirits within them; their mildness, their beauty, was overpowering. They did not offer the consolation of the lights on in the Estate, but they were the next best thing.

Galen took off his shirt, pulled out the hand lawnmower for the short patch of grass around the park bench. He was just replacing his cap when he saw Brent coming toward him through the rain of green and white light.

"I brought you some lunch. Pop, other things." Brent actually had a picnic basket.

Galen would have hugged him, but he was too sweaty. Brent was keeping his distance because of that, anyway.

"You seem a little wet, friend," Brent said.

He looked like a ghost or a sailor, all dressed in white for his P.T. job.

"I am. How's the work gone this morning?" Galen asked.

"Pretty intense," Brent answered. "Some real accident cases."

They seemed at a loss to talk further. Looking around at the hotel's windows, Brent took his hand and then let go. "I thought maybe you would have dropped this job by now."

"No," Galen smiled, putting his shirt back on, "I'm still here. My family can't afford to hire out the work just now."

"You mean you haven't bailed them out yet?" Brent asked.

"They haven't asked me to," Galen answered. "And I don't have the money yet."

Brent edged closer, and they sat on the bench. He said, "Well, like I said before, if you are looking to make a good investment, keep me in mind."

Suspicion again. And the time he had spent in L.A. nudged him just a little more toward Eugene's last end—precipitous—with a young lover who took him for all he was worth. The man's name was Lucky. Even sober, Galen didn't like remembering that, but he felt it.

The white butterflies continued to weave their patterns. Through the long strip of vertical glass, which stretched from hotel floor to hotel floor, he and Brent watched his father making his slow progress with the luggage.

"What did you have in mind anyway?" Galen asked.

"A little business venture I'm doing," Brent said. "A plan to get my own practice. Get out of Doc Hollywood's. You could come in with me. Form a partnership."

"I thought you were perfectly happy at Doc Hollywood's," Galen said.

"Doc Hollywood, as you saw, is no longer around," Brent answered.

It occurred to Galen, in that moment, that the absent doctor might have been one of Brent's many exes.

"That shouldn't really change the business, should it?" Galen asked. "Especially since you like the man who's running things now."

"It's not the same. I had this idea that you and I could work something out." He smiled, and the muscular creases in his face came together. "The dynamic duo."

"Well, I have to think about it," Galen answered. "Are you sure you're serious about this? You think you could visualize yourself in a family with me?"

"Why not? I kind of like Jacob," he answered. "And I know I like you." He touched Galen again.

"Just kind of like Jacob?" Galen asked.

"Well, the boy could use some guidance," Brent said, turning his face from him. "Could stand to lose some weight and maybe take up a sport. I've got a lot of background in that department."

But before Galen could answer, he saw his father topple, framed in the second-story hotel window.

"Fuck," Brent said, also seeing, and being younger, was well on his feet before Galen. In the midst of his race up the stairs—with Brent far ahead—Galen had a vision of the white butterflies in the glass.

When they got to him, his father was smiling, but clearly unable to get up. He was on the landing, head resting on the stair. One hand was cocked with pain and was reaching for his back.

"My friend," Brent said, gently helping him rise, "why don't you use the elevator?"

"Causes ear problems," Gregory said. "But obviously, the stairs got me just the same."

"See if you can stand, Dad," Galen said, putting an arm around him.

It was an uncertain venture, with his father going red with pain or embarrassment or both. Brent seemed thunderstruck that this man was Galen's father.

They smoothed out the chocolate uniform, while Gregory caught his breath.

"Now try moving one slow step at a time," Brent said. They still had him bridged between them.

Gregory did so and winced almost immediately. "Hip," he said. "Bad."

"Is there a place where you can lie down?" Brent asked him.

"Yes, at the end of the hall, there's an empty room," Gregory said.

"We'll take him down there," Brent told Galen.

Having scouted up Tamara, who unlocked the door for them, Galen had Gregory sit on the bed while Brent, very quickly, checked him over. Almost immediately, he found something out of place in the lower back.

"Lie sideways, please," Brent said.

They moved his father into position.

With no more ado, in two strokes, Brent pressed against the small of his back, while Galen was signaled to hold his father steady. In another second, all was done—very gently—and Brent told his father simply to lean back comfortably. He called for pillows. Since the room had none, Galen and Tamara went to find them in the linen closet. In leaving, he saw that some of the pain had gone out of his father's face.

And as he went back to the room, he felt his own heart rate ease. Returning, as Brent ordered him to place a pillow under his father's head and legs, he saw relief come over Gregory's face like a warm wave.

Tamara had gone to alert the family.

"Anything broken?" Galen asked.

"No," Brent said. "I already checked. No bruises either."

"When can he get up?" Galen asked.

"When he's ready," Brent answered.

Gregory smiled, lying there. "I'm not ready."

So they waited, quite a while, not knowing what else to say. Finally, together, Brent and Galen formed another bridge. Galen felt all the euphoria of human contact. With their arms around his father, their hands, his and Brent's, joined in a clasp.

At last, Galen introduced Brent and Gregory.

Rickety, led by Tamara, they went down the hotel hallway. "What miracle happened in there?" she asked.

"Afraid we'll have to use the elevator," Brent said.

"Go for it," Gregory said. "This is no time to be choosey."

Once they had gotten to the first floor and then over to the adjoining house and Gregory's room, Gregory could pull out his keys. Galen situated him on his bed, while Christabel, having caught a glimpse in the hall, bustled in and showed him the first wifely solicitude that Galen had ever witnessed in her.

"You're not to go back on the job today," she declared. "Not today. Not tomorrow. Not the day after—until I say so."

"What about all the catch-up work before you leave?" Gregory asked.

"We'll just have to work it out," she said.

With the silence, Galen introduced Brent to his mother. Explained what Brent had done.

"Miraculous."

"I could hardly feel unusual or special," Brent said gallantly, "being around such gifted people as you."

"Gifted for what?" Gregory asked. "Falling down?"

"Exactly," Christabel said, "and in more ways than one if you include the whole family."

"Don't you plan on being on the local talk show soon?" Brent asked, stretching his back. "Isn't that a confirmed spot? It's what I heard."

"Yes, yes," Christabel answered, quite bored. "However that's more for historical interest—what my past included—than for what is going on now. People like seeing housewives these days make good."

"Nevertheless," Brent said, "you're among the brightest stars in the local galaxy."

"I suppose you could say that."

At that moment, Ophelia and Andrew came in.

Ophelia was immediately arranging coverlets and reprimanding her father for overdoing it.

"I told you," she said, turning to Christabel, "we've been running him ragged."

"Don't look at me," Christabel answered. "I've been saying that he should have retired years ago."

"Yeah, have him do that," Andrew said, "and the hotel folds in like a house of cards or a tower with one brick pulled out. If you let Gregory go, we then have to think about the impossibility of finding replacements."

"I hope you feel appreciated," Ophelia said to her father, patting his cheek as he lay there. "What we're saying is—you go, and the New Amsterdam goes. That's how essential you are."

Galen couldn't help but notice that this was the first time his father had ever been really acknowledged —not since the time he had been revealed as their father.

"I thank you for those words, but I'm not ready to retire," Gregory said. "Not yet, anyway."

"Well, maybe not," Ophelia said, "but we'll certainly see you through this until you're on your feet again."

"I do have to go," Brent said. "I've been on my lunch break."

"Obviously a busman's holiday," Christabel said. "We can't thank you enough."

"Please," Ophelia said, taking Brent's hand, "give me your address, so I can send you a little something."

"I'm right in the Mayflower Apartments," Brent said. "100 Sanford Avenue. But what's a little something?"

"Just a little token of our esteem," Ophelia said.

"Look out," Galen said. "Your porch will become a veritable bower of roses."

He wondered, then, if Brent could be a part of this family. Somehow this perfect figure of a man did not fit in this swirl of talk.

"It's the least we could do," Christabel insisted.

"Mother," Ophelia said, "this does raise serious questions, though, about what we're going to do when you leave in a month or so."

"Don't worry," Christabel answered, "we'll cross that bridge when we come to it. I'm thinking, right now, we may have to put the place up for sale."

Ophelia was resistant. "Your whole way of life, Mother."

"Her whole way of life?" Gregory asked, putting a hand to his sloping chest. "What about mine? What about mine?"

Tamara, who had not said a word this whole time, looked devastated.

"Way of life or no way of life, talk show or no talk show, we just, plain, don't have the money," Christabel said. "We've been running on a shoestring as it is."

"But what about the family?" Ophelia asked. "Couldn't we pool our resources?"

"Excuse me," Brent said, "but I really must be going—"

"I think," Christabel declared, "we could save all this for a private conversation."

"Thank you, Mr. Brent," Gregory called from his bed, despite his upset. "Hope to meet you again under different circumstances!"

Everyone was still talking as Galen and Brent slipped out.

"Thanks for everything," Galen told him, once they were alone. "I know my family can be a little overwhelming at times."

Brent glanced carefully down the hall, then gave Galen a kiss. It felt stolen. "No problem. Like I've said, you're lucky to have family."

"But what is all this about a family?" Galen asked, holding him still. "You've got one."

Brent shook his head, standing quiet in Galen's clasp. "A mother but no father. He's dead. Look, I have to leave, because I'm sort of a mess, after taking care of an old man like that. It brings it all back."

And Brent escaped him, hurried out the front entrance with Galen trying to follow but letting him go at last. No one happened to be in the lobby at that moment, and the paintings seemed to turn their eyes in Brent's direction. Where the hell was he going?

He returned to his father's room. Ophelia and Andrew were just leaving.

"I'll get flowers to that man directly," Ophelia said.

Lying there, his father raised his hand. "Ophelia, someday I'll have enough to send my own flowers. Like I tried with Galen."

◆◆◆

Well? Well, he was reminiscing on his bike, back to Seattle, back to the days with Eugene. There was the sound of the creek which ran by his uncle's house. Galen would lie there at night, fully awake, praying that he would never have to go back to Carleton Park, because here he could be himself. He had to work, yes—Catherine Blaine was a demanding junior high school, and they had put him in the accelerated group—he had to work on his paper route, too, to help make ends meet at his uncle's. The man was a schoolteacher, not rich, but it was altogether different (altogether different) than working at Carleton Park, serving as clean-up boy at his mother's boarding house. (For Christabel had had a boarding house back then, too, a precursor to the hotel.) At his mother's, the morning breakfast table held its tribunal over him, and she never offered one note of defense. In fact, she joined in. Fatherless, he was at her mercy—prey to her constant demands that she make a man of him, that is, over into the war hero's son everyone thought he should be. Later, of course, he was to find out about that war hero stuff.

As he rode on his bike, he reached almost the top of Carleton Park Heights, where his highest-paying customers lived. He needed to make another bid on one of these places. He must get himself moving on this one, too.

But instead, he cycled straight back into those earlier years in his mother's boarding house, the days before Uncle Eugene arrived, when he had developed an imaginary playmate, or better, guardian, Klaatu, who had stepped straight out of *The Day the Earth Stood Still*. He remembered creating him the day after he had seen the movie down at the Mayflower Theatre right by the University, off Holland Avenue. He had been standing on the street corner, ready to cross for school, and he had prayed for everything to be all right, even when he had just come into that age when he was painfully aware other boys had the guidance of fathers, and he did not. In the instant, he was conscious of a strong hand in his, and in looking around and finding nothing, he still felt it. He had immediately scanned the sky for flying saucers, but there was only a white cloud, turning sort of conical against the blue. Comical? Oh, no, it's just imagination, he thought, quite consciously as a child, I'll let that be my flying saucer.

And he must remember that a man from another planet does not need to sleep. In the movie, Klaatu even survived death itself and underwent resurrection. But then, but then, after all those nights of Klaatu seeing him to bed and then keeping watch, after all those nights and all those days of undergoing the tribunal at his mother's boarding house breakfast table, Eugene appeared very suddenly from some distant point in the country. He had lost his wife and family in a fire—terrible to say, the boarders said—and he needed a room; he needed a family. He had taken a position in the nearby Briarcliff Elementary school. That moment he very smoothly and easily appeared for breakfast—the handsome man who was as lean and kindly as Michael Rennie—he spoke some words compassionately on Galen's behalf.

And now Galen coasted down a hill, with the wind around his collar, glimpsed his uncle's Estate in the distance, and thought, it might have been in the months to come I began to realize, that Uncle Eugene was being driven out of Carleton Park, ridden out on a rail, almost. Shamed the way I had been that previous Halloween for being dressed as a girl. Or the way Anton felt shamed now. It had not been Eugene's plan to leave at all. But by spring, the rumors had started. It was all mixed up with the scares over aliens and UFOs. The newspapers I delivered were full of the sightings, as well as the McCarthy hearings every night. The very first day, in fact, Uncle Eugene appeared at the breakfast table for the first time, the conversation had been strange.

Galen could feel the table sizing the man up. "You must pardon our look of shock," one of them said. "But we all thought you were Lieutenant Gregory. You're a dead ringer for a carbon copy of him."

"Lost like a god over Burma," one of the boarders—Mr. Talis—added.

"What a surprise," Eugene said. "If you're looking for a carbon copy of Gregory, you should look to Galen here."

He remembered blushing—Klaatu had been in those words. In fact, he then saw the spirit of the spaceman merge into Eugene at just that moment.

"We have great plans," Christabel said patriotically, "for Galen coming out just as heroic as his father."

"I'm sure," Eugene said, "Galen's been heroic enough already."

Klaatu had been in those words, too. Galen had smiled toward him, and Eugene had gone on, "What you say Galen comes with me to school today while I get my room ready? The principal may duck his head in, but that's no big deal. There are several things he can help me do."

He remembered feeling old enough to sense the resistance at the table. (Was that when he knew of what was about to happen?) A ten-year-old going off with a strange man. Someone his mother hadn't seen in ten years—and who looked lean and very single.

"I suppose," Christabel said, "if you're back by lunch."

"Mind you're careful," Miss Alicia said ominously, "if you go out on that playfield alone. There have been strange sightings lately. Particularly at night. Prowlers. And Flying Saucers, too. A woman disappeared not a week ago. And then a horse."

"One thing we can say for sure," Mr. Talis said. "Flying saucers have landed. The Palomar Gardens in California have been flooded with them. I have pictures in a book up in my room. Man claims to have already met a man from outer space. A creature good looking enough to be both man and woman at the same time."

At that moment, Galen was sure he was getting their drift. They didn't want him to have a father. And that was partly true. Like the bullies who plagued his every step in those days, they found it good to have certain kids around they could call orphans. It gave them an air of superiority.

But nevertheless, Christabel let him go with him to school. And he could remember, as the table broke up, as he and Eugene left, feeling protective of him. And he was elated. For on that August morning, many people on his newspaper route were at their windows or carrying things in from their porches and the underground sprinkle systems were going top-drawer. Everything was granite and rainbow. Still, there was something at the back of his mind saying this would be tentative. This man could not stay as his father for very long. He remembered that water tower facing the school glistened and looked like a flying saucer itself, ready to take off again.

And all that summer, I worked my paper route, too, dreaming of going far away. I was encouraged to dream—and at night, I thought my father had come back in Klaatu, in Eugene and the scene I remembered from my movie. The scene I waited for, pined for, and was thrilled by was the part when Bobby, fatherless from the War, too, goes in the company of Klaatu (Mr. Carpenter to him), from Arlington Cemetery and the Lincoln Memorial to the spaceship itself, to spy on the thing as though he were only an afternoon spectator. (And that's all he thought he was!). And the roving reporter says to the microphone, "And I see a gentleman here with his little boy." Over and over I would toss with that in sleep, listening to the creek, "And I see a gentleman here with his little boy," and "Mr. Carpenter" didn't deny it! This is my son Bobby.

And that summer evening, I had been out collecting on my route, with Eugene following me along on his bike. At one customer's door, the lady looked over my shoulder and asked if my father was on some exercise program, and I said no, he just liked being with me. And she, calling over my shoulder, said, "Nice son you have here!" and he smiled back and just said, "Thanks!" The nights of happiness following that! And I see a gentleman here with his little boy! He didn't say I wasn't his son!

Galen, biking down toward Mayfair's City Hall, saw in the August landscape a particular angle—a hard edge to all the plants, the nearness of a rusting autumn, and remembered, in the moment, a conversation he had heard between his mother and uncle one night. Something going way back to his pre-Seattle days. He had been in bed, trying to sleep, and the two of them were in the next room, in what his mother commonly called the "Commons," and as he lay there, soothed by Klaatu in Eugene's voice, he began to pick up on a theme of grief and mourning. Christabel said, "Some days, some days, I wake up hoping that the next call will be from him. That he wasn't lost over Burma but had ended up in a concentration camp, which they've just now discovered. It's not unheard of. So why shouldn't I wake hoping? Wake up hoping! Yes. Sometimes I'll just turn from cutting flowers in the garden and sense his shadow over there, not far from the sundial, reassuring me, giving me strength."

"And sometimes," Eugene said, "I wake up hoping there will be a call that my wife and son were not lost in a fire after all. That there was some terrible, wonderful mistake. That they're coming and will be at the door by nightfall. But they are lost, they are absolutely lost, I have to keep telling myself. If I don't tell myself that, then I won't be able to get up and go to work. And I have to get up and go to work, because the fire involved bills that I still have to pay for, and I need the work just for my own self-esteem."

"You'll remarry," my mother said. "You'll remarry and start your life over."

"No, I will not remarry," he said. "You have to understand that now—"

But he did not finish his sentence. He did not need to, as far as Galen was concerned. He was different, and he would not marry this time any more than Klaatu would.

Now, having turned in the Mayfair City Hall, Galen dismounted and got out in front of the cement construct, and he felt the full pain of that memory. For his mother and uncle had been at one in that moment. Through loss. And he began to believe that what had driven the brother and sister apart had most likely been the discovery of Gregory. That he was not dead—therefore, no sympathetic bond. And, yes, he knew, Eugene had been married once, had had a son once, and that the child and the mother had been mysteriously lost in a fire. But that went back so far. And when Gregory had popped up secretly—somewhere back then—in the 1960s, Christabel had become hard rather than mournful. Such a difference! And Gregory with all those painful memories of keeping watch over him at Catherine Blaine.

◆◆◆

The City of Mayfair had the check waiting. But his mind started bargaining with him again. It said that it would be very OK to bump Andrew out, and instead of building World Wide Workouts, as they had planned, just use the money and take up with Brent and form "Rehabilitation Associates"—Brent's alternative proposal. Of course. Of course, because it would take him nearly a year to get his massage license. But until then, there would be all this help of Brent showing him the ropes and bringing his clientele over into an office they could rent together also in the Oasis district, with Brent doing the PT work and Galen doing the massage. And he could just tell Andrew on the side someday—just as he was going out the door—that he hoped to put his $20,000 elsewhere, and would he mind dropping the idea?

Jacob went to visit his mother more often, leaving room for Brent to sleep over. One night, they decided to have dinner in, and afterwards rent a video. It was definitely an experience going to Casablanca Rent and Buy, because by then, his cousin Keystone had gotten his entire stock out on the shelves, with all the glamorous Hollywood photos on the walls, with Katharine Hepburn from *Sylvia Scarlett* and Humphrey Bogart from *The African Queen*. In the foreign film section, they had a swish looking close-up of Fellini in a trench coat. The whole place was lit up with jukeboxes and Papa Pop's popcorn machines—in a kind of red glow, which made Galen even more heady than usual, now that Brent was beside him. All headlights from the bustling cars seemed to converge on Keystone's place, which constituted exactly the right mirage for a late August night in the Oasis district. Meanwhile, Galen could hear the disco coming from the hotel lounge, with at first Human's League's "Heart Like a Wheel," and then from someone else—

> *Come on feel the power*
> *On and on, hour by hour!*
> *Wrapped up inside the mind*
> *Of Someone so sublime,*
> *So much great, big, better*
> *Better than you!*

In going through the "gay" VHSs, Galen was aware of the sensation Brent was creating among all the men, as though he were still at the nude beach. He was also aware that Brent could be called away by any one of these sirens at any moment. And me? Galen thought. I'm just a gardener. Less than a dirt farmer. And old. An ex-con with a lot of unfinished business, who's come into a little money. Amidst all these changing lights, he noticed that his skin was almost chocolate—colored from the sun. And probably by December, he wouldn't look as young as he did now.

"I know what video I want," Brent said. "Come over here to the classics section. Looks like it's just come out."

Oh, God, *The Day the Earth Stood Still*. On the front, a giant hand was squeezing the top of the world like an orange, and below, Patricia Neal, in a low-neck dress she never wears, was screaming while running from Gort.

"Ever seen this before?" Brent asked.

"Yes," Galen answered.

"Mind seeing it again?" Brent asked.

"I guess it would be all right," Galen said.

"I saw it on television once," Brent said. "It's better than any sci-fi I've ever seen. And Michael Rennie—I always thought he was such a doll."

Brent pulled off the red token below the box, and they went over to Keystone. He had three attendants working for him.

"You've got good taste, Cousin," Keystone said. "This is not one of your low-budget cheapies. It's got good sets, good acting and class."

At home, they decided to dismantle the television and tape player and bring them into the bedroom. Putting in the video, Galen undressed and got in between the sheets, where Brent lay already naked and waiting for him.

They were silent for some time as the film started. Galen thought at first—being held by Brent the way he was—that he would be inured to all the memories that might come up, and for a while, that was true. Then, after they turned for a kiss, Brent said, "I saw this film on the night my father and I had a fight. I mean a real, full fistfight. I was a football star back then. For my high school. After we fought, I thought, if only my father could be like Michael Rennie. It's obvious, isn't it, that he really loves this kid? That the kid is showing him how to survive in the world—and vice versa."

"I'd never seen it that first way," Galen said, feeling himself warming. "But come to think of it, you're right. I always thought Michael was exclusively doing the guiding."

For some reason, he just couldn't mention his uncle, although, even from here, he could see his photographs of Treasure Island, and, in fact, the light was on in the nook, brightening all the memorabilia imported from the Estate. He could just see—around the corner.

"But, still," Galen went on, "I don't understand—why a fight?"

"Because he wouldn't fund my education," Brent told him. "He refused to pay a red cent, he said. And he made good money as a mechanic."

"Why wouldn't he pay?" Galen asked.

"Why? Why?" Brent said furiously. "Guess. He had—he had guessed about me."

"What did your mother say?" Galen asked.

"She didn't say anything," Brent told him. "Still doesn't. The agreement is—she accepts me and sometimes pays me from Dad's insurance—if I don't mention it."

Galen loosened himself, ever so slightly from Brent's grasp, which had hardened. "That's a pretty high price to pay."

"I know, but it's worth it," Brent insisted. "Especially if I want to have a business of my own, like I was telling you. After that night, I promised myself I would. Before then, my dad used to be so proud of me, one of my chief fans in the stands. He and Mom would even bring pom-poms. But no more pom-poms after that, and then, I played out the season just loving to be beaten up by the other guys. They could sense it. They used to pick me up and literally throw me across the field."

"That seems a far cry from physical therapy," Galen said.

"Like I told you, that's why I'm in it," Brent answered. "I was in so much pain for myself. Why not try to help?"

Galen waited a minute and then asked, weighing his words carefully. "Is this whole sports thing of yours the reason you're so hard on Jacob?"

"Hard on Jacob?" Brent asked. "Am I hard on Jacob?"

"Saying he's fat," Galen said.

"I just said he could lose a few, that's all." He turned away, staring in the direction of Eugene's den. "God, Galen," he said, "you sure are sensitive about that son of yours."

"Yeah, that's the whole point. I'm looking after him now. And I don't like people making remarks about improving him." Galen turned away, refused to meet his glance.

"All right, all right." Brent drew an exasperated breath. "I think the answer for me would be not to hang around him too much."

A grip of fear came over Galen. He knew now why he was relieved Yvonne had taken Jacob for a while. They still had a few weeks until the start of school. The path had been made quite clear to this confrontation with Brent.

"If you ask me," Brent said, "your ex has the right idea with your son. Some Tai chi wouldn't hurt him at all. And that play he goes on and on about—that's just some Charlie Chan movie he's borrowed. It's not even his. And it causes him to sit on his duff all day writing."

Galen folded his arms against his chest. "The kid has got to start somewhere. If you didn't have your head up your ass, you'd notice how creative he is."

Brent moved further away in the bed. "He may be creative, but he doesn't have to be so irritating about it. Christ, Galen, you spoil that kid. If he's getting pushed around at school, he could stand to get some fitness training."

Fuming, Galen went back to the video. "And I see a gentleman here with his little boy" was just coming up. Galen strained for memories of his uncle, but here they seemed on the other side of the universe now. Fortunately, the picture of him with "Mr. Biggs" was in the room; if it hadn't been for that, he would have felt entirely devoid of family completely, despite his view of the den. Stranded, out on the edge of night with a man he realized he hardly knew and who was scorning his son.

Just at the moment Bobby and Klaatu visit the saucer, with all the rest of the Nation's Capitol, Brent started crying. "Dad died two weeks after I hit him. No reconciliation, nothing. It didn't matter how athletic or perfect I was. He told me he wouldn't give me any money because I was worthless. How he knew I was 'that way,' as he put it, I don't know. So there wasn't even the consolation of having told him. Being honest."

"I do believe something," Galen said, trying to soothe him, "I do believe something that might help."

He got out of bed one more time, took some Kleenex from a box on the dresser, and handed it across. "What is it?" Brent asked at last, while wiping his face.

"I believe that our relationships with the dead go on even after they're gone," Galen said. "That they improve. I'm sure mine with my uncle does. That he understands things that he never did before. And, as Uncle says, they take the form of people who are around us now."

Brent withdrew. His muscles were tense. "But you could never put yourself in my shoes. You couldn't possibly know what it's like. You have your father here alive. You have a son. You have a daughter. What you have with all three of them, I'd kill for. Do you know what I'd give to do for my father what I did for yours just a few days ago? Have any idea?"

"Maybe," Galen said, realizing that he was entering even more dangerous territory. "But maybe you could just see my father as yours in that moment. Or Jacob as your son. People are much more interchangeable than you think."

"Is this some kind of joke?" Brent asked, still hostile. "Is this more of your superstition? Or some kind of New Age BS? Because if it is, I've had enough of that to last me a lifetime. It's everywhere in my job."

"I don't know what it is," Galen answered. And he felt overexposed being naked. "It's just a consolation, that's all."

Brent folded his arms too and leaned back, ironic. "Thanks. But I'm not into handy tips."

Galen, standing by the bed—not having returned—pulled on a pair of shorts.

"Why are you doing that?" Brent asked.

"Somehow I just got the feeling that whatever we had going on in here was over. That whatever I was saying was not helping you, and definitely vice-versa."

Brent held his arms open like a child. "Hey, I'm sorry. Come over here. And take those shorts off again."

Galen complied but didn't want to come over. At last, he yielded. In bed, Brent came around from behind and clutched his back to his chest, and they seemed a continuous energy, at one, loving, very suddenly. They turned over, and Galen slid down Brent's body. In a breath of abandon, he held Brent's penis and sucked and sucked, while it stiffened and finally came. He swallowed repeatedly, as though feeding at the breast. In the next moment, Galen did not mind being taken, held, made love to. He also made love back. Fucking Brent very gently, with his full length on him, having prepared himself earlier. But in recovering afterwards—while recognizing that he had, by grace, transcended the slimmest odds he would ever find something like this any other place—he still had to struggle, in the shower, back in bed, now partially clothed, to remember who he was.

Brent was relaxed on the pillow. "That is the most any man has ever drained me. I want us to do this all the time."

"We will do it all the time."

He slept, clutching Brent, grateful to be actually sleeping overnight with someone for the first time in ten years.

But in the middle of the night, he was awakened by light in the room, and for a moment, he thought that Yvonne had brought Jacob back home. Seeing the bed was empty, he put on a robe and followed the light that was coming from the nook. Brent was sitting there, looking at the rough draft of some of his uncle's World's Fair Treasure Island material, which had been left out. Also pages of the draft of the "new" Frank Baum novel, which Jacob had printed out from his computer. From Hoover Tower.

"The man was a wizard, wasn't he?" Brent said, looking up. The light streamed across his bare shoulders.

It was still hot in the house, eighty degrees at least.

"Yes," Galen said. "But are you all right? What's the matter?"

"Couldn't sleep," Brent told him. "Haven't slept really since I decided to try Rehabilitation Associates. Ironic, isn't it?"

"Yes," Galen answered, "but that isn't much comfort, I'm sure."

"Fact is," Brent said, "I haven't slept well since I decided I was gay, and then decided not to tell anybody."

"But you're not in that spot now," Galen told him. "You're willing to be seen with me."

"Right now, yes," Brent said.

Galen came over and tried pressing against him, as Brent had done with him, but the man had become fully distant now. Galen's back stiffened; Galen had to stand apart. "What do you mean, right now?"

"Doc Hollywood is fine with whoever you are," Brent said. "But if I go into business for myself, it will be the kiss of death, as everybody knows."

"If we are partners, they will know—that will seal it sure as the world," Galen said. "You're not expecting me to go back into the closet, I hope."

For a moment, it went through his head that maybe Brent didn't plan on partnership at all. He just wanted his money.

"No," Brent answered slowly at last. "Not if you are discreet about it. It's people who flaunt themselves as a 'gay business' that customers don't like."

Galen didn't know what to say.

"Well, Buddy," Brent said, "let's go back to bed. I'll try to sleep. Sure wish I had had a childhood like the nephew in this piece. Are you the nephew?"

"If I was," Galen said, "he imagined me before I was born. But, frankly, I wouldn't put that past Uncle Eugene, either."

"Very possibly," Brent answered.

◆◆◆

They were in the steam room at the YMCA. Galen felt all the comfort of the heat. On the phone, Jacob had made it plain he had gotten his father's drift— that Galen wanted to be with a man Jacob himself did not want to be around. He would stay on longer with his mother. He had made friends in the neighborhood who liked film too. It was better for everybody. Here in this room and elsewhere, Galen felt he was going into some kind of sleep. He wanted fog and more fog.

A thin man, delicate and clearly sweating out a drunk, pushed himself off the stone seat, and padded out.

Brent fanned his nose. "Just think of the people we could turn around, if we had our own health club. You could get that man"—nodding in the direction of the door—"sober, and I could help that cripple who was in the weight room a few minutes ago. Even that schizo who comes here and stands on his head in the shower chanting om, we could straighten him out, too."

Galen ran his fingers along Brent's arm. It was a roadmap of sweat. "Getting sober isn't what you think it is. It's not just a matter of discipline."

"Then I don't know what is," Brent said. "Your father seems to be doing everything right, and it's because he's following a discipline."

"How did you know he was recovering?" Galen asked. He found himself retreating again.

"For God's sake, Galen, I've been working on people for years. You don't think I don't know when a man's got vertigo because he's tippled too much?"

"He wasn't tippling that day you helped him," Galen said emphatically. "He'd just gotten sober."

Brent stood up and went to the hose which the steam room provided. He sprayed himself, and more clouds issued. He got some water on Galen. "Hey, hey," Galen said. "Hey."

"What's the matter? Can't you take a little wake-up call?" Brent asked, smiling. He came back over, and put his hand on Galen's cheek. Galen began kissing his hand with a frenzy. When someone came to the glassed door, Brent pulled away and drew up his towel in an instant jerk.

A dark man was coming in. He must have been an out-of-towner, because no one except Galen had a tan like that from around here. He was thickish and rough-looking. Like his roommate in prison. Instantly Brent's face filled with fear, and he gathered his towel around him even tighter and was out of the confines of the room with the ceiling dripping after him. Galen didn't have time to draw up his towel. "What is it?" he asked, once they were out. "You know him?"

"Yes," Brent answered, throwing his towel over the top of the open stall and turning on the shower, "but I don't want to talk about it."

◆◆◆

OK, OK, OK. Galen was on his way to Brent's, to pick him up for a fundraiser.

OK, OK, OK. Let's just think for a moment. His uncle's journal had said—

> All this venturing sometimes brings on a memory that is still a thrusting forward into the future. It's as though I'm walking through the solarium of the greenhouse at the 1939 World's Fair. Walking with the idol within view, and I can "remember" what it will be like walking holding hands with my nephew, years from

now. I can write the book I thought Frank Baum might have written had he lived to see this fair.

His uncle had met him at the Burbank airport—so small and subdued then in 1965, and Galen, still dazzled from his first plane trip, had hugged him hard.

"We have all of the Fourth of July ahead of us," his uncle had said. "Days and days of just sitting back, taking it easy."

"You look very tired," Galen had told him. "Are you all right?"

"Will be, will be, now that you're here."

It was Galen's first time in Los Angeles, too. Seated there in his uncle's convertible Mustang, and taking in all the buildings that passed, Galen, gifted with a memory of the future as he thought back on this moment, recalled that time when Jacob and Ophelia had picked him up from prison, and he, Galen, had also felt all right, with his son beside him.

"I have an apartment over in Silver Lake," his uncle went on. "Just above the water. I think you'll like it."

Galen saw small parks with willowy-looking ironworks, and then huge restaurants, with towering plaster-of-Paris statues. One of them was of Carmen Miranda. Another was of Marilyn Monroe in her famous subway moment. All of the city seemed done up in a pink feather boa for him. Even the graveyards they passed had a certain swish to them, in their gaudily gowned stone angels, pointing up.

"I know I'll like it here," Galen answered. "I needed to get away from home. All they've been doing is working me to death at the Hotel."

"How's your father?" his uncle asked. "How's he been treated now that everybody knows he's your and Ophelia's Dad?"

"He's fine," Galen lied. For many times he had seen him drunk, had detected it. But in those days, he had learned to deny what was wrong in his family as much as he had its goodness. Still, the whole family—and especially Ophelia and Andrew—had made an effort to be kind to Gregory, even though he had kept retreating.

"And Christabel—?" Eugene asked.

"She said to send her greetings," Galen told him.

"Just greetings?" Eugene smiled his handsome smile above his driving.

"Just greetings, I'm afraid," Galen said, answering the smile back. In fact, he could see, in all the reflections, the close family resemblance. Their eyes were open to a kind of light that lit up the whole forehead. Brother and sister.

"It's hard to believe how close we all were, way back before the War. We traveled through Europe together. But, you know," Eugene said, "I may one of these days forgive Carleton Park and come back. I have my eye on the little mansion there across the Hotel, if I still score here in Hollywood."

"Oh, yes, you mean the Estate. They say the people are moving out," Galen said.

"Good deal. Well, we'll see," his uncle said.

They were already at the apartment building, which was set upon a hill with all the others. It was painted pink. A Technicolor persimmon tree, with blossoms mottled with scarlet screened the driveway. It seemed almost as if they were driving through it.

As though through a rose-colored veil, Galen walked in the back door, and, as he remembered, had a sensation of being in the Estate. "I have been here before," when, really, he was traveling forwards. It was almost as it he were coming into the unfamiliar kitchen, where he and Anton and Andrew had chased the ghost of the man who was now standing before him. He put down one of the pieces of luggage.

"Uncle Eugene, if there is anyone or anything you need to tell me about before you show me my room, you can talk about it."

His uncle laughed. "No—no boyfriends in the backroom or under the bed. All of them are back in San Francisco on Balboa. But why bring that up now?"

"I just didn't want you to be embarrassed," Galen said.

His uncle looked at him sideways, reminiscent of the days in Seattle— junior high and high school. "Really? Is that it?"

"No," Galen admitted.

Galen allowed the silence to hang as they toted the suitcases into a very nice room, really, with a view of the cactused neighborhood and other pink buildings. The scene in the window above the bed seemed in Cinemascope. Neon signs jumped in the distance. And Silver Lake actually did look very silver and blue, as though on a turquoise belt.

I accepted Uncle's invitation in '65, Galen thought, because I wanted to ask him—is this love I have for my boyfriend real? I don't even understand the question myself, but I need to ask it. Is it possible in this world? What will I have to give up? Children? The right to marry? A safe household? A job? Will we have to be on the run all the time? And even more important, if we were to live together, if we were to act as man and wife, would Nature cooperate?

With things unpacked, and the dresser drawers filled, and with my own writing materials and Dutch dictionaries on the table, I went on to the kitchen where Uncle was cooking dinner for us just as in the old days. That steamed rice with cheese! And I said to him, "I'm in love with Darren, the boy you met in Carleton Park. What should I do?"

"I don't know," Eugene answered. "If I had the answer, I wouldn't be living alone."

Letting the dinner simmer, he took me into his den, where he had been working on what Hollywood had given him. "See all that work," he said, pointing to the scripts, "that's me, trying to find a way out for us. I'm working with the idea that if I can change things in the movies, we might be able to change the world."

"I can't wait that long," Galen answered.

"And a long time it will be," Eugene said. "I was working on a script— the Motion Picture Code would just allow it—about a gay senator in Washington. He was played by Don Murray. He was in love with a man trying to dig himself out of the gay underground in New York. I was trying to write in him leaving his wife and joining his lover at the end. I tried to write a speech where he announces who he is and defends his love for his partner, insisting, over and over, 'There's nothing wrong with it! There's nothing wrong with it.' And yet as we stand here, all of Hollywood, all of L.A., and all of this country declared that I have Senator Brigham kill himself, that his partner commit suicide too for ratting on him the way he does, and that the final speech be given to his weeping, nothing wife. Close to the way it is in the book. That's where the country was, is right now, Galen, and that's what you're looking at. What should you do with your love for Darren, Galen? I don't know."

Galen had the feeling he was back in Briarcliff Elementary, now, in Carleton Park. That he was at that moment of helping his uncle pin the ABCs above the chalkboard, of seeing all the treasures of his uncle's classroom, the legacies of Alice in Wonderland. Except, now, this was even more important.

"So are you saying gays are getting a script for suicide?" Galen asked.

"That's what I'm saying," his uncle said, "but I'm also telling you you don't have to take it. You don't have to submit."

"How do I keep from it?" Galen asked.

"By not turning," Eugene said, "by not turning."

"Turning into what?" Galen was sitting forward, trying to rivet on every word.

"Turning into what they would have us be," his uncle said, sitting back and opening his hands. "Or turning our words into what they want to hear. Right now, there are hundreds, maybe thousands, of playwrights and screen players who are writing just that, and many of them are gay. Know what they're doing?"

Galen shook his head.

"They're creating the straight hero street thug," his uncle said. "That's what the public wants. Someone to knock them around. Check out your screen idols right now. The ones with all the brawn. The rough trade. They're all Marlon Brando, Attila the Hun. Mark my words, Galen, this is the wave of the future. And all created by gay authors and acted by gay actors. Most of them are drunks."

"Fine," Galen said. "I'm marking your words. Fine. But what do we do about it?"

That put his uncle into a study. "There's a meeting we can go to tomorrow night. People will be talking about what we can do."

Now, with Galen sweating in the car as he neared Brent's apartment building, he saw the funny little theatre just off Wiltshire, which had housed the meeting on the second floor. A woman had stationed herself at the window to keep watch. Crystal hung everywhere in this tinseled place, with incense and tea, but it burgeoned with the idea that they could do a sit-in on the American Psychiatry Association. In a few years.

His uncle gave them a pep talk.

"That's easy for you to say, Hon," one of the more dazzling members said. "You're just sassy tonight because you have that young dish with you."

"I'm not a dish," Galen answered hotly, "I am his nephew."

That made everybody laugh.

"Really, a nephew?" a man who looked like Noel Coward said. Sweater and wavy hair. "Is that what they call it these days? I heard their protectors called aunties once. But Hooray, Hooray for the avuncular!"

It was then, Galen thought, that I got the idea of dressing up in a Superman suit. Why not costume it up? That was my answer. To the closet! There's a Superman in me, and it'll be coming out!

That night was the Fourth of July, and we watched fireworks above Silver Lake. Red, blue, white struck the clarion aquamarine sky like snowflakes on glass. Every pattern streaking down in beauty, every pattern different. And reflected in the lake, the star shells, from golden cosmic dust flowering into a stained glass configuration of—yes—rubies. Liberation was dawning over

L.A. The movement had been started; in a few years we would converge on San Francisco.

Uncle made it big after that. He made lots of money. Hired to doctor scripts, he tried revising homophobia out of the entire motion picture system. His changes were almost always ignored, almost always turned back to the usual pattern, but they paid him anyway. He gained in power and esteem. He was able to keep two places comfortably when he eventually bought the Estate. He formed a life where he was able to be on hand for me, while he still consistently labored in Hollywood on weekends to help them once again with "difficult material." He had come so close with that Don Murray film. Some of his writer friends nearly came out themselves. Some of the stars nearly did, too. Some of the stars were nearly "out" at night. For a while, the verge was enough for him. He almost became a role model. Suppose Rock Hudson had been in one of the films and come out then?

Then Uncle got the idea of developing a violence-free helpline, which allowed you to call and vent your feelings, if you were about to hurt someone, with no questions asked. It worked. The violence, beginning in L.A., plummeted, then soon in other states, and then very soon in Europe, the world. More artistry appeared in men. They could track it. Billboards were everywhere—even in Mayfair. I see now that the solution for him was always the same—speaking out.

And me? I had to go back home to Carleton Park—to this very place.

◆◆◆

Galen got out of the car. The fundraiser was at hand.

Right in the Oasis district, his lover had something of the perfect apartment. Nevertheless, whenever Galen went there, he had the sense it had been furnished by somebody else. Maybe Doc Hollywood. The four-poster alone could have brought a price big enough to decorate the whole New Amsterdam lobby. When Galen came in this time—to catch Brent with a hug—he had reached the limit as far as giving out little sums of money was concerned. He'd have to make some choices.

Brent wasn't finished getting dressed.

"I just have one thing to ask," Brent said.

"Just one?" Galen answered.

"Just one," Brent insisted. He looked defensive and halted, putting an arm through a starched white shirt.

"Go for it," Galen said, patting him on the shoulder.

Brent put the other arm through. "How about not playing 'Mr. Out' tonight?" he asked.

"Why not?" Galen asked—and looked at Brent's posters, which were worth so much less than the frames. All cottages in the distance, with boughs, whether autumnal or in bloom, in the foreground.

"I just don't need it tonight, that's all," Brent said. "I've had a full day. I'd like to enjoy Handel in peace."

"You sound like all I do is walk around in high heels," Galen said, still keeping his smile. "That's hardly it. And at a benefit for AIDS House, there's not going to be much to worry about as far as what other people think."

Brent had his shirt tucked in by now. He put on a white linen sport coat and brightened the room. Galen himself was dressed in a sport coat and tie. "I know, I know"—he smiled as well. "But you know what I mean—there will be a lot of donors there—people with money, including you—and I'm thinking of Rehabilitation Associates. Who might give us their business and who might not."

"Well, you thinking about it is nothing new," Galen said.

They went down to the spot in back of the brick apartment building (Brent lived on the fourth floor), where the Mercedes always stood, with an empty parking space on either side. It was as though the management had designed the whole parking lot for this red magic carpet. Brent didn't want one nick on it.

However, he couldn't get it started this time, so they had to go in the white Lexus out front. The Oasis district stretched its shade over them, as they moved toward the hotel. The parks and gardens around them were lime green. That settled things, some, between them.

At the fundraiser, Galen found that he was at a higher premium than usual. He was shown directly to a table near the front, and Brent had to trail. He suspected some kind of award presentation was in the offing, since he had been encouraged by several phone calls to be sure to come tonight. They were sounding him out. The green shadow continued. He could see, in the distance, that Anton was there, seated at the back. Meanwhile, Brent seemed busy sizing up prospects.

"You know," Brent said, putting his linen napkin in his lap, "I could use that $20,000 you were going to give Andrew—and I mean right away as an installment."

"We'd already been talking about $30,000," Galen said. He didn't want a fight right now. He wanted the recovered mood to stay. He also thought Brent had had a point about enjoying the Handel in peace.

"I know, but I could use $50,000," Brent said. "Part of it could be just a loan."

However, thankfully, they were interrupted. They were being joined at the table. And wealth was definitely the cue. They had an advertising executive who had once been mayor of Carleton Park and the head of the University's board of trustees. Galen was aware that Brent now made a luminous spot in their circle. If he himself was being watched now—the impression changed from moment to moment—it was because of who he was with.

They had to join in the general conversation, but what he and Brent had talked about earlier had put him back in that final year in San Francisco, with Lucky, Uncle Eugene's "lover," barging in. Lucky had brought his "latest" lover with him.

The dinner was over quickly. Announcements were coming up and then acknowledgments. Names were rattled off, and applause came after each one. But then the hostess had to say that the greatest benefactor here was Eugene Vondel, who intended to donate his mansion to AIDS House and the Gay Alliance. Without him, there would be no hospice in the future. And they wanted to give an award in absentia to Eugene's memory by having his nephew come up.

Galen found himself standing.

Reaching the podium and very surprised, Galen said, "I'm happy to accept this award," he stammered, "on behalf of my uncle—who was also gay and devoted to larger gay causes."

Great applause.

"It's my great hope," he went on, "that all the details can be worked out so that the Estate does go to AIDS House and the Gay Alliance. But they aren't yet. But my deepest thanks just the same."

He felt better as he sat down. Of course, they were lobbying for the donation, but he couldn't make any guarantees. And they had been out of line in announcing it in advance. To top it off, Brent was pissed. "Why did you have to say 'gay also'?" he whispered. I feel like a jerk, sitting here."

"It just came out," Galen said.

"You mean you just came out," Brent retorted.

"I've been all over the newspapers," Galen whispered, almost with a hiss. "I can't figure out, Brent, what you think is going on. I'm no closet case."

Steaming, Brent looked straight ahead and signaled the waitress to pour him some wine. "They just want to get your mother to donate that house, you know."

"I asked you not to drink when we're together," Galen said. "It's hard on me."

"I asked you not an hour ago not to be 'Mr. Out.' That's hard on me," Brent answered.

"Look," Galen said, still fighting to be heard, without the others listening in, "three years ago, I had to sit through a whole memorial service where not one word was spoken about Eugene's gayness. Its time people were told, particularly when it comes to knowing who gives donations and who doesn't."

It was impossible to go on. The people at the table were only going to allow a little more privacy before breaking into congratulations and asking to see the plaque. There was a Herculean outline etched on it.

A few more drinks later, Brent stood up, looking rather rocky. "I'll be back in a minute." While he was out, there was a bomb scare, and they all had to exit to the sidewalk. It was a spellbound night, just the same, with the clouds holding still above the hills, and the lit green sign around the Hotel Oasis very subdued but luminous. Nevertheless, the people wandered aimlessly. Green neon palm trees accented the sidewalks. Galen looked in vain for Brent. What could be going on this time? And then he saw him at last, talking to some older man Galen was sure was Doc Hollywood, even though he was still supposed to be out of the country. The man looked urbane, worldly, dapper, with a meticulously conditioned body. All around, there was a mixture of joking and nervous smiles, in anticipation of the moment everyone would be called back in.

Suddenly a hand was on his arm, and Galen turned. Anton.

"Congratulations," Anton said. "I know how much your uncle meant to you. Could you feel his spirit here tonight? I thought I could."

"Anton," Galen said, "I need to tell you—all those lights in the house, all those notes, that was just my father, it turns out."

"I know," Anton answered. "Andrew told me. But he still has a presence, don't you think?" He was radiant.

"Yeah," Galen smiled. "I guess I can feel him here. Except he must be surprised by the bomb scare. Who the hell would want to sabotage an AIDS House fundraiser?"

"I don't know," Anton said. He put a hand on Galen's back. "Who the hell wouldn't want to accept people like your uncle?"

Over Anton's shoulder, Galen saw Brent coming up. He was angry and nonplussed. "I'll see you at the concert, Galen," Brent said. "Something's happened."

"Is somebody hurt? Was there really a bomb?" Galen asked.

"No—I just ran into my boss. I'll explain later"—and after glowering at Anton, he turned around and went back into the crowd.

They waited their turn to go back into the banquet room of the Oasis district hotel. "That's quite a boyfriend you have there," Anton said.

"Yeah," Galen said. "I know."

They just stood in silence before looking for their tables. "How's the coming out to your family going?" Galen asked.

"Getting better. I was going to call you," Anton said.

"Let's get together sometime," Galen heard himself saying.

"I'd like that," he heard Anton answer.

They separated at last—only a handshake.

Galen, now by himself again and vulnerable with his plaque, took his old chair and saw Anton sitting with people Anton didn't know very well, too—his great golden-red hair like an added decoration to the room. Reassembled, the banquet wasn't the same. Galen thought back to the time Andrew had first brought Anton over to help him move—and to their first talks about Denmark and the Netherlands. Then he remembered years ago being approached in Amsterdam—right on Damrak—by a male hustler, saying he just wanted to ask him just one question. Brent's requests were just like that, sometimes. Let me ask you just one question. Wouldn't it'd be OK to cut Andrew's money out from under him and go with Rehabilitations Associates?

The hostess had come back to the microphone and was telling them that they had made enough tonight to put in a nurse at AIDS House, part-time, for six months. Many thanks. And thank you all for coming.

So the banquet was breaking up with its extended applause, and he didn't have Brent—there was probably more of not having Brent to come. But they were all told to be quick about getting across to the concert as soon as they could, what with the bomb threat delaying everything. The concert, which was part of the deluxe fundraiser package, was being put on hold until they got there. In moving with the crowd, Galen meandered toward the "grand" opera house, which was featuring the month-long Handel Festival, was aware Anton was behind him and wondered if his seat was close to his. Ten to one, Brent wouldn't even show up until intermission.

Galen found his seat, and just as he did, Anton passed down the aisle, just brushing his chair. In an instant, Galen grabbed his hand, and for just a second, Anton squeezed it. Ahead of him, all seemed beneath lit candles. The curtain seemed to glow from behind. They were to have *The Messiah*.

Highlights. Galen, seated alone, wondered how long it would be before he would start drinking over Brent. If he kept on like this. Just weeks before Eugene died, he, Eugene, was still sending Lucky money. Or having Galen send Lucky money. He remembered that distinctly. By then, at his request, they had moved his uncle over into the Estate, into the bed, sent up from San Francisco, that Lucky and his lover on the side had made love in. Lucky wasn't there—wasn't there at his bedside!—and Eugene was still sending him money.

The oratorio, trimmed for fundraiser consumption, didn't take long to get to the part about the trumpet sounding and the dead being raised. Galen thought about World Wide Workouts, what he and Andrew had worked up together, as the bodies in the music came up out of the ground, throwing aside the gravestones like trap doors or coverings to storm cellars, and these dead-no-longers danced in their regained flesh.

Galen kept his eyes on the trumpeter, as the notes continued to circle and resurrect the whole world. The chords in the man's muscular neck were standing out against the starched collar. Then, in Galen's memory, Eugene's hand clutched his as his uncle sank into his coma, and instantly, here in the theatre, there was a radiance on the orchestra.

The chorus went into the unequaled finale of "Worthy is the Lamb," with the sopranos, altos, tenors, basses seeming to break into the fireworks he had seen above Silver Lake. The women's voices were distinct; so were the men's. And yet the chorus was its own voice, too.

Then the concert was over. And it constituted the finale of Carleton Park's Handel Festival on this extended night.

Out in the lobby, Galen saw Andrew, sitting at the opera information table and giving out flyers on the upcoming season.

"Our first one's going to be *Aida*," Andrew said, flagging him down. "We're going to have the teaser at the Fine Arts in Mayfair."

"Teaser?" Galen asked.

"Like a little preview," Andrew told him. "To sell tickets. The poor company can't afford the Opera House for more than three nights plus the two for rehearsal, so Ophelia and I are going to help things along by renting the Fine Arts for everybody."

"Are you going to be in it?" Galen asked.

"Just a walk-on role," he answered. "A gymnast in the finale of the second act. They're going to bring in a whole entourage for the triumphal procession. Also a real live elephant."

"At that little Fine Arts Theatre?" Galen asked. "Won't that elephant go straight through the floorboards?

"I'll reinforce them," Andrew said.

Anton joined their group. "Well, my friend," he said to Andrew, "time for opera again?"

"I was telling Galen," Andrew answered. "Just a walk-on."

"Just a walk-on," Anton said. "I'd give my right arm to be anything in an opera. You're surrounded by talent, Galen," he said, "your brother-in-law, your son, and your mother. Not to mention your sister's way with flowers."

"So I've noticed," Galen replied.

"You two have got talent, too," Andrew said to them. "You can try out anytime. You've got the bodies to be supernumeraries."

Both of them, he and Anton, laughed and took the flyers. "Well, we'll come to the Fine Arts," Galen said. "Just to see if the elephant goes through the floorboards. Can't let family enterprises go by the board."

People were making a lot of noise, going past. From time to time, it was hard to hear.

"Lucky we didn't get another bomb threat here," Andrew went on.

"What was that all about?" Galen said. "Strange thing was—everyone acted like it was expected."

"It's getting to be pretty bad when they start menacing AIDS fundraisers," Anton said. "But it's happened before."

They had run out of things to say. It occurred to Galen, and only now, that Brent had not shown at all. He couldn't decide whether to walk out with Anton or not.

But Anton was anticipating him. Lightly touching Galen's elbow, he asked, "Shall we go out together?" and then went on over to Andrew for a hug.

"This seems to be my lucky night," Andrew said, all flushed, after hugging Galen as well. "Wasn't expecting this."

They went down the stairs and back out on the sidewalk. "You know," Anton said, "the last time the three of us were together was when you moved in your new place. I've been wondering how you've liked it."

"Very much," Galen answered. "Although Mom and Dad flipped when we left. But it's like what Jacob and I needed."

"It's obviously had a positive effect on Jacob," Anton answered. "If he's writing plays like Andrew tells me."

Under the streetlamp, Anton seemed a little like the trumpeter. With him having just complimented his son—and by extension himself—Galen would have liked to have said he looked angelic, with red hair. Well, rather, he seemed to have been hustled into his gray suit, a nursery grower who was ready to go back to the soil tomorrow morning. In grabbing his hand earlier, Galen had felt the roughness of his palm. He could smell the Irish Spring on him again.

"I've been feeling better, too," Anton admitted, "now that I've been living alone."

"Living alone?" Galen asked.

"Yeah, I moved out," Anton told him. He stood a little apart.

"That's a big change," Galen said. "After all these years."

"More than anything I've ever known," Anton answered.

They still stood there, awkward.

"You seem to be missing a boyfriend," Anton said.

Galen nodded pensively. "Seems so."

"You were saying you'd like to get together," Anton said.

"Yes. Are you saying that, too?"

"Yes," Anton admitted.

"Well then, there you are," Galen said, surprised by Anton being so forward.

"I'll call you."

"Good" was all Galen could think of. And then all of a sudden, out of nowhere, Galen was going up and kissing him full on the lips, right with all the patrons rushing down the opera house steps beside them.

Anton was red from chin to hair. He looked sideways. "Well, I mean, thanks."

Galen, blushing too, could see they were the center of attention. "Talk to you soon."

People had stood stock-still and were looking at them—especially the teenagers—as they separated.

He'd walk to Brent's to get his car—the night being as beautiful as it was. At the very bottom of him, he hoped Brent would not be at his apartment.

And so what if he was—he didn't have to go up and see him. He'd just get his car and hightail it out.

◆◆◆

OK, OK, OK. Let's just think for a moment about what happened when Eugene died.

There was a bedpan. Of that I'm sure. In Mother's house. And there was the walking of Eugene to the bathroom. He wasn't especially grateful at first. Well, he was in his late sixties by then. He had one idea. He wanted Lucky back. Lucky had taken up with him down in L.A. Lucky, who was in his twenties. When I had heard about it, I couldn't believe it. I had thought Eugene, Uncle Eugene, would be more original than that. An old man with a young protégé. Oscar Wilde said it was sanctioned by the Greeks, et al, was blessed by them. However. However. It could be the kiss of death.

I think Lucky had only one thing on his mind—Lucky. At the San Francisco address, they lived high on the hog. Travel tickets, it seemed, every other week. Maybe back then—way back then—I started taking responsibility for Uncle's impending estate, and I could see that it was quickly running out. They had an adventure in Hawaii, stayed six months, with the idea that Lucky might find work there as—? Professional beachcomber. What sort of work did he do, anyway? No, to be fair, he was going to be a tour guide. On Waikiki. He was to show off his beautiful body in cool linen, walking people all the way out to the Queen's Surf. He was spending my money, I thought, sometimes. Money that I might later inherit.

Well, Uncle's hospice bedroom here in Carleton Park was no Hawaii, no Queen's Surf. I tried calling Lucky down in their San Francisco place one time, and some macho guy answered. He told me his name was Toby and that Lucky wasn't there. Lucky was out getting beer and pizza. I had images of them messing up Uncle's living room beneath the photographs of Treasure Island. Or of Toby, Lucky's man on the side, fooling with Uncle's papers. Lucky never called me back.

I helped Uncle eat in his hospice bed, fed him soup one slow spoonful at a time. His face had become as spotted as a blighted flower. So I just kind of fed this wilted nasturtium this stuff—I saw him as a nasturtium because I was probably drunk—and didn't tell him that Lucky was two-timing him with Toby. I couldn't help but think of that line from Charlie in *Charlie Chan at Treasure Island*—when he was talking about befriending a donkey and getting a kick as a reward. Just plan on it.

In changing the bedpans—one after the other, after the other—I wondered if we had Lucky to thank for this. This disease. And then there were all those meds, every hour, on the hour, it seemed. Funny, though, although Eugene seemed completely incapacitated, he sure did know how to give orders.

He got the idea that all his important belongings ought to be sent up here, especially his "den stuff," as he called it. Maybe, even then, he was getting ready for Dad's midnight sneak visits, as the ghost, into the estate via underground. Anyway, he wanted me to fly down there, "his treat," he said, and get things bundled up and moved. I caught on that he wanted to see his own "Estate" actually in the Estate before he finally died.

He also wanted Lucky with him in the Estate, and he made no bones about that, either.

So what could I do? I was hanging loose by then. Well, I was always hanging loose. So I got on the plane, left Jacob with Christabel and went to the San Francisco address. Teresa was still with Yvonne.

Lucky must have had his ear to the ground, because he wasn't anywhere to be seen when I got there. I had written permission to have the landlord let me in and close out the lease. I called Mayflower, and they came over, did their estimate. It was to all be up there in three weeks. Fine, I thought. Let Lucky come back with Toby one night weeks after this and find the lock changed. But I was nervous sleeping in Uncle's bed, supposing the two of them should surprise me there now.

And they did. I had gone to bed early one night, and suddenly Toby and Lucky were coming in.

"Who are you?" one of them asked. "What are you doing here?"

"I'm here to get Uncle Eugene's things," I told them.

I had thrown back the covers and put on my robe. I had expected them to be hostile.

"You can't take things just like that," Toby said, somewhat menacing.

"I have permission," I said. "I'm his nephew. I told you that on the phone."

"Well, nothing leaves this house until I say it does," Lucky said. "It's half mine."

"I'd like to know by whose say-so," I said. "My understanding is—he's paid for everything."

I was getting a feeling much like the one I had had when I had gone into the Midnight Mart. The danger. That these two men were gay made no difference. In fact, it made it worse.

"Doesn't matter who's paid for what. He's my partner," Lucky said.

"Then why don't you come up with me and see him?" I asked.

"I plan to," Lucky said. But he seemed no more present than a poisonous vapor.

"When?" I asked.

The word hung out there. Toby deliberately hunched his back and went over to pour himself a drink. I wanted one, too, but I said, "Now if you don't mind, I'd like to get some sleep. The Mayflower van will be coming in the morning."

Lucky looked softened. "How is Eugene doing?"

"Fast going," I said. "We don't expect it will be much more than a few months."

"I'm sorry to hear that," he said.

Just then, Toby, who looked so good in a yellow polo shirt—he had olive skin and was no more than Lucky's age—pulled him aside and started grumbling. I could hear Lucky negotiating—it was the most compunction I ever saw in him—saying that since I was here, they'd better go back to Toby's place.

Without another word, they left. I never saw Lucky again. I went back to Uncle's bedroom and slept, but I went on thinking about it at the same time in a kind of dream. It wasn't unusual when young men tried to cash in on their soon-to-be-dead older partners. What I couldn't fathom was Uncle's incredibly bad judgment in making the choice he did and staying stubbornly with it.

That night, my dreams went into Treasure Island, where I walked among some of the illustrated scenes of his children's book that Brent liked so much. Past a starry pond, for example. Under an archway. The Exhibition Hall was under autumn trees. I had the distinct impression of holding hands with him when I awoke the next morning. I had been dreaming of seeing our San Francisco times together in the pond. Toby and Lucky had been a bad dream—the rest was OK.

◆◆◆

Galen was within viewing range of Brent's apartment building. The Mayflower block was coming up, and his cousin's Casablanca Video, although shut down, glowed with its one neon mosque. The theatre marquee was off, too, but the building emblem, of a yellow, bell-shaped flower, still burned. The light was enough to allow him to see into the windows of the upcoming World Wide Workouts, up on the second floor. Andrew had done a terrific job (Galen spied in). He had heard that another health club had closed suddenly, and Andrew had pulled off a great deal to get most of the equipment in at half price. Still, it looked brilliantly new. "Opening October 1."

Galen came back down the steps and into the courtyard, which he had trimmed and mown himself. The rhododendron, though spent, still had its glossy, olive-colored leaves.

In two more minutes, he was at Brent's. The Lexus was back. But he wasn't going to trek up there and have it out with him. He didn't have to get Brent's permission to send the check to Andrew. Or to give money to Christabel to bail out the hotel. He'd go home and work on his finances now, work on sorting out the suitable donations, late as it was.

He got in his truck and started the engine. Above, he could see Brent, bare-chested, in the window. He felt a tug to go in—no two ways about it.

But only minutes passed, and he was glad to see the "New Amsterdam" sign on the rooftop through the glass. To follow it. And now, at last, he felt visited by the spirit of his uncle. It was there, all around. It had even been in the Mayflower courtyard when he hadn't been thinking about it. The telephone next to the glossy rhododendron leaves. And here the lobby was bright with the pole lamps, and here and there, on all six floors, bright squares of windows dotted the building.

Further down the block, his rental house was waiting for him. It seemed very much alive with the summer night, as though it were at one with the Oasis district signs which had directed him. He could see Ophelia inside—she had come over to look after Jacob during the fundraiser—moving around, tending. She came to attention with a start when she saw him drive in. In fact, she came out, hurrying.

"Brent just called," she said. "He said he wants you to meet him down in the hotel lobby right away."

"How's Jacob doing?" Galen asked.

"No problem," she said. "He's in bed."

He got back into his truck and turned it around. Just while talking to her, he had caught a glimpse of Uncle Eugene's World's Fair photo—the statue—hanging on the wall. He went back to that first conversation he and Ophelia had had when he'd first gotten out of prison. No talk about Eugene at the hotel. And now things had changed. The plaque was on the seat beside him, and now people were talking as though he were alive.

He had a hard time finding a space for the truck—he saw what they meant about getting a parking lot. The hotel was packed because of the Handel Festival, and he ended up two blocks from the place.

However, in the lobby, he found no one but his father, who was seated in an easy chair with his feet up. He was reading. He had never seen his father like this before. The stillest he had ever seen him was at meetings, but he seemed even more so now.

"Well, Galen," his father said, "your friend was just here. He said, if you came in, to have you wait. He just went down the street to try to track you down."

Galen stood there, dumbfounded.

"What makes him think he could do that? I could be anywhere."

Nevertheless, his father had created a comfortable niche for him to step into—right by the empty fireplace. The stars were visible through some of the open windows, and in fact, their light was visible in the glass of the paintings. Galen was aware of the calendar clock and the sound of Mozart from the console from the same south end of the lobby. Always, before, Christabel had predominated here, with her Sorceress Seamstress Shop, but that, of course, was closed.

"Sit down," his father said. "It won't be any easier waiting standing up. Besides, I want to show you something."

What he was holding up was a book on the planet Pluto. In it, there was a picture of Gregory himself, at the age of ten, beside the discoverer Clyde Tombaugh. "I was actually there for the moment he found it," Gregory said. "I was the one who went running out with the message. It's taken me years to get up the courage to open this book again. Galen, I actually went down to the city library for the first time in twenty years."

"Was it so hard?" Galen asked.

"No, not when I actually got up and going," his father told him, "but what kept me from it was, thinking about all that I had missed."

"We talked about this before, didn't we?" Galen asked. "I have to say—I'm having a hell of a time getting back on track, too."

"Really? With all that money?" His father was touching his arm.

"Especially with all that money," Galen said. "Anyway"—he went on looking through the book—"it must be great to think about what you got from Tombaugh."

"Yes, yes," his father answered. "If I don't think too much about the potential I lost, too."

The lamplight caressed his father's face in a strange way. He was inclined to think of his uncle, now.

"Come to think of it," Galen said, "I've never had the courage to look myself up, either. I mean, in the gay histories, as the Man in the Superman Suit. I wonder what's that about?"

"I can't handle anything I might be proud of," his father said. "It's like I was saying. About the underground to the hotel. My gallery. Everything hanging there was at least forty years old. Too painful to think about everything I squandered."

Sounds of the night were coming through the window.

"But that friend of yours," his father went on. "Like I said, he sure is something. He wanted to know how my hip was doing, and he even checked me over. He gave me a clean bill of health in about thirty seconds."

"Brent can be that way," Galen answered.

"He's incredible," Gregory said. "What I'd give to have a gift like that." He closed his book. "No, we've all got gifts all right. That isn't the problem. Well, I'm dead on my feet from all these customers from the Festival. I'd better get to bed, give my back some rest. Don't stay up too late, either, my friend. See you at the next meeting."

They shook hands. And for a moment, he was again aware of his uncle. Instinctively, he turned to see if there was a light on in the Estate. There wasn't.

Watching his father slowly retreat, he thought again to a time in prison when he used to be allowed out, once a week, on good behavior, to run with the running group just south of a park. Actually, they met in front of a sports store, which sponsored the community runs.

Standing there in the hotel lobby, he remembered the trees on that run, the river they had gone past in that short circuit of freedom, all spaced apart in emerald darkness. He remembered, back then, that he had promised himself that if he ever got out of prison he'd never take anything for granted again. Not one single moment of freedom.

He had forgotten completely. He had come to take everything for granted. But suddenly it had come back, the gratitude. Now he appreciated the early September sky he had seen tonight, a sky that had reminded him of the dark bright water he had witnessed on that run that seemed so long ago.

Brent came in. He was dressed in white once more. With his father gone, the lobby was unattended. "Buddy, I'm sorry about the concert. I got there late, but they wouldn't let me in."

"It must have been awfully late," Galen said.

"It was." Brent had taken his hand. "Some men from my past are back. I thought I'd take care of some old business."

So, he said, "Brent, what's going on between you and Doc Hollywood? It must have been awfully important to leave me stranded. Is he your real boyfriend?"

"Boyfriend? No." Brent held his hands up. "Doc Hollywood wasn't there tonight."

"Then where do you get all this stuff from?" Galen asked. "Lexus, Mercedes, etcetera? Physical therapy doesn't bring in that much. I know, I've started to check."

Brent's face became rigid. "I did have a few other boyfriends who were rich."

"Rich and old?" Galen asked.

"Some of them," Brent said.

"Where are they now?" Galen asked.

"A few of them are dead. A few of them found somebody else."

"But not this man you had to see tonight?" Galen said.

"No."

"And it wasn't Doc Hollywood?' Galen said.

"No."

"Then who was it that kept you? The man we saw in the steam room?"

"Yes."

"And what," Galen said angrily, "could you have to say to him that was so important—important enough to leave me by myself?"

"I didn't leave you by yourself," Brent shouted. "As a matter of fact, I left you talking with your boyfriend."

Galen could detect that, despite his iciness, Brent was drunk. "He's not my boyfriend—at least not now."

"What do you mean by that—'at least not now'? Did you kiss him?" Brent asked.

Galen backed off. "Yes, I did."

"I thought so. I could just tell by the way he was looking at you," Brent said, furious. "So don't pull your usual self-righteous on me."

Galen nodded. "All right, I won't. I was out of line for asking."

Brent cooled down. After looking both ways, he put his arms around him. "So where does that leave us?" It was ludicrous their making a scene like this in the lobby. Anyone could come in at any moment. The corners had ears.

"Where it leaves us, is that you're obviously drunk," Galen said, "and I'm going home."

"OK, OK, I'm sorry about that too." Brent let go suddenly.

"No need to be sorry," Galen told him. "It's just that I have to go home. I've kept Ophelia well past the time I said I'd be back."

"She can wait--and Jacob can wait. He doesn't have to be all you ever think about. Because there's something else I need to bring up." Brent looked business-like, despite being drunk. "That $50,000," he insisted. "I need it, man. I asked Doc Hollywood for some tonight, and he can't come up with it. In fact, he doesn't even want to talk about it. He's spent too much on going around the world. He gave a lot to the Dalai Lama. The Dalai Lama! But what kind of fucking kick in the butt is that? You've got to come up with it now. I need it, man. I'm out of options. Rehabilitation Associates."

"I'm sorry, Brent," Galen said. "No. I've decided to stay with my promise to Andrew. I'm in. Up to here." He drew the sign at his chin, and he remembered what he had told Jacob about not buying bullies off with sticks of gum.

"But you've got more—" Brent began.

"Not enough to cover you and some other plans I have, like taking my family to Holland, Galen said. "No. And I wouldn't give it to you even if I had it. Not now. Not ever. Can't you see we're breaking up?"

Galen, then, was able to spot some danger. Maybe it was the memory of Toby and Lucky. The redness came over Brent's face, and he could see that the man was making a fist. When it came right at him, Galen blocked it violently—as he had learned many times in prison—and sent Brent crashing back down onto the sofa, where he burst into tears the moment he landed.

"I haven't got anyone left," Brent said, putting his head in his hands. "No one."

"I'm sorry," Galen said, trying to let his heart go down.

"No, you're not," Brent said, still crying.

"You're right," Galen said at last. "I'm not."

He let Brent cry some more and then said, "Can I help you up?" For someone, at last, was coming down into the lobby.

"No," he said. "Fuck you. Leave me alone."

Why Brent didn't murder him right there on the spot, Galen didn't know. He certainly had the strength.

"I will as soon as I drive you home," he said. "You can't drive yourself."

"Fuck you," Brent said again and got ready to storm out. "Self-righteous asshole. Speechifying ex-con." Galen, following, tried to stop him, touched him, and at just that moment, two hoodlums drove past, took the two of them in, and yelled "faggots!" at the top of their lungs. The old woman in the lobby was looking at them, and the moment Galen turned back to the street, Brent was pulling away.

The hoodlums, coming back, acted like he hadn't heard them and yelled "Faggots" again for good measure.

"Great," Galen called back, "so are we."

Staring from the hotel's main door into the street, he had the sense that he'd better follow Brent back to his apartment. He had had a similar feeling when he had gone into the Midnight Mart. He righted the skewed sofa. Under the eyes of the scandalized woman, a *grande dame*, he checked the cash box at the desk to be sure it was locked. Then he called Tamara on the house phone to have her attend (which was her job anyway after eleven) until the midnight clerk came in. The dumbfounded customer left.

Going up the street, he wished the worst for Brent. And he imagined him with the shit beaten out of him lying bleeding beneath a streetlamp. He took a shortcut through the hotel parking lot, saw the white Lexus again, and heard groans. At first he thought it was his wish fulfillment when the body of Brent emerged, rolled up against the left rear tire. His face was bruised, and Galen was sure the hoodlums, as gay-bashers, had gotten to him.

"Can I help you up?" Galen asked.

Brent's head rolled to one side. He was looking into the sky, which still seemed friendly. "No. They kicked me. I'm sure my rib is broken."

He held his stomach, then his chest.

"OK," Galen answered. "I'll get help. I'll be back in two shakes. Just don't move."

"No problem with that."

He dashed into his house, scaring the life out of Ophelia, who was bedded down on his couch. "Got to use the phone. Brent's been hurt." He dialed 911 and ran back to the car. By then, the roaring ambulance had arrived, and two beautiful firemen in blue were bending over Brent. He yelled some, being brought to the stretcher. Galen asked if he could travel with them to the hospital, and he was met with a heavy-browed "no." Galen had to travel alone in his truck, and it was a dark, late ride, with all the sense that once again, because of Brent, he was leaving Jacob behind. He also felt guilty, having wished the worst for Brent and gotten it.

Within moments, he was sitting in the waiting room of the ER. Finally, a nurse came out and said Brent had already been checked over and admitted.

◆◆◆

Afterwards, the dreams of Brent were long and hard. The shape of the man's body was still upon him, and in reaching for it in sleep, Galen found it difficult to stay in that enclosure of dark, that sense of protection, when he failed to find the man there.

In the empty nights, when he could not get back to sleep, he would walk into the den he had made over in honor of his uncle; he would turn on the lights—his own way of creating a haunted refuge. The idol in the photograph would burn like an icon fronted by a votive candle, and beneath it, there was the plaque he had placed there. It seemed fitting, now, more in this place than at the Hotel or Christabel's. Then, in returning to bed, Galen would look toward the light streaming down the hallway and fancy, at least, he saw the iridescence returning. In fact, it may have come, after all, from the bit of prism glass now hanging from the central light fixture in Uncle's room.

Stay with me, Galen thought.

In being up sometimes at night, he had the hotel with him, too, instead of the Estate. The "New Amsterdam" in gold letters on the roof was his beacon, his friend, along with this vaguer ghost that he found in the brilliance of things. But also—what?—a pressure. Sometimes the light of his father's room—he could see it this far away—was on. That made him feel better, somehow, that they shared this. Like the crooked way they both carried baggage. Sometimes his father saw his window and called him on the phone. "Hey, Galen, just trying to stay sober tonight. Thought about Bohemian Club, but I don't think so. Went out to the hospital to see Brent. He'll be out in a few days. He's a good example of no Bohemian Club for me."

As a matter of fact, Galen had been out there to the hospital, too. The man's bruises were going down, and he was beginning to look again like the angel he had first seen on the roof of the Oasis Hotel.

"No, I know what you mean. Let's just sit through it," Galen would say to him.

It reminded him when, as a child, he used to worry about lying in bed, unable to sleep, and being the only one awake in the world. His father had been no good to him then.

But then his uncle had reminded him of the world's time zones, so that at any given moment, there would always be someone up. And of course, there was the Skywatch—people hired to scan for enemy planes through the entire night. And so gradually, with his uncle's reassurance, he began to sleep soundly in his bed in those days. He was, in fact, sleeping more soundly, now that the commotion had left the Estate. As his mother got herself and the rest of them ready for Amsterdam, he recognized that he had neglected a lot of things while he had been seeing Brent. He needed to sort out papers, books and bills in his landscaping office, as well as whether he wanted to keep the office itself. It was as though the nights, now, gave him a clear head. How much longer was he going to be in the landscape business anyway? And he felt devastated, sometimes, heartsick, thinking that he would not have that lead—Brent's mentor's lead—in his life. Wasn't the loss of one guide enough? And now, did he really want a life of helping people with their health, their bodies, or was that just something he had borrowed from Brent?

And he couldn't help but think of Eugene in his last days, the way the man had assigned his whole life over to Lucky. Eugene's journal read—

> This whole summer, I have been waiting for him to come back. I have the strongest sense that if he were to put his body next to mine, I would be healed. Skin against skin. The way I used to be. I send him letters hoping he will come through that door, but he will not. All I get is the embodiment of July. The low level of light in the dappling of the creeks (I can hear light outside this window!). Or the sound of my son's voice so many, many years ago, on a July day, when our old home went up like kindling. And this memory going off like a rocket. It never would have gone up like kindling, if I had had the money, earned the money for a proper dwelling.

And Galen saw in his own journal back then—

> It's hopeless, almost daily Uncle sends out hundred dollar checks to that asshole who ought to be the one up here walking him to the bathroom. I daily have to change the sheets, bring in breakfast on a tray, and wonder why Uncle won't spend the money on proper nursing. Christabel says he wants to die at home! But if he wants to die at home, why doesn't he get it over with, so I don't have to watch him throw his life away on that jerk?

But I remember, Galen thought, I remember taking his hand in those last hours. The grip was strong. The hand was still blue-veined.

"We're about to go over a bump, just a little bump," Eugene said—just the way he used to say it when we were on the Ferris wheel—or like he used to say when I was about to go through my next stage of coming out of the closet. "Just a little bump, but we'll be over it soon. How are you doing?"

"I'm doing fine," I answered, still gripping Eugene's hand. "But Uncle, please don't leave now. Please stay a little longer."

Three years later, I would have his letter, which would read, "I love you."

"I have to leave," Uncle answered. And he really did look like a spotted flower. I had all the windows open, as if to prevent him wilting, and now I had to call everyone to gather around, because this was going to be it.

"I really have to leave," Uncle said.

The doctor gave him a shot. "You'd better speak now or forever hold your peace."

Ophelia said, "You have been a good uncle and such a friend to my brother"—and broke into tears.

Andrew said, "Let me know if there is anything else I can do."

Christabel said, "Please forgive my neglect, Eugene. Please forgive our parting of the ways so many years ago. I will make it up to you, somehow."

And now, in light of the letter, I would have said, "I love you, too, Uncle. If it hadn't been for you, I wouldn't be alive now."

And there had been no Lucky.

Gregory said, "I'll get sober for you," and then never did until now.

So Uncle had not gone out of this world with the shape of a young man against him. Maybe he went out holding the hand of Frank Baum or some other storyteller who had passed on but had decided to come back and be a tour guide, leading him out. Who can say? But one thing is clear now, one thing is very clear, if Uncle betrayed himself then, he did it knowing full well what he was doing, and by God, he wasn't going to have it handed on to me. He knew what kind of life I had lived with Leo. He had seen my frailties, and he wasn't going to have it happen again. And so no money for me in the will—that was love—no money, because a Brent or Lucky would soon be around the corner, and I'd be sitting in a lonely bedroom which was probably in its own way a closet waiting for either one to show up again.

Do I have to think about this now? Do I have to? I can remember standing there in the Memorial Service afterwards, right there in the New Amsterdam, in the very hall Room where Mother had had her reading. I remember standing there under the arch of Ophelia's roses, the only rainbow or hint of anything gay in the room, and thinking they were shoving that man back into the closet. Do I have to remember how I remembered having Uncle hook me into that Superman outfit before going out and having me defy those psychiatrists? That a family was putting Uncle in the dark the way they put people under anesthesia. "Torturers!" "Murderers!" And I stood there under the arch of Ophelia's memorial flowers and remembered Amsterdam, which had given us all the ideas—for they had come in Anne Frank House and Vondel Park—and I had wanted to shout out, "Uncle Eugene was gay— without that, where would my childhood be?" But I didn't say anything. The people in the chairs—their stares held me back. All I wanted in that close room, with the smell of the wine punch, was to go back out into oblivion. I was too afraid to say a thing; better, I was too fragmented to say a thing. I was one of those buildings that they explode from the inside, and comes cascading down in on itself in a shower of dust.

◆◆◆

Galen stirred himself now, got out of bed. Out of the posture—at least in his mind—that he had shared with Brent. The dynamic duo. Right. The partners of the now defunct Rehabilitation Associates.

No, not today. In fact, today—October 1—World Wide Workouts was opening.

So he must up and hustle Jacob off to school. As best he could, since Jacob had walled himself off. Jacob still held a resentment that Galen had been seeing Brent for so long. Even after the break-up with Brent, Jacob had been uncooperative. But there was no time to take care of that, at least for now. He also had to clear the morning things out of the way, so he could land at Andrew's building by noon. He had decided to extend the lease on his office downtown; he still had to review whose lawn needed mowing now and what substitute help he could call in before they went to Amsterdam.

Throughout Carleton Park, autumn had not quite fully arrived. The sidewalks seemed slightly burnished with heat, but the trees above the street cafes had not yet dropped their leaves. Not in the least. The streams of fog were promising Amsterdam. There was a tentative quiet to the morning. Walking down to the old building that housed his office, he passed Milton's Books, which displayed his mother's poetry in the window. It had placed a picture of the planet Pluto as well as a stone statue of the god behind the now reissued collection. He wondered if he himself would ever leave behind anything as solid as that.

In the office, his schedule and phone messages reminded him he needed to get out to the Park area of Carleton Park once more. So he drove to one home after another and wheelbarrowed leaves and took them to his truck. A tall climbing rose upon a lattice made him think of Brent again—in a still yard, with a pond. Those long mists, like an aurora, were coming in above the hills, and he could see one vast vista of slender aspens, like an array of golden splinters, leading toward that one center of light. He dug through Mrs. Madison's vegetable garden, leaving just the pumpkins for Halloween; everything else was spent. He could stay doing these jobs forever, actually. But Ophelia wanted him at eleven, to help move the flowers to the Opening, and he could do that. His mother had also asked to see him about the last of the plans of the Amsterdam trip. But he just wanted to stay here, continue clearing, keeping up with nature, not be sent off again into the outer world. At that moment, the idea came to him that he might ask Anton to join them in their flight to Holland. The music—Bach's Toccata and Fugue—which they had mentioned (in caves, in St. Bavo's) came back.

He did, in fact, get to Ophelia's by eleven, and found Anton there. They were stacking cut gladiolas and six-foot vases into his truck.

"I also made a sign," Ophelia said. "We can roll that up and toss it in the back, too."

"I was going to call you," Anton said to him, on the side.

"It's just as well you didn't," Galen said.

"The two of you," Ophelia went on, "I need to get both of those imitation pillars in back—I would have called in Andrew to help with this, but he's over there now, checking out the offices for the tour—and I need you to get the pumpkins and pumpkin flowers and leaves in there as well."

"It's too bad you didn't tell me you wanted leaves," Galen said. "I could have brought you in a whole truckload."

"We just may as well both go in my pickup," Anton said.

"And the balloons, please," Ophelia said. "Those boxes. And the cylinder of helium. Please use your knees and not your backs when transporting. Thank you."

When they were ready to go and sitting in Anton's front seat, Anton turned to him and said, "Well?"

"Well what?"

"What about you and Brent?" Anton asked. "Andrew told me you were thinking about doing a joint business venture with him."

"No joint business venture now," Galen said flatly. "You must have read what happened to him in the paper."

"Yes. But the man sounds in even more dire need of money now."

"The reason he's in dire need of money is one of the reasons he and I are no longer together. At least he's out of the hospital."

Anton started the engine. "All right, then what?" Actually, the whole vehicle seemed fired up. With the flowers in back, with Anton's red hair, and with Galen's red shirt, they were kind of like firemen. "I mean—then what after this venture here?"

"What's next is Amsterdam," Galen said. "Which is what I want to talk to you about."

They drove right down into the Mayflower district, and it seemed to Galen they were driving straight into Amsterdam as he remembered it. The filigree which shimmied, in stone, up the buildings—and flowered—took him back to his days with Uncle Jacob, whose hotel and even whose prose style reminded him exactly of this. Ossification and choreography together.

Here was the Mayflower building, with its barbershop and Casablanca Video on the first level, and then World Wide Workouts on the second, reached by an outside staircase. The neon sign with the bellflower was on, even at mid-day, along with the dizzying green of Andrew's sign on the roof, WWW, one letter at a time. The script was a definite steal from the New Amsterdam. There was a huge contrast between the stillness of the hour, the season, and all the hubbub on the second floor.

Gregory joined them at the truck. Galen stacked both of them high with gladiolas.

"I'm ready to help you move this time," Gregory said. "Not being such a butt."

Andrew was at the top of the stairs in a green "WWW" tank top. "Hey, guys, bring those right through the front door."

Galen was holding a long-necked floor vase in each hand. "So, Andrew," he called, "where do you want these?"

"Right by the front desk."

Galen trudged behind Anton, right up the stairs. "So," Anton called back, "talk to me about Amsterdam."

"Want to go with us?" Galen asked. "Got the money? We'll supply the room and board."

"Yes," Anton answered. But looked tentative.

"Can you get ready in two weeks? Is your passport up to date?" Galen asked.

"I think so," Anton said. He was walking away again, however. He seemed relieved they were still moving things.

They ushered all the loose items into the lobby. Ophelia started arranging the flowers. She also hustled them into fixing the display of balloons outside. Just the moment before they were about to cut the ribbon, Christabel appeared, along with Cousin Keystone. A small crowd had gathered. Outside of his video store, Keystone was the family malaprop. "I'd feel absolutely deciduous if I had missed this," he said to Christabel.

As the church steeple struck twelve all the way down Holland Avenue, Andrew went to the podium and made a short speech. He thanked their aunt Evelyn, who couldn't be there, and his brother-in-law Galen, who had helped make this possible. He also thanked his Board of Directors. He was a little giddy with what they had done, and the mob applauded again while he turned red with embarrassment and started wandering through and giving the tour. With Anton at his side, Galen made his way through again a new weightlifting section, an aerobics room, and a large area for stretching and yoga classes. The locker rooms and hot tub were more than standard. Andrew had modeled it on those in his family's sister hotel in Amsterdam. The potted plants and marble around the spa were definitely "my European flavor," as he called it.

Galen, glancing here and there, wondered how Uncle Jacob, certainly no malaprop but definitely, still, a circumlocutory rhetorician, might have described it. "At angular lines, people will enjoy the windows crossing back and forth in a cross-stitch of imagination of light and darkness, finding full benefit for their bodies in machines fitted out for their use and benefaction."

His mother had caught his eye. She was with Gregory. "It's nice to see you, Anton," she told him. And on the side to Galen—"Much better than that *infant terrible* you had."

"Mother," he said, having to raise his voice against the call for a gift drawing, "I want to talk to you about your trip."

"Yes, this is as good a place as any." His father was listening while rolling down a small new red carpet to the side of him.

He was reminded of when they had all first gotten together, during Ophelia's brought-in dinner, under the Evening Star.

"Have you got the dates booked?" he asked.

"Tentatively—the 27th of this month to November 6," she told him. "The reading at the Vondel Hotel is to be November 2."

"I would like to bring Anton along," he said.

"Sure, bring him along," she answered. She was so amenable—for a moment Galen thought *she* was drunk.

From time to time, they could hear Andrew's cautious voice giving the visitors descriptions of more of the facilities.

"So that leaves five of us who are going—you, Anton, myself, Gregory, Jacob," Galen told her.

"I don't think so," his father said, speaking up. He dusted his hands, with the carpet positioned. The neon, through the glass, of the Mayflower sign was above him. Galen could also see the window of Brent's apartment. A figure stood in it, watching. The place looked like a Palm Beach hotel. Nice soft sandstone.

"You're not going?" Galen asked.

"Not solid enough sober," his father said. "Too hard on someone in their first ninety days. You go and have a good time. I'll take care of your landscaping customers while you're gone. I'm only working part-time at the hotel now anyway."

"I never asked you to do anything like that before," Galen said. And, really, it seemed like too much, and it was very odd—the idea of his father being left in charge and not going with them. Frankly, he didn't completely trust him.

"Maybe it's about time," Gregory answered. "It won't be a heavy season anyway. What do you say? Everything's going to be all right."

Tamara came by with some crust-trimmed sandwiches on a tray. "Watercress," she said, "catered by your mother." She was in her black uniform, with white apron. Perfectly starched, as always.

"You're going back to the old country, Mr. Galen?" she asked.

"Yes," he answered. "It's in the works. Do you have a desire to go? My father's not going. Perhaps I could—"

"No," she said. "It wouldn't be the same." Her eyes searched the whole upper story. Obviously, she was concerned that everybody was taken care of. Galen recognized, after years of having her in the family, how minute and sensitive her touch was.

"Why wouldn't it be?" he asked.

"The whole city would be a *standbeeld* shop for me. Only icons, Mr. Galen, only icons. I like it here better, where everything is alive."

"I often thought there was more life over there," Galen said.

"Same here," Anton said. "At least I thought that when I visited."

"Over there," Tamara answered, still standing with her tray, as though she were an icon herself (and it was so unusual for her to pause from her work like this), "you would be visiting churches. Here we get a place like this, your sister's and brother-in-law's venture. Such a place as this—one visit would cost thirty-eight gilders over there. My heavens."

"Thirty-eight gilders?" Galen asked. "How much is thirty-eight gilders?"

Tamara looked to the side. "About nineteen dollars. One-year membership would be 3000 gilders. I talked with my cousin by phone. Here your brother-in-law is offering one-time visit at five dollars, full year at $150. Ten times less. Who would not prefer to live in this country?"

She moved on ahead with her tray. Galen was about to say something to Anton, when he looked out the window again, and beneath the sign, he saw Teresa coming up with a bouquet of flowers. She had the same deliberate step as in the spring, but some of the harshness had gone out of her face. The thought of her being here with Anton almost took the wind out of him for a moment, but he could do nothing more than stand there.

He could hear Christabel exclaiming at the door. Then he saw her kissing and hugging her. "I'm here," he could hear Teresa saying defensively, "because I like Andrew, and I want to support what he is trying to do."

As he crowded to the front, he could hear Andrew answer with a smile, "Yes, physical fitness for the masses."

Shy, Galen exchanged hellos with her.

"May I take your flowers?" he asked, not knowing what else to say.

"They're for Andrew," she said, looking down.

"I know that. But I know where the vases are," he said.

Andrew was coming out again from the back room. His WWW tank top was sweaty. "Well, that's it for the tours. Teresa—how are you? It's been so long."

"Teresa!" Ophelia shouted behind him. "Teresa's here? I'm so glad she's come." She rushed over. Her green drapery nearly wrapped Teresa up as she hugged her. To Galen, it seemed for a moment that they were all just potted plants alive and growing in a greenhouse.

"Teresa," Galen said, mustering the courage, "I'd like you to meet my friend, Anton."

Taken off guard, his whole family seemed to hold its breath. Started to turn blue.

"Nice to meet you," Anton said, blushing.

"Likewise," Teresa said, also shy.

"Well," Christabel said, "this is quite an occasion. I don't believe we have been this reunited in years."

But of course the statement caused everybody to fly in different directions.

"We're leaving for Amsterdam soon," Christabel explained.

"And who will watch the hotel?" Teresa asked.

"Your grandfather—who's somewhere around here—and Ophelia and Andrew," Galen said.

She seemed very grown up, now, with more make-up; even in just a few months, she had turned more beautiful. She had a silver ring of intertwined fish on one of her fingers.

"I have been calling and writing," Galen said. "I hope you got my message. You're invited to Amsterdam, too."

"Not this time," she said. "Maybe Grandma will go again, and then I can."

She smiled. Several people had left already, and other friends had gone downstairs to the front of the building. For a moment, Andrew distributed his flyers on World Wide Workouts, and in the instant, the whole floor seemed as though it were in a processional, with the potted plants and workout equipment and Carleton Parkers all timed, in rhythm.

"Still, maybe I could see you more often," he said to her. "Especially after I get back."

"Yes." She smiled again. "Last time we had a good time."

Did we?

With WWW behind her—in that light—it seemed as though she were the young woman runner he had met on that day, with the descending white Easter clouds.

"Somehow, this day," he said, "reminds me of that time we had."

"Yes, the courtyard downstairs reminds me of that graveyard," she laughed.

"Well, thanks a lot," Andrew said from the back.

"I meant it as a compliment," Teresa answered.

When there was a moment, he took Christabel aside. He sat down on one of the bench presses. "Here's a check to clear your debts," he said. "How about letting AIDS House and the Gay Alliance have the Estate? You don't need to sell it."

"What about our parking lot?" she answered.

"Maybe you'll just have to hire a man with stronger legs to park the cars, three blocks down. Someone to help Dad," he explained. "You've been having backup men helping him behind the scenes for years anyway."

She folded the check and put it in her blue handbag, which she held by a chain around her wrist. She was looking at him with skepticism. "Thank you," she said. "I'll bethink me, as Shakespeare says."

"You've said 'bethink' before," he told her. "If you decide to keep the Estate or raze it, I want my money back."

"That goes without saying," she answered.

Further away, he could see Teresa talking with his father. Gregory looked overwhelmed. Galen was going to have to leave in a minute to pick up Jacob early from school so he could go to the last of the ceremony. Slowly he was coming around again, too, after being mad at Galen for weeks.

❖❖❖

Jacob was standing in front of Edison School when Galen pulled up. He was clutching a couple of notebooks.

"I thought you'd never come," Jacob said, bustling in.

"I said one o'clock," Galen told him flatly. "Have I ever forgotten?"

Jacob opened his notebook. Obviously, another script. Galen glanced at the watercolor illustrations.

"One o'clock wasn't fair," Jacob said, paging through. "Not fair at all. I wanted to be there for the whole ceremony. Teresa got to be there."

"She's also college age."

"But she wasn't left alone like I was," Jacob answered. He had turned eleven and was getting some down on his cheeks, as well as an edge, at times, to his voice. "I should have been able to skip school."

Galen gripped the steering wheel. "I wanted you to go to part of school today. It was a gym day. I especially didn't want you to miss gym."

"Gym is stupid," Jacob insisted. "By the way, I'm going to stop this Charlie Chan script. It's just somebody else's thing."

"Gym is not stupid."

"It's stupid. You know what 'gymnasium' means? A place to be naked. All the guys in my gym when they get naked put towels around them, and change sometimes in the bathrooms so nobody will see."

"Maybe if you keep going, you won't mind if somebody sees. You'll just be considered an athlete like the rest of them."

Jacob was obviously fighting back anger. Suddenly, and without warning, Galen had to avoid a black lab bounding across the street. His mistress stood on the porch, yelling. After the swerve, they went under the low silver branches of a Siberian elm. Galen took a breath.

"I don't want to be athletic like the rest of them. That's why I hated Brent. Why I was glad I could just go up to Forest Grove when you were with him. He was a dickhead. A total dickhead. He was an athlete that kept trying to make me into one."

"Well, I don't see him anymore, and you don't have to call him a dickhead. He's fallen on some bad times."

"Hallelujah, sing Hallelujah. I hope he got what's coming to him. Ophelia and Andrew told me all about it."

Despite what he remembered, Galen said—and with heat—"You don't rejoice in anybody's bad fortune. That's not what we do. If my prison experience taught me anything, it's that. So listen up—I only want you to go to gym so you can feel better."

"Yeah," Jacob answered with some cynicism, "so I can 'feel better about myself,' like Mom says."

"She's not always wrong."

"I thought you said she was," Jacob retorted.

"Well, then, I was wrong," Galen said, irked to his limit. Fortunately, they were drawing up to the slowly lit letters of WWW Workouts.

They had some ways to go, he and Jacob.

◆◆◆

Four a.m. when they had to drive out to the airport. Unseasonably warm, however. Galen pulled back the curtains to the surprising night of the sky, and all the dahlias were still intact just beyond the window. Their colors of red, yellow, and white-purple were in an ethereal light. The first frost had not yet come.

He was ready to get away from the Estate and presumably Uncle's presence.

At that moment, however, here in his own house, Galen drew himself up short. The dahlias seemed to have a message. Some moths fluttered up, unexpected, into the moonlight. He could hear Jacob in the kitchen, bungling through his breakfast. Across the street, Ophelia's Flowers was lighting up, unexpected once more, the green maiden taking an early morning walk across the bridge, precarious.

"Dad? Dad—where is that guidebook?" Jacob asked. "The one that tells about Vondel and his park?"

"I don't know, Jacob—let's just make sure you have the important stuff first," Galen told him.

"I found it, I found it." Jacob pulled up a stack of newspapers. "See, Dad, this beautiful Vondel Park—?"

This was the first time in many weeks that Jacob had allowed any of his enthusiasm to show again.

"Jacob," Galen insisted, "we've got to get ready. Otherwise, no Vondel Park, no Amsterdam, no nothing."

Jacob was deliberately not following orders. Christabel was trying to usher him along.

But soon, Andrew and Ophelia were at the door, helping their nephew, and Anton was drawing up in his truck, which he was to leave on the street for Andrew for ten days. Now they, the six of them, got into Ophelia's Cadillac, which Andrew had kept going through constant tinkering. To Galen, it seemed that they were departing through the hotel's underground passage, which would somehow lead them back to their original life.

No one spoke in the car. Beside him, Jacob kept turning the pages of the souvenir book. The city seemed to offer just the right amount of lights to get them to the plane. For just one moment, they passed the opera house and saw all the vans unloading the vast sets for *Aida*, the shells of the Egyptian columns rolled tight like rugs, along with tapestries, silks burgeoning from boxes, and huge wooden casements holding God knows what.

"There will be an elephant soon," Andrew said.

"But we can't have it for our fundraiser preview at the Fine Arts," Ophelia said.

"We'll have four tusk bearers instead," Andrew added. "They will be our elephant. They look fantastic in their costumes."

The car did seem, in fact, to be rolling toward some of kind of circus—and when they finally arrived at the ten-minute passenger zone at the airport, the goodbyes—which included Andrew as well as Ophelia—just seemed to be a part of some vast parade, which would get a musical background number very soon.

"Call me instantly," Ophelia said, "if anything dire happens and you want me to come. Call me long distance, collect."

"What could happen?" Christabel asked. "You're not making any dire predictions, are you?"

"No, no, I foresee all things beneficial happening," Ophelia told her. "However, if anything dire concerning Father Gregory comes up, you will, of course hear from us."

"Father Gregory?" Galen asked.

"Gregory, our father," Ophelia said impatiently.

"Greg is doing fine," Andrew said.

"Goodbye, goodbye again," Galen said.

The last person he threw his arms around was Andrew. "Here's to our World Wide Workouts."

From the puddle jump to Portland, from Portland to the huge KLM in Minneapolis, Galen settled into a railway compartment at the back of his mind, where he could look out and see, for example, his prison cell with its Rembrandt postcards. See the courtyard of the New Amsterdam, and view the memories, again, of walking up Anne Frank's stairs. On the KLM (whose landing wheels were each as big as a multi-storied house), they were allowed seats four across, and Galen felt as though they were sitting down to a long movie. In fact, eventually, they did turn the lights down after dinner, and both Anton and Jacob fell asleep beside him, then against. On the aisle where she could reach the bathroom, Christabel, however, had her light on and was writing in her new manuscript. "Well," he said, "how's it coming?"

"Faster now," she answered. "The closer we get to Amsterdam, the quicker I imagine."

Although he wanted to press her about her decision on the Estate, he fell asleep at last.

In a dream, he resumed walking up the stairs. In the attic of Frank House, he saw it—Anne's "bulletin board" of photos and artwork. He looked again and was overwhelmed. He saw Anne holding out by putting a picture of Leonardo on her wall, right there along with the family photos, the clippings, and the Hollywood glamour ladies. Now he could see the Westertoren. Yes, he had seen all of this once, before prison. That he had been young and naive and fresh, once, in the sixties, looking at that steeple. That he had been whole once, in an easy state, which was no longer true.

Then he was running through the underground of the New Amsterdam hotel, saw his father's photographs in a blur, and instinctively, in sleep, held Anton against him, even though at some level he knew they were both just in airline seats (hardly romantic!). Nevertheless, he actually drew him towards him, tight, and he saw his father's photographs and heard the Time poem,

"Geswinde grijsart die op wackre wiecken staech/De dunne luct doorsnijt, en sonder seil te strijcken."

"Oh," he heard Anton say beside him, "it's you."

Then in dreams, he was at a little cafe table on the corner of Pieter Corneliszoon Hooft (1581-1647) Straut, named after the man who had written the poem. His uncle was saying, "Should we go to the Rijkmuseum down the street? It's not five minutes," and Galen did not know how to answer, he had been so overwhelmed from Anne Frank House (for he had seen something else from the window next to the Westertoren).

But they did decide to go, and not very far ahead, the Rijkmuseum courtyard stood before him, the one that later imbued his dreams, that made prison endurable. It was opening up, even before the two of them, he and his uncle, had left the sidewalk and gone through the wrought-iron gate and passed by the statue of the lady holding the mirror high above them. He remembered going through her shadow and then up to the front of the grilled and heavily decorated front entrance, as though it were a weave of figures and windows. There, on the second floor, was *The Night Watch* and *St. Peter's Denial*—like lanterns, or lighthouses, in a long passageway. The colors had seemed to extinguish all voices. There was a musket, a girl in gold, men in plumes and sashes, white and rose, a gathering of people about to explode from the center.

"When Holland started to be bombed," his uncle said, "they hid this away."

Somehow Galen knew his uncle was referring to himself as being hidden when he said this—but how? Something he zealously protected. His journals, maybe. Or his vision of film and Hollywood. Or maybe his late-night sessions of talk, with other gays and lesbians, in the heart of Los Angeles.

And when they turned to the Rembrandt *St. Peter*, something cut through Galen. His own capacity for denial. The firelight was on the saint's face, filling up the corners. It was like a map plotting treachery. Peter, nonchalant and gray-bearded, looking sideways at the glowing Maid and saying, "Who me?"—as Galen had remembered before.

Just then, Galen awoke in the airline seat and realized he had been sleeping for hours. Anton was up and having his breakfast.

"Schiphol is just around the corner," Anton said. "Boy, were you gone. We were going to sprinkle water on you."

"That's me," Galen said, "a regular gravesite."

"Not yet, not yet," Anton observed.

Jacob was buried under a blanket and watching the Dutch film on the screen. It seemed to be about leprechauns. Christabel just sat looking straight in front of her, daubing tears.

The plane was beginning to descend at last. Hours and hours of trash were being gathered. Christabel anointed herself with a Wash-and-Dry, and tried to look brave, and Galen reached across Jacob and patted her shoulder.

In Schiphol, all was gray, but people were talking about how unseasonably warm it was for late October. It was nine a.m. in the morning. It seemed as if the entire city existed against slate-colored sand dunes in the sky, but certainly there would be a sudden flowering.

"Uncle" Jacob Jr. was there the moment they cleared customs, smiling and speaking very clearly in English, along with his father's souvenir-book syntax. The first Uncle Jacob, of course, was no longer living, but this adopted son, who ran the family Vondel Hotel, was a very close second. Physically "Uncle" Jacob seemed a lot like Patrick, back in Carleton Park. "Ah, you must be so very tired, after all those chronological ellipses. However, we have rooms all ready for you, and my son, Theo, he is young and strong, and will be ready with the car for your luggage. We take the car out very rarely for ourselves, you understand."

Christabel was still crying. "My Dear," she said, "I had forgotten how very much like your father you look."

"Well, maybe accidental," he answered. "Because I am, as they say, added on to the family from other parents."

He also reminded Galen of Patrick because he had entirely taken over as a guide. He hustled them into baggage claim, while the clouds outside still seemed to have a mind of their own—was winter on the rise at last?—and then out again, speaking in Italian, English, and Dutch, when Christabel's one paisley valise could not be found. With that many languages, it was possible to pass the message on down the line, and of course it was retrieved, at last. Theo drew up the van outside Schiphol. Overhead, a huge sign lit up the temperature and time. Unfortunately, Galen had forgotten the conversions for Celsius and Fahrenheit. Nevertheless, he knew it was still balmy in Amsterdam; his heavy coat already was too hot for him.

The van, clearly, had been borrowed from the hotel. "We have many rooms for you," Theo said. "One for you and Anton, one for Christabel and Jacob."

"Jacob," Jacob said, correcting the Dutch pronunciation. "And my dad and I were supposed to stay together."

"Ah, I thought that you and Anton were, as they say, married," Theo said.

"Theo," Uncle Jacob said, "that is not to be talked of here."

"It's all right," Anton said. "We don't have to share the same room. May Christabel and I stay separately?"

"Yes," Uncle Jacob said. "And in the old part of the hotel, too, with the rest of us. Which is preferred."

They moved, now, between the packed houses, the lines of ornamentation being just as Galen had remembered. He started looking for an iridescence somewhere, and it dawned just above the *Koninklijk Paleis*, with Theo saying, "Ah, there you see the creatures of the sea in the facade, and the lady, who is Amsterdam, who wishes to pay honor to them."

Galen thought he saw Ophelia in her. She seemed to have life gathered around her, as though it were a bouquet or banquet.

"Isn't the War Memorial close by here?" Anton asked. "Could we stop for just a moment?"

They did stop at the War Memorial. Anton took Galen's hand. It seemed all right. On the obelisk, the figures rose out of the stone, acquiring muscles and flesh, as though the trumpet from Handel had caused these gravestones to be thrown aside, too. The resurrected bodies had moved in a gesture of thanksgiving toward the heavens. The National Monument seemed to outweigh World War II itself—the scales tilted—and Galen remembered trying to write that in his original uncle's (Jacob's) guidebook. "The stone urns which the monument encapsulates significate those beloved departed dead who gave their lives in twelve different regions on behalf of our country."

"I brought my grandmother here one time," Anton said. "She had been in the occupation, too."

"I left before then," Christabel said. "But I received letters from those who bore through it." She wiped her eyes again.

"Ah, we must not stand here for such a long time," Uncle Jacob said, still looking supervisory. "This is long enough. We show you a few other things from the car, and then we take you home."

The day was beginning to break open. The warmth was putting them back several months. The sun and retreating shadows accentuated the lines of the compressed houses along the canals. There was window box after window box of beautiful geraniums. And at the street corners, Galen noticed the bulbs for sale, marked with bright-colored photographs of the perfect yellow tulips and the marvelous parrot variations, flecked with green and red.

"The soil here," Theo said, "is very expensive. That is why we have to crowd so many things together. And here in this crowd we have the house where Rembrandt died poorly."

They rushed by; Rembrandt's place had a marvelous-looking door.

"I have a poem on that door," Christabel said.

"Let's go by that again," Galen said. "Many, many times."

It seemed, once more, that he was getting out of prison. That the day was presenting all of this to him, to them, like jewels set out on a tray. Only this time, he did not have to guess what was going on in the minds of his fellow travelers, as he had that day in the car with Ophelia driving, way back in February. Anton's hand was closing over his, again, as the midway of Damrak avenue opened up before them, with the trams going by so fast and close, their hats would have been knocked off their heads, had they been wearing any. Galen remembered the hand which had been his uncle's when they had been going through Anne Frank house, and along the streets as well, and Galen was nearly overcome with a sense of family, not just as far as the Vondels were concerned, but also the whole of Amsterdam itself.

Amstelredam die 't hoofd verheft aan 's hemels as

en schiet, op Pluto's borst, haar wortels door 't moerars.

It did seem that all was rising out of Pluto's breast, as Renaissance Vondel said; Galen remembered, back in Oregon, some nineteenth-century poet searching for a way of seeing Aeolus as their god of continual wind and rain, and sometimes, yes, close to the river, he was aware maybe of some greater force, vaguely associated with Olympus, but here, for sure, there was no doubt Pluto imbued all, rising up from the very expensive soil. The gods were everywhere. Even in Tamara's *standbeeld* shop (Galen looked into the window, passing), which seemed to carry the pagans as well as the Christs and Marys.

Pluto was, in fact, in the courtyard when they got to their hotel. They had a view down from their rooms. Uncle Jacob had seen to everything. They were grouped at one end of the hall, and considering what Europe usually offered, they had a great deal of space. Near the bureau, Galen could actually see what he was sure was Anne Frank House.

"We have many things we wish you to visit," Uncle Jacob said. "We have what you would call treasure or legacies from your uncle."

"Writings?" Galen asked.

"Yes, from your uncle and my father," Uncle Jacob said.

"Are they in Dutch or in English?" Galen asked.

"In English. We all speak English now," Uncle Jacob told him.

For some reason, Christabel and Jacob had gone off to her room. So it was just Galen and Anton and his cousin he was addressing.

"I wish to show you my Culture Club—not far, not far, you see. It has to do with making the body better, which you wrote about doing. It's like your WWW, which your mother wrote us about," Theo said.

"Ah, a health club. Didn't Andrew get some of the plans from you?" Anton asked.

"That is correct," Theo answered. "My cousin who married my cousin. Congratulations on the opening."

For a moment, Theo's face matched very much a portrait of Keats which Galen had seen years ago. Maybe there had also been a study of his hands, which seemed to fit as well. Their room was very high up. Theo threw open a window, and all the smells of Damrak came in. It was the odor of soil, as in Brandsmark Gardens. The Coburg Hills. The world was a little less odd, taboo.

"So we leave you for a rest," Theo said.

Christabel and Jacob had come back.

"We meet for dinner tonight," Uncle Jacob told them. "Five p.m., as you say."

"Don't forget the Culture Club," Theo said, his tanned body very much alight. "We'll talk about your work."

When the others were gone, Jacob rubbed his eyes and said, "I slept through most of that leprechaun movie." He smiled. "They should have had my play on that video instead. It would have been more exciting."

He lay on the bed, and Galen got on his. He was sure he would never sleep, with the fatigue weighing him down so much.

"Do you think, Dad," Jacob went on, "do you think we could go out and look at that statue of Vondel today? The one that I've been reading about?"

"It's my understanding," Galen said, "it's right where Grandma will be reading her poetry. I'm sure we'll get to it sometime soon, but probably not today."

He could see Jacob's face become luminous. "And I want to see—and I want to see if we can find some plays of Vondel's, if he is our ancestor. The ones we couldn't find back at home."

"Maybe we could check some bookstores out by the University," Galen said. "By Tamara's *standbeeld* shop. We were out by there coming in today."

The roars of the Damrak entered the room.

"Wouldn't it be something," Jacob went on, "if we could put on something of Vondel's back in Oregon. Wow!"

But Galen was finding to his surprise that he was almost asleep. "Yes, well, you have to wonder, though, about Oregon going for the works of a classical Renaissance Dutch playwright."

So they all took naps, even though they had planned otherwise. Galen awoke at one in the afternoon. He had been aware that something had been screaming in his head, but now it was gone. He had gotten past some rage. Jacob was still fast asleep. He walked over to Christabel's room, and found her at the small escritoire, hard at work at her manuscript, still.

"Jacob's still asleep," he said. "I'd like to have a look around. Do you mind going in there every now and then and seeing he's all right? Just keeping an eye out?"

"No, I don't mind," she said, looking over. "I'm almost done."

He must see the Pluto courtyard. He had remembered the other one with the lady. He went down in the lobby and through the courtyard, sitting at last on the bench. There was vine maple all around, red-veined, as though brushed on by the hand of Keats. Euonymus, turning even more scarlet, was along the perimeter, and above him, the walls of the hotel loomed down, just as they did back home. The whole design was, in fact, a reflection of what he had known back home. Instinctively, his eyes sought out the tool shed, where he and his father kept their equipment, as though it would be here, too.

For some reason, he was avoiding Pluto's stare. The statue was life-sized, and the plaque, one side in English, said it was modeled on an original by the sculptor De Vries, "the Dutch Michelangelo." Good, strong-veined hands held a wand, as Pluto stood at attention, just the way, now, he remembered it—so this was the source of the marble image in his mind—his back roped with muscle, his chest massive and arched, as though he had just arisen from the earth itself. Galen was reminded of Brent and the time they had spent together in the courtyard of the New Amsterdam, that one afternoon when his father had fallen. To imagine that man's white, glowing touch—his genius, and its loss. Or to imagine Leo. All aglow, with his blonde beard. Gone, too. Yes, yes, he did remember this statue, this courtyard now. He and his uncle had stood on this very spot—he was sure of it—after visiting Anne Frank House. It had been on a day filled with random, breaking clouds, just like this one. A shadow, in fact, passed over them just at this moment. As he sat there and closed his eyes, he was aware, very suddenly, of hands caressing him, just as on that day in the loft in the Estate. He felt his whole body, weary from the journey and trying to reconstruct the wreckage of so much that had transpired, begin to relax.

He looked up again; the clouds had started to clear away completely. It was noon, time for things to begin happening. He could hear, now, the revolving hotel door swish again and again out in the entranceway, and now the combination of voices—he must have been listening to it all along—begin to rise up. For the first time, almost since he had gotten out of prison, he found he had nothing to do. One of his first still moments.

op Pluto's borst

But there were hands again, real this time, this time kneading his shoulders. Instinctively, Galen held them, even without knowing for sure whose they were.

The palms were still rough. "That was a rest I needed," Anton said. "Did you rest also?"

"Yes, surprisingly, I think," Galen answered.

"About the different rooms," Anton went on, "I'm sorry. But I didn't know what else to say. It was awkward the way it was."

"It's right the way it is," Galen said, "Jacob needs to be there with me."

"But I would like us to be together," Anton said, "sometime."

Pluto's stretched arm, beneath the sun, seemed to turn the courtyard into a clock, and the pendulum that swayed somewhere was the rhythm of his mother's recollected poem. "I would like to live together," Galen answered. "When we get back."

"So that we could form a joint business?" Anton asked with some archness. "Like you and Brent?"

Galen smiled. "I didn't say that. We'll see."

He stood up and Anton allowed his face to be held and kissed.

"I don't remember this courtyard at first," Galen said. "It's strange I'd forget."

"Not strange at all," Anton said, running his hand along the statue's leg.

Galen touched the statue as well. He was aware that there was a small likeness of Triton, too, over in the corner. He would have said "west" if he had been sure of his directions.

"I did sort of ask you a question," Galen went on.

"Did you?" Anton asked.

"Well, I said, I would like to live with you. I was hoping you'd be saying that's what you wanted, too."

Anton turned away, his long neck taut. The usual blush was coming up as well.

God, you red-haired people, Galen wanted to say. But he was still rattled.

"You know the situation at home isn't too swift," Anton said, sitting down on the bench, apart.

"The situation at home? Your living by yourself?"

"Right. That's what I mean," Anton said. "I've got another negotiation going with my father and stepmother. They know about you—this trip sealed that. But I had to appease them with the idea that I would be meeting some of Father's relatives and be digging up Grandmother stuff when I went to Haarlem."

"Appease them?" Galen asked, angry. "What is this? The Inquisition? What do they have to do with it?"

"Well, give them time, Galen," Anton said. He waited. He was gripping the bench. "This is new for everybody. You have a whole hotel full of family. There and here. Who know about you. I don't want to lose what I've got."

"I'm getting tired of waiting," Galen said, smiling. But he was thinking about the accusations Brent had made of him.

Anton was in no mood for reconciliation, even though, obviously, he had entered the courtyard very rested and exhilarated. "You know, all you can think of is yourself. You've just gotten off the Brent bandwagon, and now you want to get on mine."

"Brent was a poor facsimile," Galen said. "Of you. I was aware of that the whole time."

"Somehow that doesn't make me feel any better," Anton said. In his distraction, he had stood up with his legs against the bench.

"I can understand that—and part of it was," Galen confessed, "just for sex."

"And I'm no giant in that department," Anton said. "No giant at all. So don't get your hopes up, so to speak. We're just going to have to take it one step at a time. All my experience up until now was those barroom years which I don't have anymore and which I can't remember. So don't get your hopes up."

"I'm not talking about fucking," Galen said. "I'm not even talking about foreplay. Just lying together." And finally, he held him.

Anton gently pushed himself away. "I know, I know. There's nothing more I want. But when I'm ready. Let me make the passes. Just once, Galen, all right? I'm tired of following your lead all the time."

"Seems reasonable enough," Galen said, backing off too and trying to look cheerful. But this whole courtyard, this whole city, this whole nation were having the same effect on him as before, years ago; it was taking the lid off, and he liked being the one to make the passes.

"Shall we go and see how Mom and Jacob are doing?" Galen asked at last.

The day advanced in quantum leaps. Galen felt himself experiencing moments that seemed to have wide gaps between them, and each time he looked at his watch, another two to three hours had passed. Young Jacob dragged them all out onto Damrak, with his camera taking in everything it could find. They found a small bookshop on a side street, which of course, knew of Vondel but had nothing by him. They followed other leads, until they made their way down a cobbled alley to a full-blown Tower Books type store, which had three plays of Vondel in English—*Lucifer*, *Mary Stuart*, and *Gijsbrecht van Amstel*, in separate editions. Jacob was beside himself.

"See, Dad. See, Anton," Jacob said. "They come out of Britain and Canada. You couldn't get them back home. We have imports! Not even available on the computer!"

There was something in the air, an ease so utterly foreign to home. They had rounded a corner, and one street had led to another and then to another, to a parade of arcane shops with rainbows of stone above them. They seemed to be going to the end of their treasure hunts. Under the rainbow, which would bloom, sometimes, into the colors of suspended flowers. Gladiolas, the harbingers of an autumn, like Ophelia's in Carleton Park.

Jacob and Anton wanted to go back to the hotel gift shop, and Galen, staying to linger over a rack of bulbs at a street vendor's, sent them on ahead. He was reading the fine print on the packages—comments about customs—when a young hustler, in a tight white t-shirt, approached him. His face was finely cut, with a short beard defining a hard jawline. His eyes were like the blue of an Oregon butterfly, the one that alights on lupine.

"I need to know something," the young man said.

Galen looked at him.

"Do you know the way to *Thermos*?" the young man asked.

"*Thermos*?" Galen stood very still.

"Yes," the beautiful man said, "*Thermos*, the Baths."

"No," Galen answered. "I don't."

"I take you, then." The stranger grabbed his hand. "You looked like you were looking for them."

Galen was still consuming the definition of the young man's body. He had been through this kind of invitation a thousand times before, especially in prison, but he was appalled to find how easy it was to give way. As in the time he had wanted to shower money on Brent.

"It would be fun to go with you," Galen heard himself saying, "but I have no time. I have to get back to the hotel named after my mother."

"Which hotel?" the young man asked, smiling.

"The Vondel."

"Ah, yeah, yeah, the Vondel," the stranger said. "I meet you there later."

"You see," Galen went on with difficulty, "my family is with me. *Ik ben Galen Melville. Mijn moeder heet Christabel Vondel.* My mother is to read in Vondel Park. Where they have the poetry."

"Your mother?" the young man asked, his neck tight and his face falling. "You could not leave her for an hour to go with me to *Thermos*?"

"No," Galen answered, "We came together from America—my mother, my boy, and my—*mijn man*, friend."

"No, then, no family," the young man said, and turned away, into the hubbub of the street. "No *man*." Galen was amazed by how pulled he felt. He had been starting to sweat.

◆◆◆

Evening found them in the upstairs dining room of the Vondel, a small, neat floor with paintings and etchings in the shadows. A frieze, not clearly visible either, hung on the north wall. Unpleasantly, the few people who were at the tables were smoking, which would have scandalized the whole populace of Carleton Park back home. Christabel was clearly annoyed and mentioned her allergies.

A cousin, who was their waiter, took their order. It was to be the cold salmon salad, which was the specialty of the house back home. For dessert, they had parfaits. With his eyes adjusting to the faint light, Galen was able to see the etching closest to him was one of Rembrandt's Goldsmiths, which brought a flash in his memory of his time with his uncle, here, on this very street. However, he had not remembered it to be in this hotel.

"Your uncle," Uncle Jacob said, "left much with us."

"Well, he grew up here," Christabel said, "at least part of the time. As I did."

"But he left behind more than you did," Uncle Jacob went on. "Like I said—these notebooks."

"He seems," Christabel said, "to have left them everywhere. They raised a whole hurricane back home."

"Hard for you," Theo said, in his direct way, looking at Galen, "because you had just come out from incarceration. We do not incarcerate people here the way you do there."

"Yes, in so many ways you don't," Anton said.

"It was hard for you?" Uncle Jacob asked. "Hard for you being away from little Jacob and little Teresa and your mother?"

"I'm not little," Jacob said, drinking his water noisily and stuffing bread. "I write plays and work a computer."

"Yes, hard," Galen said.

"You made money on that time, though," Uncle Jacob said. "They paid you back."

"If anything like that can be paid back," Christabel insisted.

"And where did the money go?" Theo asked.

"I hardly know," Galen answered.

"Your Uncle Eugene, our Uncle Eugene," Theo said, "he would have known what to do with it."

"Yes, he always had an instinct about that." But Galen wasn't altogether comfortable saying it.

"My father," Uncle Jacob went on, "tells a story about when he visited you and your mother at the boarding house."

"Yes," Galen said, fearful about the story.

"Please," Christabel said, clearly sharing his train of thought. "That's not anything that should be gone into here."

"But it's a good story," Uncle Jacob said. "Father told me about when you came back to life."

"I'm not altogether sure Jacob should—" Galen began.

"You tried to"—Uncle Jacob grasped his throat and tilted his head with his tongue out. "You know." He made a squeak.

"Off yourself," Jacob said, frightened.

"Yes, suicide," Uncle Jacob agreed. "But Eugene caught you. You were in a dress. You wanted to hang from the belt."

"I was trying to get attention. I was dressed for Halloween," Galen said.

Christabel looked terribly mortified.

"Father said you were ashamed for dressing up like a woman," Uncle Jacob explained. "For Halloween. The boarding house people made fun. Later, he said, you made up for it by being in a Superman suit to tell people gay people could not be treated poorly."

He remembered again the belt around his neck—red. He remembered that. People barging in had thought it was blood at first. Christabel had passed out straight on the scene. The focus shifted from him to her—once they were sure he was all right.

"Dad, did you almost die?" Jacob asked him, still looking frightened.

"No, no," Galen assured him. "I was dramatizing it. I made sure people would walk in and think I was hanging there."

"I did more than think," Christabel said.

He remembered unwrapping the cord from his neck. It was like letting go of a snake. Eugene and his Uncle Jacob Sr. hauled him up into their arms, and Christabel revived. He had wanted to feel Uncle Eugene or Uncle Jacob carry him in their arms, when he was deemed too old for such things. He had passed that point when touch between men had been allowed.

"Yes," Galen said. "That Superman suit in San Francisco more than made up for it."

"You guided the people," Theo said. "You gave them direction."

"I did at one time," Galen answered.

It was not surprising Theo would say this. Ever since they had arrived, Theo seemed to be wanting to give them a message. "Father did not mainly talk about that, though," Uncle Jacob said. His spectacles and beard, now, did make him look, very much, like Jacob Senior. "Not that, though, when he talked about your family. He talked about Eugene's loss of his little boy when he lived somewhere in the south of America."

"Arkansas," Christabel said, her eyes filling. "He refused to talk of it. But I do know what state it was in."

"He said that all was lost in a fire. Married for a short time, one child, fire. All gone," Uncle Jacob said.

"Sad," Jacob said. "Dad, do I still have to stay at the table?"

"We're all nearly done," Galen told him. "Hold on just one more minute. I doubt you can find your way back to our room."

"Oh, yes I can," Jacob insisted.

"A sad man at heart, then," Uncle Jacob said. "A man who died. And of Acquired Immune Deficiency Syndrome."

"Not sad," Galen said. "Or not very. Not after he left Arkansas."

"You must know," Theo said.

"Yes," Galen answered, "I do."

More candles in the room had been lit, now, and the smokers had left. The air lifted some. In the shadows, or better, from out of the shadows, the frieze came to him, one of Vulcan, clearly, at the anvil, surrounded by his men. His body seemed in a great hurry to get to it, as he stroked down, his shoulders, chest, and thighs were caught in a still-life of folded muscle, as though a garment had been caught still in mid-air. Nearby, his fellows lifted, or turned, in coordinates of sinewy motion, while all along the metal steamed and settled into shape. Over in the corner, Venus with Cupid watched from the sidelines.

"We must say goodnight, all of us," Christabel said. "The jets are catching up with me, at least."

"Of course," Uncle Jacob said.

As they stood up, Jacob grabbed for Galen's hand. He was silent all the way back to the room.

"Why would you try to kill yourself, Dad? Were you my age?" Jacob asked

"Yes, I was your age." Galen took off his sport coat. He expected Jacob to change immediately, for he hated his "scratchy pants," but he just sat there on the bed.

"Well, why did you?" his son asked.

"Oh, I was only trying to get attention, I think," Galen answered.

But Jacob, all dark eyes now, and very uncharacteristically brooding, seemed to demand more of an explanation.

"I don't know how to explain it," Galen said hesitantly. "Except that I lived in a very big house, a boarding house, where other people ate and slept, too, and they didn't always approve of me."

"Why not?" Jacob asked.

"Because I didn't fit what they thought I should be." He was coming to an explanation himself. "I wasn't very much of a man in their eyes."

Jacob's face changed. "Bullies?"

Galen thought for a moment. "Yes, yes, just exactly. It would be like living with a bunch of bullies."

"Well, then, I understand, then," Jacob said, getting up and taking his pajamas to the bathroom, "except I wouldn't try to hang myself. I'd tell them to fuck off. Just like I did back at Edison when you came to pick me up."

"I believe you would," Galen answered, smiling.

◆◆◆

Galen turned in his sleep. After Jacob had gone to bed, he had been up for several hours with the notebooks Uncle Jacob had delivered over to him. In his dreams, he escaped hanging many times. Dropped straight through the noose. His uncle had written—

> The perfect corner of Pieter Corneliszoon Hooftstraat. The smoke from the cafes goes up into a gray sky, richly blended. I will sit here and write all day, undisturbed. Let America across the waters collapse into street fights if it needs to. I am oriented and coordinated into exact points of time. I am fixed into an October of rich trees, a grandeur of woods, surrounding the Rijkmuseum, where the Flemish masters, flaming in paint, ride roughshod over the walls in noiseless splendor. Beyond, not very, very far is our family Vondel Park, where Joost the poet and dramatist sits surrounded by his heavenly host of stone muses. I will sit here and dream, as though by my earlier brook; I will let the centuries make their turn on this street named for the Poet of Time, our ancestor's contemporary. And I will think of what our poet Vondel wrote in *Lucifer*—

And in dreams, Galen was in a railway car, which made the sound of the trams outside the hotel—down in the street, below. It was just a train in summer, with the windows open and no one else in the entire car. Somehow Galen knew he was on his way to death once more, but he knew the train was being driven by someone, an intelligence—someone was at the switch—and when the conductor came by, he said they were going to Miss Bell's summer art class. Not long and the train was pulling into the station, and there Catherine Blaine Junior High was, with his uncle waiting for him on this hot July morning, just the way he had waited for him time and again when they had been living in Seattle.

But there was a change of lights suddenly—he was aware he was in his bed in Amsterdam—it was a flickering, he was certain, somewhere in the street. He was sure he was getting up and going to the window, and not three blocks away, Anne Frank House was all lit up, as on Holland Avenue—the Estate—back home. Darkness drew up to the house from the canals, but here the light was, like a candle, giving shape to the entire city. A tram rattled past all of a sudden, then more stillness. Then an ambulance went down the avenue with its reds flashing. But not a sound. Uncle said, when they were at the top of the house, "It can't be the same after this. No one's the same after this. Open a window, if things get too bad. Open a window!" And in the prison cell, he couldn't open a window, but he could, like Anne, pin cards to the wall. He just preferred Rembrandt to Leonardo. Open a window!

It was almost morning now. Soon everyone would be up. A new day and a new time. Back home, it was just midnight. And now, the light of Anne Frank House was extinguished. But there was her ghost. Her ghost which had imbued itself clear around the world. A cultural monument hovering, with unusual weight, over whole seas and land bridges and continents, and changing the entire drift of the universe, through a few lines, nearly forgotten in a notebook.

But it was time for him to get up. Jacob didn't have trouble hauling himself out of bed here, but Christabel, who tapped at the door, said she felt dizzy and on tilt. Nevertheless, they needed to travel today to Vondel Park, to review the setting for the reading. And Jacob's heart was set on it.

"Oh, yes, I feel unsteady," Christabel said, "and I may not be strong enough to ride today all the way out there. You may have to do it for me." She sat in their room, waiting for them to go down to breakfast. "As it is, you're going to have to help me get to the elevator."

"We do that easily," Uncle Jacob said, coming in. "We do that with two— what you call porters."

"I'm sure that Anton and I can manage," Galen said.

"No, we call the porters," Uncle Jacob said. "That's why they're here."

His orders brought in two middle-aged men, with black hair combed back wet. They looked smiling and vulnerable, like Gregory. Between themselves, they formed an iron bridge as they helped Christabel down the hall. Three doors down, and in the middle of the entourage, he knocked shyly at Anton's door.

"Just coming," Anton said, buttoning up his Pendleton beside the closet. "What's up for today?"

"Vondel Park," Galen answered. "That may be it, the slow way things are getting started."

"Your foot hurt?" Theo asked Christabel, once they were in the dining room. It was right by the swishing revolving door. Outside, all seemed powdered with white mist, as if they would never see the sun again.

"Yes, as though my whole right side had slipped," Christabel said, clutching herself, "and I was leaning on it."

"We take you to my Culture Club then," Theo said. "There I will perform manipulations on your foot and leg. To make you feel better."

"I really must prepare for my reading," Christabel answered.

"No good, your reading, if you don't feel well," Theo insisted.

It was decided, then, that Galen, Anton, and Jacob would ride by tram to Vondel Park and have a look at the gazebo while the rest of them ferried out to the Culture Club. Galen was urged to join them, as soon as possible, to be shown the way of physical therapy in Holland.

"Well, I have an idea about it already," Galen said, now sitting with a full platter in front of him. They were at a regular Roman banquet of breakfast foods. "I wonder if I couldn't model my part of WWW on it."

"You come anyway?" Theo asked.

"Yes," Galen answered. "We won't be long."

More Dutch words were coming back into his head, stamping themselves in his mind like firm wooden shoes, and he was realizing how much his whole outlook had been framed because of them. Why shouldn't he feel perfectly at ease going in a little streetcar across town to Vondel Park with Anton and Jacob? Already he was starting to get oriented just looking out the window. He had, after all, worked as a stand-in messenger boy for that time when the two of them, himself and his uncle, had come here. He was sort of that now. But, still, Galen felt afraid, and it was because of Anton. He sensed the man pulling away again. Because of yesterday's move on him, maybe. And Galen feared what he himself might do if he continued to feel shut out, especially in Amsterdam, which seemed like an American city but with the lid missing. Already those two porters had turned him on, and there had been the hustler yesterday. He just despaired of himself sometimes.

He, Jacob, and Anton left for Centraal Station almost immediately, and, looking over his shoulder, he saw the hotel, which he realized now was turreted and infinitely involved and complex. He remembered it had been fashioned there with a watchtower to look out on Amsterdam's harbor.

The square in front of Centraal Station exploded with pigeons. Up they flew, shimmering jade and rainbows, shadowing the hundreds of travelers boarding the trams, which left every five minutes, most of them. The people swung off the sidewalks, not rude, just unmindful of one another, the languages babbling up like sounds from a brook and ultimately a gathering ocean. Nearby the Station's brick facade, city mimes stood at attention with their coin boxes in front of them—one of them a metallic witch with her pointed hat, covered from head to toe in metallic gray paint. She could have been the Tin Woodsman, nearly. Also close by was a man with a hurdy-gurdy complete with intricate dolls that bowed and curtsied beneath the overcast, which would not bring rain after all but sun as before, breaking.

Galen felt the heart rise inside him as they boarded the tram which Uncle Jacob had designate. And it was not just because he remembered all the tram rides he had taken so he could help his Uncle Jacob write the guidebook. It was all the young men around him now, blonde, shock-haired and all the old men around him, grand, bearded, wide-thighed, their eyes close on their newspapers, also of many languages. And then the beauty of Anton himself.

They stepped into the tram—the glassed door received them—I am out of prison. Have been for eight months. More Dutch words Galen had known flew up. Borst, standbeeld, doorsnijt. He felt he was in such strange command in this strange city. In Jacob's paperback *Lucifer*, there had been the passage—

> *Let him be content*
> *With that rich Garden as his element*
> *Where, rising and setting, sun and moon*
> *Divide the months and years. Let him attune*
> *His life-style to the stars' bold revolution—*

"Is this where we get off?" he suddenly asked one of the travelers, as if they would know. "Is this near the Rijkmuseum?"

"The Rijkmuseum?" the strangers asked, clearly not knowing English. And the pronounced "muse-a-him" came straight across. "Yes," they went on, and pointed to the door.

So here is Vondel Park, he thought, getting off, and here is the long pathway through, with sun now breaking over it, seeming to raise the branches of the maples. Birds, noise, and people perfectly at ease. Galen felt the lift to the morning. Beyond the wrought iron fence, volleyball was already happening, and here were two men sitting on a bench, leaning against each other, watching the games. It was as if the couple was fashioned to sit in the park like this for the rest of their lives. He took Anton's hand, then Jacob's, and moved toward the monument to Vondel.

And Galen noticed the remaining hollyhocks around the stone, pink and carmine spears.

"There's Joost!" Jacob said, backing up. For Vondel seemed enthroned upon a minor mountain. "A whole place named after us!"

Anton smiled toward him. "Just remember, if you get famous, who your friends were."

"I will, I will." Jacob climbed to the top of the monument, using the Muses who held the statue of the poet up as steps. "Just look at his fans below him."

"Those are goddesses, Jacob," Galen said.

"Well, I know that," Jacob answered. "I was trying to make a joke."

Galen could now see the gazebo just beyond the green knoll, and the two men who had been watching volleyball had now moved to another bench. They had moved apart.

Since Anton and Jacob didn't care about the gazebo, Galen went on ahead. The shadows from the trees made a drift through the park, and he could sense an influence emanating from the direction of Vondel's memorial. He watched Jacob and Anton together over there. Jacob was trying to climb on to one of the muses' backs. Anton was giving directions.

Galen stepped inside the gazebo.

◆◆◆

They arrived at the Culture Club with time to spare. They sat in the lobby among the potted plants and waited. All around were sketches of the body—its pressure points and junctures, as though they were charts for mariners. Galen thought of a medical notebook he had seen—kept by Keats. There had been a page capturing a lecture on the head. The poet had fashioned all sorts of poses, front and back, made the man smiling, while a whole garland of leaves and flowers had been embroidered down the margin. His entire body seemed to feel the weave of what had been on that page—and the diagrams captured the hustler's physique, too, front and back, with all its trigger points. What did I give up, Galen wondered, when I turned down that body? And it wasn't hard to get an answer.

"We are back," he heard Theo say suddenly. "We and van Gogh met. And with great success."

"My leg is better," Christabel said, pleased also. "From what Theo did. So we went over to the van Gogh museum. And what did you think about my gazebo? Will it do?"

"It will do," Galen said, "if it's a small party."

"We'll have reporters tomorrow," Uncle Jacob said. "The reading is announced. But the newspaper report will help."

"It will accommodate fifty," Galen said. "It's more than a gazebo, really. A summerhouse."

"Then we are all right," Christabel said.

They were standing in the lobby and blocking the way of some arriving patients.

"So you will look here quickly?" Theo asked Galen.

"Very quickly," Galen said, "because it looks like the crew is tired."

"Not me," Jacob said.

The tour did go quite fast, however—it was like a flash between time zones, one European, one American. Galen was struck by the fewness of the rooms—only five in all, and this club, according to Theo, was the most distinguished one in Amsterdam. The center had been carved out of an old building, many centuries old, so that the hallways turned very suddenly and led into coves of workout equipment, whose spareness also surprised Galen. His own Jacob got on one of the stationary bikes, whose instructions lit up in Dutch, to his delight.

Christabel became tired and wanted to sit down. As the rest of them went on, Galen could hear his son starting to tell her, point for point, everything about the visit to Vondel. He went ahead, followed by Anton into Theo's examining room, where his cousin pulled out a manual. "Here is my muscle energy book," he said.

He flipped through for them, showing various moves—through photos of patient and therapist working together.

"We do not press anyone—force anyone," Theo said. "We correct gently."

"By any chance," Galen said, "have you heard of a Doc Hollywood? His real name is Edward Tyson."

"Yes, yes, of course," Theo said. "He was here. He learned this technique from us. How do you know him?"

"He taught"—Galen was aware of Anton—"my...friend some of these moves, and he applied them on my father."

Anton looked at him with irritation.

"This is a special invention," Theo said. And, once more, he looked like Keats, his hands fine and carefully made. As though touched with genius, too. The supreme simplicity of the room, with the one anatomy chart on the wall—da Vinci's—and the vase of gladiolas in the corner, seemed to invite in any guiding ghost who wished to appear. "A very special invention," he went on. "If you come back and visit us. I'll teach you."

They were quiet in the van returning to the hotel. Jacob actually fell asleep against him the moment they got in. Surprisingly, Anton took his hand once more, even though they had nothing to say. They passed the Rijkmuseum, which they had not yet had time to see.

"Come," Christabel said when they were at the hotel again—it was nearly four o'clock—"I'll write once more in your room while Jacob paints or does something else. I have much to correct and add after seeing the van Gogh."

After attending everyone back to the hotel, still, he and Anton went out into the city. Galen, remembering the hustler, put his arm around Anton. Again, no one noticed. They walked until they got to Anne Frank House, and, buying tickets, went up the narrowing stairs, as the voices on recorders and on television sets (videos of Anne's life and associates) guiding them, as though in an underworld. They went behind the bookcase, ventured up to the secret flat, past Anne's photos and clippings that were, still, on the wall, and they were able to see the diaries themselves, beneath glass, the handwriting grand and slanted.

12 Juni 1942

Ik zal hoop ik ann jou alles kunnen toevertrouwen, zoals ik het nog ann niemand gekund heb, en ik hoop dat je een grote steun voor me zul zijn.

12 June 1942

I hope I will be able to confide everything to you, as I never have been able to confide in anyone, and I hope you will be a source of great comfort and support.

They stood now at the windows and looked out. Every canal of the city seemed visible to them, and busy, everywhere, fingers, Renaissance fingers and medieval fingers, and modern ones, were at work, as if in his mother's Sorceress Seamstress's Shop, creating and recreating and undoing the past and present of the city, the nation.

Galen led him back down into the street, over the canal and beside the Homo Monument, a plain slab with a pink triangle, which jutted out into one of those many canals. In the next moment, they seemed to be in the courtyard of the Rijkmuseum, sitting upon the stone bench at last, and taking in the goddess lady who stood at attention with her mirror. From window to window of the museum, his uncle's ghost seemed to be moving, as though with a lantern. They were enclosed, solid and secure, within a perfectly trimmed hedge.

As evening fell, they rounded the final arc of their walk and were home again, back in Anton's room, with time to spare, actually—as had just been true of the morning—and this time Anton was picking up the phone and ordering distilled water. At fourteen gilders! When Galen came out of the bathroom, Anton was standing there naked.

Galen stepped forward, and his hands moved over all of him, across his pectorals, down to his buttocks. Anton, taking the lead as promised, planted his mouth over his and kissed him hard. Helped him undress.

I remember the Coburg Hills, Galen thought, when I drove over and saw you there, in your gray sweatshirt. I could see your forearms, and the dirt on your hands, like mine. The outline of your body.

He took the palm that was before him and kissed it. Caressed the red nape of his neck. Drew his own hand backwards across his rough cheek. And again.

Anton, in the light from Damrak, through the thin white curtains, lowered himself slowly on Galen. Very slowly after Galen had also made himself ready.

He felt he was moving along those hills again, their contours, forest their contours, both forest and sandstone. The grandeur of a forest, the gathering of water, cascading down a canyon.

He felt Anton was red and tan, and himself, tan and brown, mixed like two kinds of sand. They could lie there, spent forever, like ashes, like compost, the remains of Pluto, spaded into the roots of the flowers at the foot of his statue.

They separated, got into bed.

Then Galen waited for the loss of spirits to fall on him like an impending doom, but nothing happened. He stayed this way, as himself, even through showering, through dressing again, through getting ready for dinner.

"I love you," he said.

"Yes," Anton answered. He laughed. "I have never felt anything as strong as this since Grandmother."

◆◆◆

The next morning, like two lovers in a World War II movie, they caught the train out to Haarlem, taking their child with them. In fact, they were told that Haarlem Station had been the set for countless films. With many romantic hellos and goodbyes.

Anton's relatives, a stout husband and wife, with burnished hair, met them when they arrived. And immediately, they were driven to St. Bavo's, which was where Anton wanted to go.

"We have not seen you since you were in your twenties," Anna, his cousin, who was American-born, said. "Not since we visited and saw your grandmother."

"How that brings back memories," Anton answered. "That was when Grandmother set everything right after Mother died."

"Are we going to get sad again?" Jacob asked.

"Maybe," Galen answered.

But they were allowed to go their own way once they got to St. Bavo's. Jacob was transfixed by the golden statuary above the organ. Ladies with trumpets and zithers, leaned against the mahogany pillars. And then towering above, in silver and marble, the Saints played their harps. Meanwhile, Toccata and Fugue sounded beneath. His uncle wrote:

> July 18, 1969.
>
> Galen and I have just been to Anne Frank House. We looked out the window and saw the formations for the Homo Monument below. This is a safe world for us, an inspiration to move toward in the future. Imagine if we could create an island, if only an island, like this for ourselves back home. I am driven now by the presence of saints and artists everywhere—Anne Frank, Rembrandt, Vondel, and the great martyrs who died with pink triangles on their chests. Life is rich with expression and martyrdom here; it flowers in the very trees, in its music. The light step of Mozart, too, is not far off.
>
> And somewhere in this dank nave, below the statues, with the music playing, he could sense the movements of Mozart, only ten years old, as the guidebook said, approaching the loft of the organ all on his own.

Anton and his relatives returned to them shortly. They took a brief walk through the town itself. Galen and Jacob, feeling subdued, let Anton talk on and on about the time his grandmother had set their own household in order back in the Coburg Hills. His mother had died, and it had been Christmas, and even the poor tree, in the aftermath of what had been a traffic accident, had gone to smash, upended. His grandmother had set everything to rights on that frightening night.

"And she had said," Anton went on, "that once all this was over—she was tucking me into bed—once this was all over, she would take me to a museum. And for some reason, that was the greatest consolation she could think of. And it was."

The promise of rain brought their time quickly to an end. Anton checked the schedule and saw they could get an earlier train. Although both Anna and her husband invited them to stay and see their home, Anton seemed satisfied with the few hours they had spent. It was quite clear that everyone was coupled. Galen was not just a friend.

On the train back to Amsterdam, with Jacob on one side, Anton on the other, Galen saw that Anton had bought four packages of tulip bulbs, all of them—according to their pictures, which he asked to see—red and yellow and feathery. As he looked out at the passing fields and windmills, his memory traveled up the loft of the organ.

When Thursday came, in the gazebo, Christabel's new poems told the story of her brother.

(All were there in the audience, young Jacob, old Jacob, Theo, Anton, himself, the bookstore people who were funding the reading, and many from the staff of the hotel. Strangers packed the room as well. Many were standing.)

She told the story, first in Dutch and then in English, of a man who had been through a fire, and who had lived through a dark adventure, too. He had lived here in Amsterdam during the early part of the occupation, and he had helped the students who had refused to sign pledges to the Nazis. They had been cut off from their education at the University of Amsterdam, because they had not made that commitment, and so Eugene had helped to teach them in the underground.

Their own mother and father had been no longer living at that time, and so he had been an orphan, in a way, among orphans.

But he had escaped to America—that was when the fire had come and the loss of the wife and child. She, Christabel, was already living there.

(There was, in fact, she told them, a poem about her view, in 1939, from Carleton Park, when she had heard how the Queen of Holland had fled by ship for London and had placed the seat of government there. Orphans! All of them!)

She told of how Eugene became the man of the house, in a way, of the boarding house she had kept, and how she had wanted him to stay, but she had been ashamed of what her tenants might think. She told of how he was Pluto, with "an earthly coming" into the dining room every morning with spring rising in the windows like light flowering in a dish or in the tulip fields of her beloved home. He was their Pluto at the door, coming home from teaching his children. With chalk dust on his hands, with sadness in his eyes, and a kind of cape of hauntedness mantling his shoulders.

He could not tolerate the sham. So, he changed himself into a bird in flight, and moved to the larger city, taking not his son but a child who was her son with him. And then to another larger city, and then another, and another. Soon his Plutonic touch was spread around the globe, the flowering, evolving, light—borne touch. Meaning that people were beginning to move and breathe more in a new presence, one which allowed for the bonds between men and women to be freer, if only just a little. And between men and men. Of course. He was in the rhododendrons and throughout the leaves of the park, her park, Carleton Park. He was in the winter roses, and in the fragrant viburnum, earliest of spring. He was in the azaleas, white and orchid purple; he was in the tulips, brought over from his native country. She lost her boy to this presence, as Ceres did with her Persephone, but then he came back.

This man was a Teacher of the Underground, as he had been for the University of Amsterdam students, the moment their own Queen Mother had left, fleeing, for London. One must take up, Christabel read to the group in the gazebo, one must take up that which causes a flourish.

He is, in fact, Carleton Park. He is the town and its sheltered nature. He lives in the veins of the streets, in its lit windows, just as he lives here in every corniced room and every easeled or mounted painting. He belongs in the lines and nerves of Vondel's poetry, his ancestor, whose extraordinary stars of light are like Roman candles, shooting out, creating new words, new voices, in the shape of Lucifer, Samson, Adam, which crossed the channel and into the remarkable citadel—through the belfry towers—of the mind of Milton, creating new lines, new configurations, new changes. He was in the house of Anne Frank, one stair at a time, up, up to the Westerkerk, down again, over the canals, leading her son especially away from her, to a new direction she could not create. This was all she could muster—this, this poetry too late, in the park of her ancestor.

Galen, sitting there with Jacob and Anton on either side of him, closed his eyes and felt all the pain of Teresa, of Yvonne, and of Gregory. How could poetry do that, create that—that both at once? The October Dutch moon came through the windows, cold, made the room, perhaps, a little warmer? The portable heaters, brought especially for her, made a small whirring sound, but no one was distracted; everyone was listening. Even the bookstore owner, who sat in readiness at the sales table (mounds and mounds of *Pluto's Bounty* in English but also, now, in Dutch) did not take his eyes off her.

And somehow, somehow, Galen thought, because of this reading, it will be easier to go back home.

◆ ◆ ◆

One day more, and they would need to pack.

Galen, having returned after the reception at the gazebo, was checking what clean clothes they had left. Jacob was already in bed, asleep. Galen wondered if he had ever gotten adjusted to the time shift, and he was determined to let him sleep in tomorrow as long as he needed. They would have to get up extremely early the next day.

He was too restless to try to sleep, but his eyes were too tired to attempt the Dutch books—many of them—which he had gotten from the family. He actually had, as well, a Dutch review of his mother's poetry, which he wanted to puzzle through before someone helped him out.

He went to the window. He could not make out Anne Frank House now. Only the slow lights of a few trams, and a very few passersby, making their way through a light mist, punctuated by lit statues.

Sitting down, he took up a few sketches Theo had drawn of the muscle energy techniques belonging to the circle of himself, Brent, and Doc Hollywood.

A moment later, a light tap came at the door, and there stood a young man, dressed as a valet and holding a letter. His uniform, too, was chocolate-colored.

"This is for you," the young man said. "Was today," he smiled, "but you weren't here."

"Yah, yah," Galen answered in the Dutch manner, despite himself, seeing the young man as his own reflection twenty-one years before. "Thank you"—and gave him a ten-glider tip.

"Thank you very much sir"—and seemed to be waiting for something else, but Galen closed the door.

The envelope was covered with postage, so it would reach him in time. From his father. Galen would have known it even without seeing the return address, since he now recognized the block letters from "everything's going to be all right." His father printed:

My dear Galen,

I just wanted to tell you how sorry I was not to be able to see all of you to the airport, but my hip was acting up from the day before, and I didn't think we could all quite fit in the Cadillac anyway. But I want you to know that I've already checked with Andrew, and he's letting me use the car to pick you up. I'll be there. I'll be there, and while I know I could have called or just shown up, it's important for me to write you, the way I never did when you were in prison.

Also I wanted to let you know that all your gardening accounts are in good order and good shape. I was out at Mrs. Ward's just yesterday, and some of her roses are still doing fine. I edged all along the driveway (it's been years since I edged), and my back and I came through OK. Her golden lab sat with me through the whole operation, seemed fascinated with what I was doing. Then when I took the clippers and started in on the flowerbeds, he leaned against me the whole time. Every time I'd get up and move a little further down the line, up he'd get and plop down where I settled.

I wish in many ways, I could be with you. I love that hotel. Although it's been decades, I still remember it. Is that statue of Pluto still standing in the courtyard? If it is, please pay my respects. It was the sight of him that made me think about the planet. I mean, your mother and I came to her old country for our honeymoon and we stayed there. One night, I got up and sat down in that place. It was the statue that made me think of the planet, and my experiences with Tombaugh all those years before. I felt a lot of promise in those days.

But I'll tell you something. Remember when you were in Seattle and I kept a watch over you? As Mr. Biggs? Like we said. You were one of my lights, but also I used to think of the work I had done, that astronomical work, as one of them. It was like a landmark, figured out in my mind. I'd float around old 1950s Seattle, doing odd jobs. I did all sorts of odd things—even repair swimming pools and build fences—and I'd think of where you might be at any given moment, and I'd also think about my work. Where you'd might be would be beneath that old water tower, where Eugene lived. Sometimes I might be way over in the east part of town, but I could still see it there on that bluff. Eugene's Tower, I would think. And then you, and the promise of my work. That I never followed up on.

I wanted to close by saying that I mean to follow up on my studies now. I'm going to the library. At the University. It's open late. I can walk there, now—it serves me well! I can stay up until midnight, while all the students are cramming for mid-terms! I just sit there at the window looking out at the quad and I can see the sign of the New Amsterdam, and I can think about the Vondel Hotel, too, with its courtyard of Pluto.

I'll be looking for you, Galen. I'll be there at the airport. And I'm still sober, thanks to A.A. Look for the small man in the crowd. Mr. Biggs! He'll be there.

Love, Dad.

P.S. Your Teresa came by my room the other day. Said she wanted to get to know me better. Actually took me out to coffee. She's a beautiful child, Galen, and I know she'll come round.

P.P.S. The Gay Alliance and AIDS House young people came by to get the key to the Estate. They've been given the go-ahead to start taking over. So Christabel must have changed her mind.

Galen just sat and listened to the sounds of the hotel. The flushing of a toilet, the banging of a late arrival down at the end of the hall. Someone upstairs and two rooms down must have been practicing dancing. In the street, there were voices, now, and they seemed practicing, too. Singing? So Christabel had changed her mind.

The letter seemed part of the muted voices. Like the emphatic rests between notes in a musical piece. As in *Jack and the Beanstalk*—way back in the early piano days. It formed its own line of music, and it seemed at last that it was shaping a bridge back to a place he could call home. And Teresa? He hoped that sometime maybe his father's prediction would come true.

◆◆◆

On the return flight, Galen, to while away the time, took out the Dutch review of his mother's poetry, along with the article, also in Dutch, covering the reading. He was stumped on some words.

"What does this mean?" he asked Christabel. "*Doorzichtig en toch weerspiegelend?*"

"'Transparent but reflecting,'" she answered.

"Does that seem right?" he asked. "About the way you write?"

"Close, I guess," she answered.

"And what about the article in the paper?" he asked. "Did you think it was just?"

"Fairly much," she replied.

"And what is this?" he asked, pointing to a phrase. *"In een sobere stijl met ingehouden lyriek?"*

"'In a lucid style with restrained lyricism," she said.

"Seems to me accurate, too?" Galen asked.

"Yes, I hope so," she answered. She looked sad. And considered. "Tell me," she said, after a moment, "have you ever forgiven me for throwing Eugene out of the boarding house? I've been thinking about it ever since the reading."

"Yes," he answered.

"When did that happen?" she asked.

"I can't tell you," Galen said. "It just happened. Maybe in prison."

"Why prison?"

"I don't know. But the day I got out—do you remember it?"

"Yes."

"When I came home and saw you there. It was like that had been wiped away. Sometimes you have to be apart from it to know. And maybe I was thinking about how Eugene had taken me into his home. That was the point, wasn't it? And then there was Eugene's letter."

Christabel looked rueful. "Yes, Eugene had to take you into his home. I know what you mean—I know you mean it kindly. But that will always sound to me like a judgment, too, because I couldn't keep you."

"You took me in after prison," he said.

She smiled. "I suppose, but it's harder to remember all this when you've given so much money to bail out the hotel. In some ways, I feel like I ought to be exiled."

"No," he said. "And you've signed over the Estate—Thank you," he was about to add, having said it before. "Thank—"

But she stopped him. "Never mind about that," she said. "It's a payment you deserve."

"No payment, no payment," he told her. "It's not me, anyway."

That Saturday morning, he explained to himself, yes, that one Saturday morning, Eugene was hounded out of the boarding house, but before he was, I was allowed one last trip to his room, where he was putting the last mailing labels on some boxes. As I opened the door, I seemed to be entering, truant, a cave of spring. The heavy forsythia outside the window flashed its yellow at me, and the magnolia, visible from his side of the house, dripped dew like a rose bush. Small puffs of Saturday clouds made their way overhead, sending shadows into the deserted room—all packed up and waiting.

"There's a couple of things I want you to have," Eugene said. And he went over to one of the boxes, not yet sealed for mailing, and handed me a print of *The Night Watch*, along with a small thin volume.

Pluto's Bounty. Later, I must have lost it.

Did I ever take any time, then, to realize it was my mother's poetry? Ever take time to read? Where is that copy now? Valuable beyond belief.

"I want you to know," Eugene went on, once we were on the stairs, "that if you ever need a home, a place to stay, you can come up to Seattle and live with me."

And then he disappeared.

I used that invitation as my security, my safety net. Because I took him up on it. Why shouldn't I let go of all of that? It turned out for the best. He allowed me to get through the 1950s, because I had a standing invitation to his planet. And later, at Uncle's house, I learned more about painting, music, and writing. Perched on its hill in its stucco light, it was a veritable museum, with roses and lily ponds on its knolls on the side. He had opened a prison door, letting in the light.

Galen, realizing they had been silent several minutes, fished about for something else to say. Christabel was looking at him.

"What was it like knowing all those celebrities in the old days?" he asked. "After getting that prize?"

She closed up her reading, as if to settle this for a while. "It was nothing," she said abruptly, "in comparison to meeting your father, which happened soon after." She turned out her lamp, also with abruptness. "You look like you could rest, too," she said. And she gazed over at Jacob, who was reading Vondel in translation. "And better get some sleep," she added to him. "Enough of this for now. There'll be a lot to do once we land."

"I don't need to sleep," Jacob said. "This is incredible."

Galen followed her orders to rest. Movements through the Rijkmuseum. Through the Rembrandt hall. Through the Rememembrandt arena. Once again, he imagined clutching Anton, who was in the seat beside him again. One-eyed shapes rushed past him, in the unearthly light of his dream, in the unearthly light of the plane—winging its way through a night that broke down the hours, putting the travelers ahead of themselves—as though if it found just the right speed, it could stand absolutely still, in time and space.

Figures crouched their way through, an impression of the very day before, when all of them had gone through the museum, as a farewell, just after Galen's A.A. Meeting—in English, actually. The shapes of *The Nightwatch*, reds against the black, yellows—the young girl again with her birds this time—circled around them, as though holding lanterns. St. Paul's face, in the painting opposite, lit up against the fire, and Galen, then, as well as now, was brought back to that moment when the young girl had visited him in Forest Glade, her neck encircled by the rainbow rings.

Let me lie here in the museum, beside the stone effigies, let me fall asleep as though in a recovery room. Somewhere, buried in their luggage, was one of his uncle's treasures, a catalogue from the Rijkmuseum from the days when they, the two of them, had visited, *Rembrandt, 1669-1969*, little sketches, one of Cleopatra, and then the paintings, with a detail of Aristotle's hand resting, in full golden light, upon the head of Homer. The veins seemed to rise beneath the skin in the light from the pigment's lamp.

A hand, a flower. Teresa had given him one when she was a child. Jacob had given him a sketch of one. If I lie here long enough, I'll be conveyed back to prison, sleeping in my cell. But that will be all right, because I'll dream of the way I had dreamed then, of Amsterdam, of the courtyard, of the street corner. As though in a stereo viewer.

I'm sure now nothing—not death nor life nor angels nor principalities, nor powers, nor things present, nor things to come, nor height, nor depth, nor any other creature—can separate me now from the great love of Eugene.

For the day Eugene was given notice to leave, both on seeing me as his nephew and on keeping his job, the silence seemed impenetrable once we came down to the boarding house dinner table. Everyone seemed to know he had gotten the ax.

One of the boarders said, "Did you read about that groundskeeper? Caught stealing. I knew that man used to work out at Funland Amusement Park. Saw him watch a woman at the Spook Ride take money and put it in her apron. He kept his eye on that pocket all right, and I knew what he was thinking. Stealing. Same thing this time around."

"Ah, the culprits," another said. "All over the town. Being caught red-handed. And even now, the flying saucers are picking them up. Damaged souls caught in the act. Just like in Ghost Riders in the Sky."

I sat there looking sour at them all. I knew they had been speaking again in the direction of Uncle Eugene. "Has anyone thought," I said, "there might be something wrong with this town? Just seems like one big beating up to me."

After dinner, Eugene caught me in the hall, and he told me he would have to be leaving, that he would be packing up his things upstairs and never coming back.

"But Uncle Eugene," I said, "you're like a father to me. You can't leave."

"I won't be far away," he said. "I'll see to it we stay in touch."

"But why do you have to go?" I asked, starting to cry. "School isn't even over."

"You'll understand when you're older," he said.

But I wanted to answer, I understand now. Alice in Wonderland. Songs of Chopin. Color crayons. Rembrandt. All the things that belong to your planet, where I can be allowed to be myself. For just a few days ago, at recess, I had been caught trading cards of the Great Masters in the back of my own classroom, and Christabel had reprimanded me later not so much for breaking and entering, when the room was supposed to be closed, but for not being out on the baseball diamond with all the other boys. For after all, I had been doing the trading cards with girls.

Years later, I'd be putting them up on the walls of my cell. Years later, Eugene would be zipping me into my Superman outfit, and I'd be going out to do the demonstration against the psychiatrists. You can't keep us down. Not anymore.

Uncle, I'm coming out. And I'm going back. In the darkness (they had changed planes), he knew that they were nearing Carleton Park just from the shift of weight on this flight. Let me wake up one more time.

He sat up at attention, and saw that Anton, Christabel, and Jacob, were getting ready for the descent. The pines of the town came into view, through the mist, then the waters of the river, and even the lines, surprisingly visible, of the autumnal rhododendrons, some of them still in flower. His eyes scanned for the hotel, the way his father's eyes must have scanned for the water tower in Seattle. There the sign was, "New Amsterdam," lit for the early afternoon. And somewhere in back, their own house, with its own miniature courtyard and Vondel Park, must be waiting.

They were on the runway, and Galen was held in suspense for an instant, wondering if his father would in fact show up. Anton and Jacob seemed to be feeling the same. The plane drew nearer; some sun, bright for November, struck the glass of the airport, and there, he could make him out, a small man, in chocolate colors—still looking like a porter, but definitely smiling as they came off the plane—a man alive, sober, and waving, at the window. Present.

ABOUT THE AUTHOR

Henry Alley is a writer of fiction and literary criticism. His background includes over sixty stories published over the past fifty years, in such journals as *Seattle Review, Cimarron Review, The Virginia Woolf Quarterly, Harrington Gay Men's Fiction Quarterly*, and *Virginia Quarterly Review*. In addition he has five other novels: *Through Glass* (Iris Press, 1979), *The Lattice* (Ariadne Press, 1986), *Umbrella of Glass* (Breitenbush Books, 1988), *Precincts of Light* (Inkwater Press, 2010), and *Men Touching* (Chelsea Station Editions, 2019). He is also the author of a collection of stories, *The Dahlia Field* (Chelsea Station Editions, 2017) and was included in *Best Gay Stories 2017*. He was the recipient of a Mill House Residency from Writing by Writers.

He received his B.A. from Stanford University, and his M.F.A. in Creative Writing and Ph.D. in Prose Fiction from Cornell University. He grew up in Seattle, Washington, and has lived in a variety of places in the U.S. As a professor of English and Literature, he taught for forty-four years in the Clark Honors College of the University of Oregon. He has written numerous scholarly articles, many on them centered on George Eliot and Virginia Woolf as well as the classics, and they have appeared in *Studies in the Novel, Kenyon Review*, and *Twentieth Century Literature*. In 1997, University of Delaware Press published his scholarly study, *The Quest for Anonymity: The Novels of George Eliot*. He lives in Eugene, Oregon, with his husband, Austin Gray.

ACKNOWLEDGEMENTS

In Memory Of Jody Procter, husband, father, writer, best friend. And with many thanks to Jane Smiley, James McConkey and Patricia Henley for their help and encouragement.

Portions of this book appeared as stories in *Clackamas Literary Review* and *Harrington Gay Men's Literary Quarterly*.

The quote from Pieter Corneliszoon Hooft's "Sonnet to Time" is from Martijn Zwart's and Ethel Grene's *Dutch Poetry in Translation: Kaleidoscope* (Fairfield Books). I have also quoted from Joost van den Vondel's *Lucifer*, Noel Clark translation (Absolute Classics), and from Anne Frank's *The Diary of a Young Girl* (the Otto H. Frank and Mirjam Pressler edition, translated by Susan Massotty, Penguin Books, also from Otto Frank's and Mirjam Pressler's *Het Achter Huis*, *Uitgeverij* Bert Bakker), and from H.I. Onnes-de Groot's review of my novel *Through Glass*.

CPSIA information can be obtained
at www.ICGtesting.com
Printed in the USA
JSHW050733050622
26645JS00002B/8